BLOOD RED

THE CONNECTION TRILOGY - BOOK 1

ANITA WALLER

www.bloodhoundbooks.com

Print ISBN 978-1-914614-33-0

ALSO BY ANITA WALLER

For Mum
Edna May Havenhand
08.05.1921 – 01.11.1953

Would have been 100 years old on 08.05.2021
So dearly loved

No matter what the colour of your skin is,
we all bleed red.
— **HH Younus AlGohar**

While the rest of the species is descended
from apes, redheads are descended from cats.
— **Mark Twain**

PROLOGUE

MONDAY 21ST AUGUST 1995

The tears continued for an hour once the realisation hit that Evelyn was dead.

It was Evelyn's suggestion that they had a talk, she had things to say. She wanted to go public with her love for a man, a different man to the one whose engagement ring she wore.

'It will be fine, but we need to talk. I have to tell you my plans and those plans involve me going to live away from Eyam.' Her voice was cold, almost brutal, as if she couldn't believe she was saying the words. She sounded almost scared to say them but she knew exactly how much her words were hurting.

'What?'

'You heard me.'

'But...'

'No buts. I've made up my mind.' There was pain in her voice, her face flushed a deep red. She turned to walk away.

'This isn't happening, Evelyn. You're mine. You can't leave! I decide when that happens, not you.'

It was so easy to pick up the heavy object and swing it

towards the back of the head of the woman who was loved too much. Evelyn tumbled to the floor, like a fan folding all on its own, slowly and carefully.

The killing object, rounded and heavy, hammered again and again before sliding with a thud to the floor, to lie beside her inert body.

Everything was red. The whole surrounding area underneath and by the side of Evelyn turned more and more russet as blood pumped out of the huge crater in her skull... the glorious red hair so admired by all who knew her was now vibrantly scarlet.

The pulse in her neck was non-existent; she was gone. One rash movement, the uncharacteristic anger, had taken her away.

And the tears flowed.

She was wrapped in a picnic blanket and wasn't difficult to manoeuvre into the boot of the car. Evelyn had to be hidden until logic could plan the next move, and remembrance of schooldays and the outhouse round the back of the disused shop in the middle of Eyam appeared as if those memories were a film script. They had gone there to smoke, but only the three of them knew about it, knew where they hid the key. The last tile on the roof was loose, reachable and a safe place. If it was still there, she could be hidden in that disused spot until the next move could be thought through. She certainly couldn't be kept in the boot of the car. Time, time to think, was what was needed.

The key was still there, and the door creaked as it was opened for the first time in an extremely long time. The risk of parking the car outside the front of the shop had seemed a reasonable one, as it was the closest point for getting Evelyn to the shed.

She was lying on the ground wrapped in the blanket while the search for the key was undertaken, but once the door was open wide enough the body was heaved inside; the door was quietly pushed, closed and locked. Deep down, Evelyn's killer knew there would never be a return to move her again, so the key was thrown as far as possible into the tangle of grass and shrubs that extended way beyond the outhouse.

Eyam and its residents were asleep by two, and Evelyn Pearson was hidden for twenty-five long years.

1

Tessa Marsden sank down onto a bench facing the beach at Cleethorpes, and let the icy wind, blowing straight across the Humber Estuary, whip through her shoulder-length dark hair.

She felt numb, and it was nothing to do with the freezing weather; it was more shock at how her life had changed so much in such a short space of time. Two weeks ago she had been a detective inspector with the Derbyshire police, and now she was a partner in the Connection Investigation Agency, and looking forward to a different chapter in her life.

She watched as a boat chugged up the river heading towards Grimsby, and knew she had been right to blow all her cobwebs away by this spur-of-the-minute trip to the coast. It felt liberating.

She thought back to the night she had gone to bed and been hit by the realisation that she couldn't return to the discipline of a police life. A meeting with her superintendent the following day had put in motion the future for her, and a conversation with Beth Walters, at Connection, had sealed that future.

And now, here Tess was, sitting on the seafront at

Cleethorpes, a smile on her face, tears in her brown eyes that weren't all down to the bitterly cold wind, and a packet full of fish and chips in her hands. She dipped into the paper and pulled out a vinegar-sodden chip. Possibly, she thought, the best meal she'd had in the last couple of months. Time to come back to life, to face an unexpected career opportunity.

Luke Taylor pulled off his beanie hat, pushed his dark hair out of his eyes, looked around at the wreckage that used to be called an office, and slowly shook his head. Everything in his life seemed to be happening at considerable speed, and he had decided to drive down to Eyam village centre and drop into the office for an hour. He wanted thinking time, and this place was his future for sure now. Twenty years old, and a partner in a business...

Beth Walters owned the building, and the recent acquisition of Little Mouse Cottage at Bradwell had allowed her and her partner Joel to move out of the upstairs flat. It had only taken them two days to pack up, move out and get Stefan Patmore, their builder friend from the village, on board with converting the entire building into much bigger accommodation for the Connection Investigation Agency, jokingly referred to as the CIA by its owners.

The builders were at work despite the early hour; Luke could hear thuds and bangs from upstairs, and he walked across to where the lift had already been installed. This was such a bonus. They needed four offices, plus a kitchen area upstairs and downstairs, alongside toilet facilities on both levels. With a lift, they could offer wheelchair access throughout the building, and the old stairs that had led to Beth's home above had been utilised to accommodate visitors who preferred to use stairs.

They hoped to be able to move in properly within about ten

days, but in the meantime Luke was keeping the business semi-open by working in one of the old downstairs rooms that still had four walls. He eased himself around a pile of cladding, and headed for the desk that was always covered in dust. He sat down, rubbed his shoulder which didn't seem to be healing as fast as the break in his lower arm following a road traffic accident, and opened up the computer. He guessed he might have a window of about half an hour before the electric was disconnected for work to be completed, so he thought he would have a glance through emails, send replies to whoever needed them, then go home. His mum was still a bit precious about him, having so nearly lost him, and she'd been as happy as a pig in muck when he said cases were on hold while they had renovations done.

His door opened and he looked up in surprise.

'Fred! I thought you weren't starting till next week.'

'I'm not, but because I was owed holiday time, I finished with Playter's last weekend. Thought I'd pop in, see what's happening.' Fred Iveson was a tall, grey-haired man with a somewhat craggy looking face and the most piercing of blue eyes. He looked around, then at his watch. 'It's only seven. The builders are here already?'

'I arrived about five minutes ago,' Luke said. 'They were beavering away then. Beth said he was good, but he's really cracking on with it. That lift's fully working, so they can get stuff between the floors easily.'

There was a crash from upstairs, and Luke grinned. 'Ouch. Hope that didn't hurt.'

'So I'm in this room?'

'You are, but it will be bigger. We're moving walls down here, taking part of the office next door and adding it to this one. Then we're using what's left of that room and the old kitchen and toilet to create a new kitchen and toilet. We can add a couple of feet of that space to enlarge Beth's office. She wants to keep it, not move upstairs. Upstairs will be two sizeable offices for Tessa and myself, along with toilets and a kitchen area. Where reception was before Stefan dismantled it, will be a new reception desk that will no longer be open-plan as it was when I started on reception, it will be in a cubicle-type of little room. I think, after we were made to realise the dangers of the work we do, that we wanted to at least feel secure in this environment, so we're all going to have to learn to live with that. And then, of course, we'll need a receptionist.'

Fred nodded, absorbing what Luke was saying. 'I'm really chuffed to get this job, you know. I've known of the agency for a long time, and never expected a place to open up here. I wanted to leave Playter's anyway, and this happened at the right time. I think Beth was right too, when she asked us to call her Beth from here on. It sounds much more professional than her nickname of Mouse, and I wouldn't have felt comfortable calling her that.'

Luke laughed. 'It took me ages to get around to calling her Mouse, but I feel totally at ease calling her Beth now. She's definitely no mouse, I can tell you. I watched her fight at the dojo a couple of weeks ago, awesome. She's a black belt, fifth Dan, I believe. I go to the same dojo, and I wouldn't stop going for anything. Although I can't fight yet,' he waved his damaged arm and shoulder, 'I can still go and take in the atmosphere, listen to the instructions, watch the others. We've some little ones there I would hesitate before going up against. But believe me, Beth is a true expert.'

'Have we still got a kettle down here?'

'We have. They've not started in this area because, according to Stefan, this is the easiest part. I bought the milk yesterday, so unless the builders have used it, it should be in the fridge.'

'I'll make us a drink. Tea?'

'Please.'

Fred disappeared to inspect the kitchen, and Luke leaned back. His thoughts drifted. Things had changed so much in such a short space of time.

Beth's proposal had been that he buy into the business as a partner, commit fully to his future with Connection. At first he had laughed. 'I have just short of two thousand pounds in the bank. I'm sure that won't buy me a partnership on a market stall, never mind in Connection. But thank you for offering, you know I'd do it in a heartbeat if I could.'

And she had solved the problem. His compensation, whenever it came through, for the horrific accident that was the result of attempted murder, would be high, so his solicitor said. We can talk money when you get some, she had said. In the meantime, we make you a partner, give you a sense of security for your future.

And that was when the biggest bombshell of all had happened. DI Tessa Marsden was leaving the Derbyshire police and joining them as the third partner in the business. They both knew how bad a year Tessa had had, but when Beth told Luke that Tessa was going to be working with them on the private side of the detective industry, he had been shocked. And glad.

Fred returned carrying two mugs of tea, handed the one that said Gopher to Luke and said, 'I hope I got the right one.'

'You certainly did,' Luke said. 'We eat a lot of doughnuts, also chocolate digestives. They all used to say, "Luke will you go for" and Beth appeared one day with this mug for me.'

'They're good to work for?'

'I've never regretted my decision to apply for the receptionist job. I've all sorts of qualifications, and I'm a partner. What made you want to leave Playter's in the end then?'

'If I'm honest, it was that last job. We left the premises as soon as the arrests were made, and that poor woman...'

'It haunts me,' Luke said quietly. 'We had no idea she was on her own. We knew Tracy and Kaya Worrall had left, but she had that new carer.' Luke shivered as he remembered back to the last case of twenty nineteen for Connection.

'It woke me up, that case. I didn't want that impersonal thing anymore. I wanted to be part of something like this, and I contacted Tessa to say how sorry I was about the way it all ended. We had a long talk and I mentioned I was hoping to be moving on from Playter's, and she said "leave it with me". Thankfully, you all were in agreement, and here I am as security for Connection.'

'With a roving remit,' Luke said with a laugh. 'Don't forget I started as a receptionist, with a sideline as a gopher. Really, there's only Beth who sticks to her designated job. She's in recruitment, sees to all things corporate. What she earns the business is massive, probably offsets our lack of earnings, but our reputation is first class.' He sipped at his drink. 'Simply be prepared for anything, Fred. I am.'

2

Eyam was devoid of all Christmas lights, clear of banks of snow and everyone had drifted reluctantly to work after the long Christmas break. Children were back at school, and several people in China had caught a strange kind of flu that had killed a few people.

Connection was, at the most, a week away from being fully functional once again, and Stefan and his crew were exhausted, yet proud of what they had achieved in such a short period of time. The upstairs was finished and the downstairs was on its way to being two offices instead of three.

On that Monday morning the air felt as if it wanted to release a mountain of snow, and Joel Masters waved and blew Beth a kiss as he left for the journey to Manchester. His routine of travelling to the office every Monday and Thursday and working from home on the remaining days was an excellent compromise; the route was a nightmare on snow-covered roads and he hoped it would hold off with the white stuff until he was back home again. He drove down the hill from the cottage and onto the main road leading out of the village of Bradwell, then put his foot down. He wanted to be home early; the importance of the day for Beth was clear. Today Connection was reborn.

Luke was the first to arrive. Luke was always the first to arrive. Stefan had left the front door on free access, so Luke figured the men must be having to go in and out on a frequent basis. He pushed open the door and looked around him. He hadn't been in over the weekend but apparently Stefan's crew had. The rooms had been divided, doors installed giving access to the rooms and it almost looked smart. Apart from the pile of rubble in the middle of the floor.

He looked up from his inspection of the rubbish as he heard Stefan speak.

'That'll be cleared in ten minutes. It's the remains of the back wall, and you've got a fire door to get outside at the back, and easier access to that brick shed thing. We're going to smarten it up for you once we've worked out how to get inside with no key, and we can make that into your storage area for the folding chairs you keep for clients.'

'We haven't a key?'

'No. Beth always said it was too much trouble having to go right round the building to get to it, so nobody ever thought it might be locked. It is. I've left young Mick trying to pick the lock. Now you've got your smart new back door leading from the kitchen to the outside, you might as well make use of it. We'll clear all the spiders out, give it a lick of paint and get you some shelving. The chairs can stack underneath the shelving.'

'Sounds good,' Luke agreed. 'But don't mess about, if Mick can't pick the lock, batter down the door. What's a new door added to the bill that this little lot is costing anyway?' Luke said with a laugh.

He turned as he heard the front door open, and Beth and Fred entered together. He could see Tessa outside with her head in the boot of her car and he knew his first day as partner was about to start.

They convened in the completely finished office allocated to Beth, where four champagne flutes stood in the centre of her desk. She produced a bottle of champagne from the fridge in the kitchen, and poured four drinks. Handing them out she said, 'To us, to Connection, to friendship.'

They toasted, and then sat around the desk. Luke handed out four pieces of paper. 'This is a CV. I think we're all agreed we need a receptionist, and yesterday I think I found her, accidentally. Do you remember, Beth, a year ago I took an afternoon off to go to my neighbour's funeral?'

She nodded. 'Only young, wasn't he?'

'Thirty-seven. His wife is Cheryl, and she was a solicitor at one of the big practices in Sheffield, but when Keith was given the terminal diagnosis, she left. He died six months later, and for the last year she's stayed at home. Her kids are thirteen and fifteen, so she doesn't need to be there for them coming home from school or anything, and she's decided to look for a job. She wants something local. She's far too qualified for us, but as she says, they're her qualifications, and she can use them where she wants. I asked for her CV, and she knows the salary we're offering, so we need to talk to her.'

'Is she nice?' Tessa said.

'She's lovely. And quite happy to run errands, do junior duties alongside more senior ones. I think she'll be perfect, but you all need to meet her.'

'Is she available this afternoon?' Beth asked.

'I'll text her. Two o'clock?'

'That's fine by me.' The other two agreed, and Luke took out his phone.

A minute later he opened up the reply and laughed. 'It's fine by her,' he said, 'but she's told me off for using the letter 'u' instead of y o u. She has this phenomenal range of words, brilliant at crosswords. My nan is always messaging her with clues she can't get, but Cheryl always knows the answers. Anyway, the upshot is that she'll be here at two, and thanks you all for the opportunity.'

There was a muted cheer from the workmen downstairs, and Luke laughed. 'I'm guessing Mick has managed to pick the lock of that outhouse. Didn't you get a key to it, Beth, when you bought the place?'

'I didn't even know it was there. I've never been round the back, and don't forget there wasn't direct access other than walking all the way around the building until Stefan put us the new door in this weekend. I wouldn't have gone in anyway, it will be full of spiders.'

With the exception of Luke they all read through the CV, quietness filling the downstairs office.

A knock on the door disturbed their thoughts, and Luke, being nearest, opened it.

Stefan stood there, his usual smile absent. 'Sorry to disturb you, but you might want to come with me. We've opened that door eventually, but there seems to be a body inside.'

Mick was looking sheepish, while directing a hosepipe at a pile of vomit. 'Sorry about this,' he muttered, 'but I was first in. We've got one or two who're scared of spiders, so I offered. I'm a bit scared of bodies, I reckon. Never seen one before.'

Tessa slipped on the nitrile gloves she had grabbed as they

moved downstairs, and tentatively reopened the door that Mick had slammed shut.

'I checked,' Stefan said. 'It's only bones, so they've been there some years, I reckon. No wonder there's no key.'

Tessa opened the torch on her phone and swept it around the small outhouse before lowering the beam of light to the floor.

The body was on its back, and was a definite human shape. There appeared to be sizeable remnants of a blanket, along with bits of clothing around the bones. For a moment she had hoped it would be a dead dog but her hope was immediately dashed. She took photographs as best she could in the dim light, then moved aside to let the others stand in the doorway. 'Don't go in,' she warned them, and switched off her torch app, ringing DI Carl Heaton in one fluid movement.

'Tessa? You okay? Opening day, isn't it?'

'It is indeed, and what an opening day it's proving to be. Can you come? And you'll need a forensics team.'

'You've killed somebody already?'

'We haven't, no, but I'd venture to guess somebody has. I don't know if you know or not, but there's a little brick outhouse round the back of the offices. One of the workmen has managed to get it open, and lo and behold there's bones.'

'Bones?'

'Been here a long time, I suspect.'

Carl sighed. 'We'll be there in half an hour. Thanks, Tessa. Put the kettle on.'

'How long?' Carl knelt down by the side of Rory Thomas, the forensic specialist in bones.

'It's definitely a guess, but I reckon at least twenty years. However, it's not a guess when I say I suspect foul play.' He gently rolled the skull, and the indentation in the side of it indicated something heavy had come into contact with the fragile bone structure.

'So whoever it is didn't accidentally lock themselves into this outhouse and simply die because they couldn't get out?'

'No, it's definitely not that convenient, I'm afraid, Carl. For a start, it's the sort of lock where you have to turn a key, hardly conducive to an accidental locking in, is it? Somebody put this body in here, either dead or nearly dead. I'll arrange to get it moved, and then leave the lads to go over this place with a fine toothcomb, see if we can help you in any way.'

Carl nodded, and stood. 'Thanks, Rory. I'll wait for your report.'

'This is where Tessa is working now?'

'It is. This is their first day of the re-opening. That's why it's builders who found the body. They're going to make this little outhouse into a storage facility for them, according to what Luke's told me.'

'They'll have to delay that,' Rory said, feeling his knees creak as he stood. 'It's a crime scene, so we'll get it sealed with tape. Nobody in or out, for any reason. Can we leave somebody here?'

'You think we'll need that level? The bones are old...'

'This news is going to spread like wildfire round this village. There's a raft of police cars out front, so the villagers will all be speculating. And somebody might, at this moment, be covered in sweat because they know who it is, and what the circumstances are. Whether it's twenty minutes or twenty years, we need to protect this scene for a couple of days.'

'You're right, of course. I'll sort it. Is the body cleared for removal?'

'It is. I'm going back now, and I'll make a start as soon as I get

16

it on the table. I believe it to be a woman, before you ask. The hips are wider on a fully grown female, so it's not a teenager, older than that. I'll know more when I run some tests. Give me a call about four, might have something for you by then.'

Carl nodded. 'An ID would be good.'

'And that's merely a taster, Fred,' Tessa said, a wicked grin on her face. 'Bodies materialise here.' She turned to Beth. 'You've never once been in there since you bought the place?'

'God, no!' Beth's response was fast and emphatic. 'Did you see inside it? Black as pitch, and cobwebs everywhere. There could be rats, mice, anything, but definitely tarantulas, black widows, trap door spiders...' She shuddered. 'The estate agent said there was no key to it, and I remember saying I would never need one. He thought it was funny, but I bet he's not laughing now, because he could end up being questioned about this. Those bones have clearly been there much longer than I've owned this property, so that takes me off the suspect list. Doesn't it?' Her voice rose in a hopeful query.

'Not if you've had the bones stashed somewhere waiting for a good hideaway spot.' Fred spoke quietly, trying to keep his face straight.

'We'd best not set the alarm tonight,' Luke said. 'Carl said he would put a man on duty, but if we leave him the back door open he can at least get a warm drink, and get some shelter from the cold. He'll be frozen. All the front of the shop can be locked as usual.'

Beth stood. 'Speaking of warm drinks, I'll make us one. Coffees?'

They all nodded, and she went in search of the necessary stuff to make the drinks in the newly kitted out kitchen. She heard the buzz of the office door opening followed by the ping of the old shop doorbell they had preserved, and a woman was standing there holding a huge bunch of flowers. There were roses, chrysanthemums, gypsophila, ornamental cabbages – far too many to identify without scanning them through the app on her phone, and she gently kissed her engagement ring. 'Thank you, my love,' she whispered.

The florist handed them to Beth with a smile. 'You know who they're from?'

Beth nodded, then thanked her before reading the card.

For Beth, Luke, Tessa and Fred, congratulations on your new venture,
and best wishes on your first day of working together. All my love,
Joel. Xxx

She stepped back into her office and laid them on the table. 'From Joel, to all of us. We now need four vases...'

3

The office was busy with members of the forensic team scurrying backwards and forwards once the bones had been carefully and respectfully removed from the premises. It seemed that once the black van had driven away, it was a signal for the hustle and bustle to start. White-suited men and women took over the ground floor as they used the corridor leading through to the newly installed fire door at the back.

Stefan took out his notebook and made alterations to the work programme, guiding his men to finishing the downstairs offices. He checked the weather forecast to see that snow was still promised, but probably not until the following day – his idea of doing the preparation work on the outhouse to avoid bad weather conditions had now flown out of the window, so his rethink was to finish the interior as the outhouse looked like being out of bounds for a couple of days at least. He grinned as he realised the forensic team would probably get rid of all the spiders for him. Every cloud...

With the upstairs fully completed and therefore not the noisiest place on the planet, Beth decided they should chat to Cheryl in Luke's office – it was the furthest point from the clatter in the outhouse, and not directly above the finishing jobs being done in the reception area and Fred's office.

Luke's pride was overwhelming him, and he sat behind his carefully chosen desk, in his carefully chosen chair and surveyed his kingdom. Four quickly purchased glass water jugs had been bought from the Co-op across the road, and his vase of flowers stood on the windowsill behind him.

The resignations of two partners had given him a future he could never have dreamed of two years earlier when he'd joined Connection as their junior member, but hard work and total dedication had earned him qualifications that now equalled Beth's, and he cast his eyes over the certificates, uniformly framed and hanging on his wall.

His little corner of the Connection world prior to Christmas had been the reception desk downstairs, but suddenly everything had changed, and now he would be part of the team interviewing for the successor to his post.

He heard the lift door open, and within seconds Beth led Cheryl into his room. The lift brought Tessa and Fred up on its second journey, and Luke poured coffees for everyone, before sitting down.

'Cheryl, welcome to Connection. Everybody, this is my next-door neighbour, Cheryl Dodd. From your left, Cheryl, we have Beth, me, Fred and Tessa. Everybody has read your CV, so we'll open up to questions.'

Cheryl sat quietly, her long curly blonde hair looking a little windswept. She had put on a touch of lipstick, more to give herself confidence than anything, and she turned towards Beth as she asked the questions.

'First of all, Cheryl, I apologise for the noise. We have builders in, but only for a further three days now. We also discovered a body in the outhouse this morning, so there's a forensic team in, causing disruption for a couple of days. I can assure you we don't normally have bodies on the premises and we certainly hope this is a one-off. Okay, your CV is excellent. You're way overqualified for this position, and I could place you anywhere you wanted to go, as I deal with recruitment. Why us?'

Cheryl gave a half smile, as if she had known the question was coming. 'When I finished work to care for my husband in his last months, it gave me a lot of cause to think. I was travelling from Eyam into Sheffield every day, and the stress of that eventually begins to tell. I got up the morning after I'd left work, and it was as if a bolt of lightning hit me. I knew then my career in the legal world was over. I would never go back to it, and no matter what your decision is today, that will remain the same. I don't need to work – my late husband was a clever man, and he left me well provided for, with the mortgage cleared and funds for seeing our two children through university if they decide to take that route. I have taken a year to grieve this wonderful man, but now I need something in my life. I have seen how this company has been so good for Luke, and we had a chat about how things were changing for him. Again it was the old lightning bolt, and so I updated my CV and took it to him. And here I am.'

'You specialised in Public Law?' Fred liked the woman, and hoped it showed in his question. He had been quite prepared to sit quietly, but suddenly he felt he should take part.

'That was my role when I left, but I started in Conveyancing. I gradually moved onwards and upwards as I qualified, but it was Public Law I always wanted. Now I don't want it at all, but I do bring my knowledge to this job, even if it might not be needed.'

Luke smiled. 'Anything could be needed at any point when you work for Connection.'

Twenty minutes later Beth asked Cheryl if she would mind waiting downstairs, and within one minute they sent Luke down to bring her back up. The decision had been unanimous.

Cheryl settled into her car with a huge smile on her face, her mind going through her wardrobe trying to decide what she would wear the next day. She spoke to Keith in her head every night before going to sleep, and she would finally have something really good to tell him. If only he could speak back to her...

'Nice woman,' Tessa said. 'I'm glad we were all in agreement. And she didn't seem a bit fazed by the body found this morning. In fact, it's quite disconcerting that none of us are fazed by it.'

Fred smiled. He'd always liked Tessa. 'You have to take off your police head now, Tessa. That was the part I found the hardest when I went into the private sector. In the police we would go into full investigation mode, but when something happens like this has happened today, it's not our case, we're not getting paid for it, so DI Heaton will be clearing up this one. Old bones, though, never easy.'

'To be honest,' Beth joined in, 'since calls have been directed to my phone while the work was underway, I've got quite a long list of stuff we will be working on from tomorrow. I suggest we're all here by nine as that's when Cheryl's starting, and meet up in Luke's office again for an allocation talk, go through who's taking what, contacting the ones who've said they can wait until we get back to them – Fred, you'll be pleased to know there are three surveillance jobs on the list. The actual investigation side is down to you three – I've a mountain of stuff to do that's really built up over Christmas on the corporate and recruitment side, and believe me when I say we don't want to lose this work.'

'Is nobody curious about this body?' Luke asked. 'I am.'

'I don't think we're likely to learn much about it,' Tessa said. 'If it had been a body still with flesh on, maybe that would have made a difference, but this is a really cold case. All they have is bones, and a few scraps of clothing and a blanket that looked to be underneath the body. Maybe Carl will pop in and fill us in, but I doubt it, and to be honest it sounds as if we've enough work on to keep us busy anyway. This is really funny, you know, because I've spent the last two or three years telling everybody at Connection not to produce any dead bodies, because murders and suchlike seemed to always happen around them, and yet here I am, day one as a partner in the business, and we already have one.'

Luke had taken some work home and decided to go through it in their television-free room. He was sitting at the table, papers spread out around him, when he heard the doorbell peal. His mother's voice blended with the visitor, and then suddenly the door opened and Cheryl walked through.

'Sorry to disturb you, Luke. I wanted to bring you these.' She placed four cans of lager on the table, leaned down and kissed his cheek.

The surprise showed on his face. 'Thank you, but why?'

'For giving me the confidence to apply for the job, and for being part of the decision-making to offer it to me. If I could have described the perfect job, one where I can continue to study, one that will pay me a good wage, one where I was specifically told if I needed time off at any point for the children, to ring in and let you all know, this job would be it. And Beth has rung to say we're all in a meeting at nine tomorrow to discuss who's doing what with the jobs that are some sort of list she has. Apparently this will be a big part of my job, handling the phone calls and appointments. I suddenly felt overawed by how lucky I have been that this job not only came along, but came along at the right time in my life. I simply wanted to say thank you for the part you played in it.'

He grinned. 'You're welcome. Let's hope you're still saying that at the end of the week. It was unanimous, by the way. Everybody wanted you as our receptionist, everybody saw what you would bring to Connection.'

She moved towards the door, and Luke spoke again. 'You said the opportunity to study?'

She turned. 'I did. I saw all those diplomas on your wall, and while I have quite a few of my own, I don't have the ones you have. I will.' She winked, laughed and went towards the kitchen to find Luke's mum.

PC Ray Charlton moved in and out of the Connection kitchen all night long. It was bitterly cold, and although snowflakes fell they didn't last. It amused him that it was simply too cold for snow.

He made numerous cups of tea, heated soup up in the microwave at midnight, and watched the little brick-built hut with the eyes of an eagle. He wouldn't be there for the briefing, he'd be fast asleep in bed, but he knew he would be ringing the station in the afternoon getting all the updates on how long the body had been a body and not a human being.

He was on his sixth cup of tea, wrapping his fingers around the hot mug, when he thought he saw movement, but when he heard the soft miaow he relaxed. He wouldn't be putting the black cat into his report. It wandered into the kitchen, and he put down a saucer of milk. The cat lapped at it, cleaning the saucer effectively before walking out and leaving Ray to his lonely existence.

Ray's replacement arrived a little before seven, and Ray had nothing to report. A quiet night and here's the kettle was almost all he had to say.

The cat watched him go, then wandered around the back of the building and into the kitchen once again. The little animal was offered milk on a saucer, and it was gratefully drunk. Sometimes opportunities had to be grabbed with all four paws.

4

Cheryl parked up in the Co-op car park and walked across the road to the front door of Connection. Luke greeted her with a smile and a good morning, as he held open the door for her.

'I'll do you an entry tag before you go home,' he said, 'and sort out a set of keys for everything else. Giving you access to the main door is the biggy in case you're here before the rest of us.'

'The others are here?' She glanced at her watch and saw she was fifteen minutes early.

'They are, but on the investigation side the hours are much more flexible. Beth doesn't really work out in the field so tends to keep regular hours, but the rest of us come and go whenever we need to. You'll get used to it, simply make sure if they're going out you know exactly where they're going and what their plans are. It took me a year to get them to do that. There's lots of safety features I need to show you, but we'll concentrate on the main items today. Half of it the others don't know about, it was my own way of making sure they were safe, or undisturbed when they were working on stuff that was a security issue, and I'll take you through all that as time goes on. Today it will be basics.' He

26

pointed towards the Co-op. 'The main thing you need to know is that we buy buns and biscuits, tea and coffee, from that shop, and we have petty cash for it.'

'We need some now?'

'No, I stocked up a couple of days ago. Let's go up to my office, grab a coffee and find out what delights Beth has been collecting since we finished on Christmas Eve.'

Laughter drifted out of Luke's office as the lift door slid open, and Luke and Cheryl walked through the door to see Tessa, Beth and Fred already seated and drinking coffee, an open tin of shortbread biscuits in the middle of the table, alongside a plant in a pretty container.

'Good morning, Cheryl,' Beth said, and pushed the plant towards their new receptionist. 'That's a welcome gift for your desk.'

Cheryl laughed. 'Thank you, that's lovely. I'll treasure it. It will die, my fingers are more purple than green, I think, but I promise to try to keep it alive for as long as I can. What is it?'

'Don't ask awkward questions on your first day. It looked pretty in the garage where I get my petrol, so I bought it to brighten up the reception. Did it need to come with instructions?'

'Kind of. I'll research it,' Cheryl said with a grin. 'I'll talk to it every day, that apparently helps. And it is beautiful, at the moment.'

Tessa passed her a coffee and all five of them settled around the table.

'Okay,' Beth began. 'This is a pretty momentous occasion for Connection. There have been many changes since Christmas, but apart from a body in the outhouse it has all gone smoothly. Stefan Patmore is a miracle worker. I rang him the day after

Boxing Day within a couple of hours of finding out how much our work life was going to alter, and asked him to meet me here to sort out structural adjustments. He gave me a four-week estimate, and he has definitely kept to that. In fact, he's in front. By the end of today, despite there being strange police personnel walking in and out, everything but the outhouse conversion to storage will be finished. From tomorrow we'll all be in our own offices. Any questions on that?'

'Not on that,' Luke said, 'but can we skip back to the body. Do we know anything?'

'A little,' Tessa said. 'I spoke to Carl last night, and it seems the bones have been there for about twenty-five years. It was a woman, twenty to thirty age range, and they're running DNA from bone marrow. There was a little bit of clothing, and that's going through all sorts of tests currently. She was a size twelve, according to a label in the back of her skirt but so far, that's it. Carl said they're going to go on the evening news with it, asking for anybody who knows of anyone either reported or unreported as a missing person to come forward. They've got somebody going through mispers from thirty years ago, and onwards.'

Luke looked a little crestfallen. 'Nothing we can get our teeth into then.'

Tessa laughed. 'Not really, it's a police investigation. Beth, for goodness sake give him something to do, he's chomping at the bit here.'

Beth grinned and pulled out a piece of paper. 'Before I do, I want to say welcome back, Luke. We've missed you, and don't do anything dramatic with that arm, I know it's still hurting you.'

'It's not!'

'It is. I spoke with your mother yesterday afternoon in the Co-op.'

Naomi Taylor worked on the checkout tills in the

supermarket, and all of them knew her well, much to Luke's chagrin. There and then he decided he had to imbue his mother with a sense of worth, and talk her into upping her career inclinations. She could do so much more than work on a checkout till. She could maybe work in Baslow where she wasn't likely to bump into anybody from Eyam…

'Before I hand these out,' Beth continued, 'there are going to be changes made. This business is growing and we may need to take on an assistant for my side of the business. I have, over Christmas, signed contracts with three new lucrative companies, courtesy of Joel. There is no reason for this to stop at three, he can filter lots of stuff our way, but there is a limit to my brain capacity.' She laughed and looked around the table. 'I hate to say it, but we may need Stefan back to discuss a third small office being installed as part of mine, but we'll cross that bridge when we get to it. What I'm really trying to say is that everything is looking good, and I'm in the process of preparing a report about it which I'll hand out to everyone as soon as it's complete. That, however, is only my side of our business. The investigation side has ten pending jobs that are ready to go tomorrow. As Fred has expressed a wish to be outside rather than in, I have put surveillance work on his list.'

There was a smile and a brief 'Yeah!' from Fred.

'Currently there are four jobs, Fred, and three of them are errant husbands, one an errant wife.' She reached down to her feet and brought up a package. 'Camera,' she said. 'Don't ask me how it works, but the man in the shop said it was perfect for what I wanted it for. Familiarise yourself with it. There's also some other stuff – listening devices, surveillance cameras and suchlike.'

Fred's eyes gleamed. He thought Christmas Day had been three weeks earlier but it seemed it was actually today. 'Thank you, boss.'

'I'm not your boss. I'm Beth.'

'Okay, boss.' It was obvious Fred wasn't really listening, he was looking at the picture on the front of the box, his fingers itching to delve inside and reveal the item that matched the picture.

'Tessa, there are two on your list. Both these cases came in at different times, but I get a feeling there's a connection. It's a stalker situation, but whoever is doing the stalking is possibly targeting two different women. Either that, or we have two stalkers. However, the women live in Bakewell, so when I was speaking to the second woman, two days after the first, it made the hairs on the back of my neck tingle. Both these calls came in last week, and I told them we would have somebody there to talk to them this week.'

Tessa reached across and took her list. 'I'll be on this tomorrow. I'll phone them this afternoon and make an appointment.'

'I'll need to know.' Cheryl's voice was clear.

They all turned to look at the previously quiet member of their group.

'Simply saying,' she continued, 'if you're not sitting behind your desk, I want to know where you are. It strikes me that there could be a modicum of danger inherent in your jobs, and therefore I need to know where you're going, any appointments you have, even personal ones, so I can facilitate the collection of your body should you end up dead.'

Luke punched the air with the arm that didn't hurt. 'Yes! I knew we'd got the right one for our receptionist. I tried to explain in the couple of minutes we had downstairs before coming up here this morning that I kept tabs on everybody. Most of the time you didn't know it, but I did. And she has an upgraded lighting system for signalling when you don't want to be disturbed, so use it.'

'There you are, everybody,' Beth said with a smile. 'We have our instructions. And what's more it makes perfect sense. Cheryl, if this arrangement starts to slip, you hound them until they comply with whatever you want your system to be. I'm sure you're more than capable of organising an efficient online diary system, that we can all access to see where everybody is.'

'Thank you,' Cheryl said, scribbling a few thoughts into her notebook that had, as if by magic, appeared in front of her.

Beth pushed a list across to Luke. 'And you got the others, Luke. There's a proper mixture in there. Four different cases, and none of them too stressful. Possibly easy to clear up, possibly not. I want you to pick up any slack. You're not one hundred per cent yet, so I'm bearing that in mind.' She held up a hand towards Luke as he opened his mouth. 'Don't argue. You almost died a month ago.'

Beth paused and looked around the table at her colleagues. 'This is the start of a new chapter for all of us, and I now officially resign as telephonist. All calls from this moment on will go to our super-dooper new switchboard thing that Cheryl has about five minutes to learn, so there will be no lists coming from me ever again. Thank you, everybody. Shall we have another coffee and a biscuit?'

Luke and Cheryl closeted themselves into her small reception area and worked out the telephone system between them. They also made a list of any stationery that was needed, and set up an account with a large company in Sheffield that would deliver, negating any trips out for printer paper and pens.

Both of them punched the air when Tessa rang from her office to give details of the appointments she had made for Thursday with the two women who had complained of being stalked. It felt like a victory for common sense, albeit a small one.

Fred also informed Cheryl of his activities, which he intended starting that same afternoon. A conversation with the wife who was employing them confirmed her husband was away and not expected back until the following day, so Fred had agreed to a visit armed with a contract, and she could tell him all about her problem. He needed a photograph of the straying spouse, and a deposit to confirm she accepted their terms. He had smiled when she said never mind about accepting terms, get the lying little bastard out of my life.

Fred left the office with a wave and climbed into his Land Rover. It felt good to be working again, and although he had enjoyed the morning getting to know everybody a little better, he was most comfortable when he was out and about. His new chapter was definitely beginning, and he couldn't be happier.

5

The forensic team left, extending their grateful thanks for all the teas and coffees they'd enjoyed. They gave permission for the crime scene tape to come down, and for the planned renovation to go ahead. They also guaranteed there were no spiders left in the shed.

Stefan organised two members of his team to remain on site, gave them specific instructions for the work that was needed to complete the job, and handed the invoice to Beth. 'Pay it when the job on that outhouse is complete, and you're satisfied with everything we've done. Any queries, ring me. I'm taking a couple of days off, the wife says, because she's got stuff she needs doing at home, but I can soon pop down here if there's anything you need sorting.'

Fred put the Great Hucklow postcode into his satnav and drove away. Amy Barker had told him to park on the drive; it was a double one, and there would only be her car there. He took his time. He had left himself half an hour to get there, but he fancied stopping for ten minutes and taking in the views. The hills around Great Hucklow, famous for facilitating the landing and taking off of gliders, had been a place of solace for him after losing his Jane in twenty-zero-one, and today he wanted to go there and think about his good fortune in starting work at Connection.

He had enjoyed his time at Playter's, but that had been a security business. Connection was the real thing, an investigation agency; investigating was something he had excelled at when a DS, but the time had come to say goodbye to police work, to start a new life. He would stop on the top of the hills and sit for a few minutes before going to see his first client.

Amy Barker opened her front door and waited for him to exit his car. The house was a large detached building with a double garage, along with a spacious driveway that could accommodate three cars if needed. She smiled as he walked towards her.

'Lovely place to live,' he remarked, extending his hand. 'Fred Iveson, Connection.'

'Come in, Mr Iveson. You know the area?'

'Extremely well. I've spent many hours at Great Hucklow, contemplating the state of the world.'

'Let's have a cup of tea, and then we'll talk.'

'That would be good. It might be a beautiful place to live, but it's also a cold place.'

She laughed, and her brown eyes sparkled as she did so. Her elfin features and the short dark brown hair made her seem much younger than the age he guessed her to be. 'We get used to it. It's a windy area, and in winter it becomes a cold windy area. We'll sit at the kitchen table if that's okay with you. It's the heart of our home, the kitchen, the warmest room, and it's where the biscuits are.'

Fred smiled. He liked this woman. He followed her through

an impressively large hall, with wide stairs that led to the first floor. She led him down the hall to a door at the end, which proved to be the kitchen.

She pulled out a chair for him, and turned to switch on the kettle.

'Tea? Coffee?'

'Tea, please. Milk, no sugar. Thank you.'

Five minutes later they were both seated, both nursing large mugs of tea and dipping ginger nuts into the brew. He knew he was going to get on with her.

Fred opened his posh new leather folder with Connection Investigation Agency stamped in gold on the front, and wrote the date on the top sheet of the replaceable notepad. He made a mental vow not to doodle on it, at least not in front of clients. From the pocket on the left of the folder he removed a contract and passed it across to Amy. She glanced through it and signed it, then handed him a cheque.

'Thank you, Mrs Barker. Now let's get down to why I'm here. You believe your husband is being unfaithful?'

'Please call me Amy. And anyway, if I'm right, I won't be Mrs Barker for much longer.' She pulled her phone towards her and scrolled through her pictures. 'This is the most recent picture of Tony.'

Tony Barker was tall, at least six feet, muscly, and was tending to a bonfire in the garden. He must have realised Amy was taking his photograph because his head was turned towards the camera, and a smile was on his face. His dark hair was short at the sides, but his fringe flopped forward on to his forehead. A handsome man.

Fred handed back the phone and pushed his business card towards her. 'Can you send me that picture, please? I'll print it back at the office. His name is Tony or Anthony?'

'Sorry, it's Anthony. Anthony James Barker. He's forty-eight, the same as me, owns an IT company with the head office in Tideswell specialising in business programmes, but he's recently opened a new office in Bakewell, a small one at the moment, where they're launching new games onto the market. Everything Tony touches turns to gold, he's highly successful. And up to six months ago I would have said he was also faithful. Not so now.'

Fred waited, letting her gather her thoughts. She scrolled through her phone, then sent him a second picture. 'That's Orla Sutherland. She works at the Tideswell office, started there about nine months ago. She's twenty-two, obviously a looker, and I believe they are currently together in New York. She's certainly not at work, and hasn't been in since Tony flew to the US last week.'

Fred looked at the picture. Long blonde hair, eyes of indeterminate colour, and a slim figure – definitely a woman you would look at and want. 'Did you feel anything was happening between them prior to this New York trip?'

'Kind of. He started working later, going for a drink after work, that sort of thing. One day it suddenly occurred to me I was spending a lot of time on my own, and we seemed to have stopped talking. He would always discuss work with me, but that's dried up now. I can't progress on suppositions, Mr Iveson, there's a lot of money going to be involved in this divorce, if it comes to that. I need proof. Photos, anything that will confirm what he's up to.'

'Please, it's Fred, not Mr Iveson. When does your husband return?'

'Tomorrow. He lands at four, Manchester, and his car is at the airport. I'll send you a picture of it. It's a Jaguar, midnight blue.' Once again she scrolled through her pictures and clicked send.

Fred made further notes, then gathered everything together and closed his file. 'Tony hasn't strayed before?'

She shook her head. 'Not as far as I know. He's extremely work-minded. We couldn't have children, and I think that's one of the reasons he became so deeply involved with the business. We decided adoption wasn't for us, so I found myself occupied with a couple of charities, I paint, and I have quite a fulfilling life. We enjoy holidays and we have lots of friends, but it was always about the two of us. Now it isn't. Don't let me mislead you here, Fred, I don't want to find out Tony is having an affair, I want you to tell me it's all in my head. But I don't think it is. He's changed. And this Orla is cropping up far too frequently when he does say anything. He gave me the briefest of kisses when he left for the airport last week, and within the hour I rang the office and asked to speak to Orla. I was told she had booked a week's annual leave. He goes to America a lot, and normally I'd go with him. He didn't even suggest it this time, said it was conferences and meetings every day, so I would be left on my own.'

Fred stood. 'I'm heading back to the office now to start a file for you, and if I have any further queries, I'll ring you. I'll only ring your mobile number, so if you can't answer, disconnect me and I'll wait for you to get back to me. I can't see this taking too long if your thoughts are correct, and if you change your mind about pursuing this investigation, contact me.'

'I won't change my mind. It's taking over my life, and that's not how I want to live. Thank you for your time, Fred, and I'll look forward to hearing from you after tomorrow's flight lands.'

Fred was back at the office shortly after three, and he wandered up to Luke's office for assistance.

'I need to know that I'm keeping files correctly, so can you take me through the method you use?'

'No problem,' Luke said. 'Bring a chair round this side of the desk, and I'll talk you through it. You'll devise your own system in time though, I did. You okay on computers?'

'I'm fine. I want to be careful to keep it to your routine system, because if I do it as a police report, it will probably be all wrong for here.'

'Doubt it, I picked Tessa's brains to make sure I was getting it right, so our method probably is the police method.'

They spent a pleasant half hour going through various aspects of the admin required to keep Connection on the right track, then Fred thanked Luke and headed back downstairs. He handed the contract and the cheque to Cheryl, who looked at them and picked up the phone to speak to Luke. Connection's new employees were on a learning curve.

Once Fred had completed his report he closed down his computer and reached into the bottom drawer for the new camera. The little instruction book that came with it seemed quite thick, and Fred sighed, but the sigh was soon forgotten when he realised he had a mere four pages of instructions in the English section, with at least twelve other languages tagged on in the rest of the book.

He spent some time learning his way around it, and then went out to Cheryl.

'Slip your coat on will you?' he said. 'I want to take your photograph with me across the road and you outside the office. I need to see how clear your face is on the picture.'

She laughed and obliged, remembering to slip her entry fob into her coat pocket. It wouldn't look good to have two employees locked out. Fred strolled across the road and stood outside the Co-op. He turned, took a couple of shots of her, then headed back to the office. Cheryl was already hanging up her coat.

'It's freezing out there now,' she said. 'Let's hope we don't get any snow.'

Fred laughed. 'I certainly hope we don't, I've to go to Manchester tomorrow and you know what the roads are like between here and there in the snow.'

She frowned at him. 'Have you told me you're going to far-flung places?'

'Oops. No. But I would have…'

'No you wouldn't. You'd forget. So, tell me now.'

'I'm leaving around one to one thirty, depending on weather conditions. You're unfortunately right, it could snow. I'm meeting a plane that's landing at four, so if it's a straightforward run I'll be drinking airport coffee and reading for a couple of hours. I'm hoping they've cleared customs by half past four, and I'll be taking photos of them. Then I'm coming home. I'll be in the office all morning, setting up appointments, and setting up files. Do you need to know anything else?'

'No thank you, that's pretty comprehensive. One thing – don't forget your wellies.'

6

Luke, as usual, was first to arrive in the office. He brushed the few snowflakes off his jacket before hanging it up and sitting at his desk. The coffee was soon filtering through his machine, and he opened up his computer.

The banging on the door was loud and it startled him. He could hear shouting, a woman's voice, and he ran down the stairs instead of waiting for the slow descent of the lift. Outside was an elderly lady, still hammering on the door.

He cautiously opened it, and she pushed past him.

'I've been watching for somebody to arrive. Is it her? Is it my Evelyn?'

He stared at her. 'I don't think I understand...'

'I've been told you found a body. Is it my Evelyn?'

Luke took a deep breath and glanced at his watch. Eight-oh-five. 'Look, Mrs...'

'Pearson. Harriet Pearson.' Her breathing was slowing, and the panic was leaving her.

'Mrs Pearson, we don't open until nine. I'm the only one here.'

'I only need one.'

40

Luke stared at her. 'Shall we have a cup of tea?'

'Please.' She seemed to crumple as she said the word, and Luke led her towards the lift.

'Come on. We'll go up to my office, and have a drink.'

Five minutes later she was sitting opposite Luke, her hands wrapped around a mug of sugary tea, and trying to start her story.

'She told me,' she said. 'Nosy Nora, we all call her. She's my neighbour. She told me you'd found a body. I want to know if it's my Evelyn. Twenty-five years she's been gone, never a word.'

A chill ran through Luke. He'd assumed now everything was cleared away that the whole thing had been dumped in the laps of the police, but here he was with a somewhat-distraught possible relative of the bones discovered in their outhouse.

'Tell me the story,' he said gently, 'and hopefully my partners will be in by the time we've finished our drink. They may be able to shed some light on things, but I doubt it because it is a police investigation. We can help you with that, though, put you in touch with the right person.'

She gave a slight nod. 'You're young to be a boss.'

'I'm lucky, but I do work hard. Is it okay to call you Harriet?'

'Hattie, I'm Hattie. I'm seventy-four now, and I honestly thought I would go to my grave without knowing what happened to my Evelyn. Evelyn was born in nineteen seventy, and about six months later my husband was knocked off his bike while going to work, and died. It was always the two of us after that. This is her.'

Hattie pushed a photograph towards Luke. The picture showed a headshot of a woman of around twenty-five, with startling red hair and deep brown eyes, her lipstick a vivid red, her mouth curved into a smile. A beautiful woman.

ANITA WALLER

'Evelyn met a man, Alan he was called, and I'll admit I was dreading the day she would leave home. And then she did. No note, just went. I never heard from her again, and she's been missing twenty-five years. That Alan seemed as baffled as me, called two or three times to see if she'd come home, and even reporting it to the police didn't help. She simply vanished. When I heard...'

'You thought it might be Evelyn. You live in the village, Hattie?'

'I do, near the plague cottages.'

'So tell me about Evelyn. What did she do?'

'She worked in a shop in Bakewell. Arts and Crafts place it was. Still is, different owners now though. She was clever with her hands, made things to sell in the shop while working there. She loved her job. It's why I couldn't believe she'd simply walk away. I live every day of my life hoping she'll walk back through my door.'

Luke heard the soft whirr of the lift, and then Tessa's cheerful *good morning, Luke,* as she passed by his door.

'Tessa. You got a minute?' he called, and his door opened.

'Come in, Tessa, and sit down,' Luke said, 'I'll pour you a coffee. This is Mrs Hattie Pearson. I think we need to talk to you.'

Tessa listened carefully to Hattie's story, and, like Luke, felt they had the answer to the identity of the body.

'Hattie,' she said gently, 'I have to notify a colleague of this, a DI in Derbyshire. This is a police matter.'

'They'll not want to know, will they?' Hattie's tone was bitter. 'They didn't want to know when I first reported her missing, and they've not wanted to know for the last twenty odd years. Why can't I pay you to investigate this?'

Luke looked at Tessa before speaking. 'It will be expensive. And the police will investigate.'

She snorted. 'No they won't. What can they find out with their limited resources? It will end up back in the cold case department, where she's been for all these years. Please, help me.'

Tessa leaned forward. 'If we do take on your case, it will have to be with the full knowledge of the police. We will have to inform them of everything we find...'

'I don't care who you inform as long as I'm first,' the old lady said.

'Look, let me make you another cuppa, and Tessa and I will go and have a chat. We'll let you know quickly if we can do this,' Luke said with a smile.

Hattie signed the contract and took out her debit card. 'I'm good for whatever it costs. Find who killed my beautiful Evelyn. And don't forget, as I'm paying for this, you have to tell me before you tell anyone else.'

'Our clients always come first.' Luke smiled. 'I'd like to visit your home, maybe get a feeling for your daughter's life, have a chat about her. Will that be okay?'

'Oh, I can do better than that,' Hattie said. 'She used two of our bedrooms. One is her art space, where she did a lot of her creative stuff, and the other is her normal bedroom. Since the day she disappeared I haven't touched them, apart from a quick flick around with a duster once a week. I always thought she would come home one day...'

Fred stood at the arrivals area with images of the man and woman he was seeking etched into his brain. He didn't doubt he would be able to spot the slim attractive blonde, and a tall handsome man by her side would confirm it was them.

In the end he almost missed them. It was Tony Barker he recognised, and Fred snapped their picture before following them to their car. He'd already found the dark blue Jaguar earlier by the old-fashioned method of simply walking up and down aisles of cars, acting as if he was a returning tourist looking for his own car. He managed to get a couple more photographs before they drove off, and he took his time driving back home, deep in thought. Tomorrow would be soon enough to report to Amy, tonight there was a film he wanted to watch.

The snow started as he approached his home, but he didn't think it would settle too much. He put his car in the garage, and sat for a moment. He felt he knew the woman who had been with Tony Barker, but his mind wouldn't give him any answers. He took out his phone and rang Cheryl.

'I'm letting you know I'm back and you don't have to send anybody out to recover my dead body.'

'Thank you.' She laughed. 'Did it all go to plan?'

'Kind of. I'll not keep you now, I'll tell you about it tomorrow. I'll be in the office before I go out to see our client. Did I hear right that we've picked up the dead body case?'

'We have if the ID proves to be who we think it is. Tessa is taking Mrs Pearson in for a DNA swab tomorrow, so they can test it against any they might get from the bones. She's a feisty lady, I'll give her that, our potential client. I liked her. She's signed a contract with us, but we're not taking her deposit until we have the proof it is her daughter. Then I think Luke will take it on, as he was her first point of contact.'

'You're settling in okay?'

'I am. It's so different to when I worked in a solicitor's office, and I'm loving it. And tonight the kids had cooked our meal to save me having to do it, so I could really get to enjoy this new career.'

Fred laughed. 'I'm going in to put a frozen lasagne in the oven. See you tomorrow, Cheryl.'

He disconnected, and climbed out of his car. His back felt stiff – too much driving and sitting around an airport tended to cause havoc with a spine – and he locked the garage door, then the car before he went through the door that led directly into his kitchen.

It was warm. The heating had been on for about fifteen minutes, and he poured himself a small beer, before sitting down. He thought through his day, then took out the camera from the smart leather bag it was in. He glanced through the photographs, and scratched his head. Unless Orla Sutherland had visited a hairdresser in New York for a makeover, this was definitely not her clinging on to the arm of the tall man laughing down into her face. Amy Barker was way off with her suspicions as to who he was seeing, but seeing somebody he definitely was. A dark-haired tall woman, her hair in a ponytail, was clearly blowing a kiss towards the lips of the man she was with, and he was responding with a laugh. This would make for an interesting conversation the next day.

Luke was thinking about bones. He was aware that they would be able to extract DNA from them, and as Hattie believed the body to be her daughter, that DNA only had to partially match Hattie's to prove the identity of the skeleton – to say for definite it was Evelyn Pearson. He was torn in his hopes; he wanted it to be Evelyn so Hattie's mind would be put at ease, but in another way he wanted it not to be so Hattie could continue to believe her daughter would return home one day. In his heart, he knew the answer.

Tessa had left the office with Hattie to go and have a talk with DI Heaton, and Luke didn't expect her back for some time. Carl and Tessa had been friends for too many years for such a visit to be over so quickly. Hattie would be whisked away to have her DNA taken, and Tessa would use the time to fill Carl in on the happenings of the morning. Then it would be cups of tea all round once Hattie was returned to Tessa.

Luke stood and walked over to the window, staring down at the brick outhouse that had caused all the problems. The workmen had finished, and although none of them had been to inspect the work, Mick had handed the key over that fitted the newly replaced lock and said it was finished. He'd slipped it onto his set of keys with the intentions of getting copies made for the others, and he went downstairs and out the new back door, holding the key in his hand.

The outhouse door unlocked easily, and he went inside. They had put shelving on two of the walls, and had left a space to store the folding chairs they used for large meetings. The walls had been painted white, and a bright white light had been installed in the ceiling, quite dazzling, necessarily so because of the absence of a window.

He looked around and stood quietly. It didn't feel strange, he couldn't sense the presence of anything despite bones having laid there for at least twenty-five years. He was glad it had been refurbished – he knew Hattie would want to go to the place where Evelyn had been found, and it was good that it smelt of fresh paint and new wood. He nodded, knowing he could comfortably bring her here.

He switched off the light and locked the door, then entered the kitchen through the door he had left open. A small black and white cat was sitting in the middle of the floor, almost as if it was waiting for him.

'Hello,' he said. 'Who are you?'

The cat miaowed.

'Really? You want some milk?' He crossed to the fridge, found a small dish and poured out some milk. The cat lapped quietly, clearing the dish, then walked around the kitchen as if inspecting it.

'You have to go now,' Luke said, kneeling down to stroke the young animal. 'I'll bring some food in tomorrow for you in case you drop by again.'

The cat looked at him for a moment, then walked towards the door, and outside. Luke locked everything up, and headed home.

7

THURSDAY 16TH JANUARY 2020

'Mom, is it okay if I take a box of cat food?' Luke called upstairs, where he could hear his mother trying to persuade his young sisters to get out of bed.

There was a moment of silence. 'Luke, I would have made you some sandwiches if you'd asked. But if you want cat food, help yourself.'

Luke grinned and reached up to the top shelf in the pantry for a box of Whiskas. He stashed it into his backpack, and called bye as he left the house.

Fred was in before anyone else, and printing pictures off when Luke walked through the door.

'Morning, Fred. You got a result then?'

'Of a sort. Yes he was with someone else, as his wife thought, but I'm as sure as anything that it's not the woman whose pic she sent me from her phone. That woman was younger than this one, and she was dark-haired not blonde. I could be in for an interesting morning.'

The office front door opened with the sound of the gentle ping of the shop bell, and Cheryl called out, 'Morning, boys.'

Fred lifted his head. 'Boys? I like this woman.' He watched as Luke placed the box of dry cat food in a cupboard. 'That your lunch?'

'Don't you start. I've had enough sarky comments from my mother. No, a little cat came in last night, so I gave it some milk. I've brought this in because it might pop in again. I like cats.'

'If you've given it milk,' Fred laughed, 'I can guarantee it'll be back. I'll watch out for it, we'll not let it starve. Might be a good idea to nip it across the road to see if it's been chipped though. The vet can scan it and tell you.'

He gathered up the printouts, placed them carefully in a cardboard folder, then switched on the kettle. 'I'm having a coffee before I head out to Great Hucklow. You want one?'

'I do. I'm hoping Tessa will be in early, to fill me in on yesterday. She took Hattie for a DNA test and to meet Carl. Then I'm going to Hattie's house, I need to ferret around in the rooms she's preserved. I'm taking a recorder, I reckon she'll have lots of information to pass on that she's not considered yet. She was too distraught yesterday to think straight, but I'll get her chatting properly today.'

'I'm seeing Amy at half past nine, then I'll probably come back here, grab a sandwich and head off out to two appointments this afternoon who've also got errant significant others. The fourth one on my list has cancelled. She actually caught hers on the job, so to speak, so doesn't need us. She's booted him out. You got a girlfriend, Luke?'

'Nope. I did at school, but we drifted our separate ways after we finished there, and since then I've worked odd hours, no time to meet anybody, have a date, anything. I did evenings in a restaurant before I got the junior job here, and once I'd started here I seemed to fill every hour there was, my choice. I took exams, so studying and the job took all my time. Working here, we come across a lot of failed relationships – it sort of puts you off a bit.'

They took their drinks, and sat at opposite sides of Fred's desk. Luke sipped at his coffee. 'You don't have a partner?'

Fred shook his head. 'You know the old saying that there's one person in the world that is meant for you? I found mine.' For a couple of seconds he closed his eyes. 'In September 2001 Jane had to fly to New York with her job. She was to be away for a week, had lots of meetings booked in, and I couldn't get time off to go with her. She was at a breakfast meeting on the eighty-seventh floor of the North Tower when the first plane hit.'

'Oh my God, Fred, I'm so sorry.' Luke's eyes were wide. 'Me and my big mouth. I shouldn't have asked.'

'I don't hide away from it, Luke, not now. I did for the first year, but eventually I went to the monument they've built and it settled my mind. The anger went; it was destroying me. I made my peace while I was in New York, and I can talk about it now. I loved Jane, there'll be nobody else. I became immersed in my job until one day I thought enough is enough and walked away from it. I had a couple of months getting my garden into some sort of shape, then went to Playter's, and finally to here. So don't ever be afraid to mention nine-eleven, I'm over that. You want me to find you a girlfriend?'

'No, I'll find my own.' Luke laughed. 'Thanks for offering.'

They finished their drinks, and Fred stood. 'I need petrol, so I'll get off now. See you later?'

'Probably.' Luke collected the two cups and took them into the kitchen. He rinsed them and dried them, and was about to walk out into reception when he heard the miaow.

He unlocked the back door and the little cat walked in as if he had every right to be there. 'Hi,' Luke said. 'You want breakfast?'

The cat waited. Luke put some of the dry food into a dish and poured milk into another one. He took note that he'd better replace the milk the cat was drinking.

He was sitting uncomfortably on the kitchen floor with the cat on his knee when Cheryl came to find him.

'Oh,' she said. 'Is he ours?'

'Not really. He arrived last night and I gave him milk, but he's come back today for breakfast. I brought cat food from home in case he did. I'm going to nip him across the road to the vets to see if he's chipped. We don't want to go stealing somebody else's pet.'

Cheryl gave Luke a hug. 'Sucker.'

With the cat zipped inside his coat, he ran across the road and into a place he hadn't been before, Eyam Veterinary Practice.

'Hi, Luke.'

He stared into the bluest eyes he'd ever seen. They were emphasised even more by the merest touch of blue eyeshadow, and a genuine smile.

'Maria? Maria London?'

'You didn't recognise me?'

'You used to wear glasses,' was his lame excuse.

'I've had laser eye surgery, don't need them anymore. So who's that under your coat?'

He stammered his way through explaining about the cat, and she laughed. 'That's saved you a vet bill. This little cat has been in before to have a chip check. It's definitely not chipped, it's looking for someone to love it, and take care of it. Is that you? And if it is, slow down on the milk, or buy proper cat milk, but water is better for him.'

He grinned, somewhat ruefully. 'Looks like it could be me. If he's still with the office in a week, we'll know he's made his mind up, and we'll book in to have him chipped. I work across at Connection.'

'I know. I've seen you come and go. It's been good to talk to you again.' She brushed back the blonde hair that had fallen forward onto her face. 'Are you going to the reunion?'

'Are you?' He had no idea what reunion she was talking about.

'I am. Maybe we could go together, then I won't have to talk to anybody I didn't like when we were all at school together.'

'Good idea. Remind me, when is it?'

'Saturday. Seven o'clock start... at the Drovers Arms.'

'I'll pick you up.' He took out his notebook. 'What's your address?'

She took the book off him, wrote down her address, and put a kiss at the end. Then she added her phone number, told him to ring it, and she added his to her contacts. 'There,' she said, 'we can contact each other if anything crops up to stop us going.'

Nothing, absolutely nothing, he thought as he raced back across the road clinging on to the cat, *will be allowed to crop up to prevent me going.*

The cat tried to escape as Luke fiddled to get his key card out of his pocket, but eventually the pair fell through the door.

'He doesn't belong to anyone then?' Cheryl said. 'Do we now have an office cat?'

Luke grinned. 'Seems so. He chose us, we didn't choose him. I'll sort him out. Food and stuff.'

The door opened and Tessa and Beth walked in together. They stopped, taking in the sight of Luke with a cat in his arms.

'I can explain,' he said.

. . .

Fred reached Great Hucklow a little early, so as on his previous visit he stopped for a few minutes to breathe in the fresh air of the surrounding hills and valleys. He loved Derbyshire, loved living and working there, and pondered the possibility of buying a house in Eyam. He liked where he currently lived, but life would be so much easier if he didn't have to drive to work on the days he was office-bound. When Jane had died he had been the beneficiary of her considerable assets and insurance payouts, as they had named each other as next of kin. It had enabled him to pay cash for a small house in Baslow, but starting at Connection had felt like a whole new world was opening up, and he needed to move on to keep up with it.

He took a deep breath before getting back in the car. *Six months*, he thought. *If things are going okay in six months, I'll start to find somewhere new to live.* He pulled out of the layby and drove until he reached the Barker house, where he waited until he saw Amy come to the front door and wave, their arranged signal confirming Tony Barker had left.

Fred drove onto the drive, and gathered up the cardboard folder with his leather one before leaving his car.

Amy smiled warmly. 'Coffee's on. Tony's at work, so we're good to talk. You had breakfast?'

He nodded. 'I have thank you, but a coffee would be much appreciated.'

He closed the front door behind him and followed his client through into the kitchen.

8

Fred took a small sip of his drink before opening the file. 'What I'm about to show you may come as something of a surprise. Yes, your husband was definitely with someone else, someone who blew him a kiss, but that doesn't tell us anything. However, one thing I am sure of is that this woman isn't the same woman I have on my phone, the picture you transferred to me a couple of days ago.'

The look of surprise on Amy's face was genuine, and she held out her hand for the picture Fred was holding. He passed it to her.

He watched her face drain of all colour as she saw the moment Fred had captured the kiss blown between the two subjects.

'You know her?'

'Oh, I know her all right. It's my fucking sister. Excuse the language.'

Fred thought that if it was indeed her sister, the bad language was totally understandable. And now he understood why he had felt he knew the woman. She shared the same facial structure with her sister.

'Your sister?'

She lifted her head, misery etched into her eyes. 'Yes, my sister Vee. Vanessa Noone. Married to Will but separated.' She held her hand out for the other pictures, and sat quietly looking through them.

'She's been with him before,' Amy continued. 'Vee is the company solicitor, and she occasionally has to accompany him to see clients where the projects are going to need complicated paperwork. The difference this time is he didn't tell me. He didn't say Vee is coming. And Vee is so professional. She would never have behaved like that, blowing kisses, and holding on to his arm. And this last picture, where they're standing by the car, is a full-on kiss.'

Amy placed the pictures on the table and stood. She walked across to a cupboard and took down a bottle of whisky. She offered it to Fred, who shook his head, then she poured some into her coffee. 'I need that,' she explained, before picking up the pictures.

Fred remained silent, knowing his client was thinking things through, and wondering what was coming next.

Finally she spoke. 'I don't know what to do. This isn't about Tony having an affair anymore, it's about destroying my mum. We're really close, especially since Dad died, because there's only the three of us: Mum, Vee and me. How in hell do I deal with this without Mum finding out? If it turns out to be exactly as it looks on these pictures, I'll lose my sister, my husband and possibly my mum. She has a heart condition...'

'You didn't know Vee was out of the country?'

Amy shook her head. 'No. We only speak if it's something we need a quick answer to, normally we text. I've texted with her a couple of times over the past week, but obviously didn't know she was three thousand miles away when she was replying. Shit, Fred. Tell me what to do.'

'Did Vee know you had concerns about Tony's fidelity?'

'No. I didn't want to say anything until I had proof. She would have been the first one I told, we're that close.' Amy wiped away a recalcitrant tear. 'I've never felt so completely alone.'

'Suppose it's a one-off?'

'One-off or fifty-off, if I can't trust him I don't want to be with him. Will and Vee have two children, two kids who adore Uncle Tony and Aunty Amy. I don't mind telling you, Fred, finding out it's Vee has floored me. Never in a million years—'

'I'm here to get you thinking straight,' Fred interrupted. 'You need further proof if you decide you can't ignore what's happening. You told me when I first came to see you that a lot of money was involved in any sort of divorce settlement. You are going to need more than these pictures. I suggest you create an opportunity to catch him out again with your sister, I'll be taking the pictures and then you pick an excellent divorce lawyer.'

She sighed. 'You're right. I'm going to have to be a damn good actress to get through the next few days while we're catching them together again, though. Really all I want to do is shoot the pair of them.'

'That's not allowed in this country,' Fred said with a smile, 'so I don't recommend it. What I suggest is that you treat you and your mum to a trip to the theatre, maybe in Sheffield, and stay overnight in one of the theatreland hotels. If this is a new relationship between Tony and Vee they'll take full advantage of you being away from home. I can set up a small motion-triggered camera in the bedroom and the lounge, plus I'll also be waiting outside with a camera for Vee's arrival. We can nail this... situation... in one evening if everything goes to plan.'

. . .

Luke stood outside Hattie Pearson's house and looked around him for a moment. The plague cottages, where so many had selflessly isolated themselves and given their own lives to save others, were across the road, but slightly higher up the hill. He had parked in the village car park and walked back round onto the main road, where he finally knocked on Hattie's door.

She greeted him with a smile. 'Come in. Cup of tea?'

'I'd love one. And you can talk to me about Evelyn.'

Hattie led him into the kitchen that looked out onto the small back garden, and he sat at the table while she busied herself making the pot of tea. Eventually they nibbled on biscuits and sipped at the brew, and she talked.

'She was a lovely girl, my Evelyn. She didn't have lots of friends, but the ones she did have were good ones, close ones. I asked them all if she was with them when she first went missing, but nobody had heard from her or seen her. She had this boyfriend, Alan, but I couldn't make up my mind about him. He seemed to care for her, but I think I was frightened he was going to be the one to take her away from me. It had always been the two of us, you see. I must say, when she first disappeared, he was genuinely concerned. But he gave up. I didn't. That's the difference with love, isn't it?'

'It certainly is,' Luke agreed. 'When she disappeared, had there been a change in her? Was she suddenly quieter? More outgoing? Anything at all that you noticed...'

He saw hesitation on Hattie's face, in her eyes. 'I didn't tell the police this because it sounded daft, still sounds daft, but she sang a song all the time. It was in the charts that year, but it seemed to mean something to her. It was the way she sang it, as though it referred to her.'

Luke waited.

'"Common People", by that Sheffield band.'

'Pulp? It meant something to her, you think?' Luke wrote in

his notebook. He needed to look up the lyrics, see if that could possibly lead them anywhere.

'That's the one. I know it meant something, but I don't know why. It wasn't anything to do with Alan, he didn't like it.'

'Did you ever feel there could have been somebody else in her life?' Luke was frantically trying to recall the words of the song but all he could remember was something along the lines of wanting to sleep with common people like you. Could she have met somebody with money? Somebody who sang the song to her?

Hattie sighed. 'I don't know. I know she seemed to be committed to Alan, she wore his engagement ring, but maybe there was somebody else. How you'll find out now, I've no idea.'

Luke put down his empty cup. 'Can I go through her room?'

'Rooms,' Hattie corrected. 'She had a craft room and a bedroom. Everything is as she left it, I flick a feather duster around occasionally. I can't bring myself to throw anything away. I'll leave you alone, I know it will hurt me to see you going through her stuff, but do what you have to do, Luke. Top of the stairs, first two doors on the right are Evelyn's rooms.'

Luke pulled on nitrile gloves, opened the door of the first room and saw it was a crafting area. He closed it quietly and moved onto the bedroom. The deep red curtains were closed, and he walked across to open them to allow some natural light in. He looked down onto the pretty back garden with its summerhouse and shed sited at the far end. It was a long garden, and the path wound its way down the length, connecting the back door with the garden boundary. Two bird tables held food, and a bird bath was close to the wooden building. Flower beds were scattered indiscriminately and he imagined in summer the colour would be dazzling.

He turned away from the window and looked around the room carefully before touching anything. The bedding had been removed from the double bed, but it was folded neatly and placed at the end of the bed, ready for Evelyn's return at any time. The bedhead was made of wood – oak, he guessed – and the base was an ordinary divan base. He lifted the mattress and winced at the pain that shot through his shoulder. There was nothing to see, and he was pleased he'd got that issue out of the way. He checked the drawers built into the base, but they only held jumpers. A flick through them revealed nothing.

The wardrobe matched the bedhead and he went through it carefully, checking all the clothes still hanging there after twenty-five years. In the pocket of a raincoat he found a couple of tissues, and on three coat lapels he found brooches. He took out his phone and photographed them, before closing and re-locking the wardrobe door. He then clicked merrily away making sure he had pictures of every corner of the room.

One chair, in front of the dressing table, had a jacket draped over its back, and he checked through its pockets. It was a blazer style, in black, and once again sported a brooch, although he suspected it was more of a badge as it had initials on it. He made a note in his book to remind him to find out what it was.

The dressing table revealed a diary, although he didn't get too excited about the find; from January to August when she disappeared, there were maybe only a dozen entries. He would take it back to the office and scrutinise it carefully, but she had clearly been no Samuel Pepys.

The drawers in the dressing table held underwear in the top one, and nighties and pyjamas in the bottom. He lifted everything out, then removed the drawers, checking nothing had been taped underneath or on the main body of the piece of the furniture. The drawers stuck slightly and he smiled to himself. *Needs a candle,* he thought. He put the clothes back, the underwear mainly white cotton, with the exception of one pretty bra and pants set in red, silky and sleek. He checked the label, realising these weren't what she normally wore, and gasped. The label said Harrods. They hadn't been removed from the pretty white hanger they had been bought with, so he photographed them along with every label attached to them, picked up the diary, and moved onto the craft room.

He wasn't sure how to go about tracking down a twenty-five-year-old purchase, but he was going to try. He closed the curtains and left the room as it had been when he entered it, wondering why the police, all those years ago, hadn't done anything about the diary or the underwear set.

9

The craft room yielded little, other than confirming what a talented woman Evelyn had been. Paper was carefully stored on shelving attached to the wall, and although it was brittle with age and faded at the edges, the colours were still bright. Luke flicked through a couple of the stacks, then moved on. There was a box containing handmade cards for all occasions, and he was astounded at the quality. He hoped she had sold them for what they were worth. There was modelling clay in bins that he suspected would be dried out and useless, but the part-finished figures she had been working on were miniature works of art. He quickly came to realise what a talent the world had lost when somebody had taken her life.

Luke felt intuitively that she had been happiest in this room; this was her private place, her escape to a world of creativity. Hattie had clearly encouraged her, and was still waiting for her to return to reclaim her domain. Two of the walls had been painted red, with cream on the two remaining ones, and he couldn't help but feel red was important to Evelyn. He filed it away in his memory to check it out with Hattie.

He spent half an hour in the craft room, but found nothing

of any help. He checked it looked exactly as it had when he entered it, before photographing the entire room. He repeated the action in the bedroom before quietly closing the door as he left to head downstairs.

Hattie looked up with a smile. 'You have time for a cup of tea?'

'I do.' Luke placed the diary on the table. 'Didn't the police see this?'

'I gave it to them, and the young chap, sat where you're sitting, flicked through it and gave it back to me. Said there was nothing much in it.'

'There isn't,' Luke agreed. 'But that's at first glance. I'm taking it with me. Everything else is exactly as it was in those two rooms. I've taken lots of photos because I didn't want to remove anything. If the DNA proves the body is that of Evelyn, they're going to take those two rooms apart. It becomes a murder investigation and that's a different ball game to a missing person investigation. It's also a different ball game to how they would have treated it twenty-five years ago. DNA seems to solve everything these days. Do you know where she got that pretty red set of undies from?'

'No, and I don't think she'd had them long when she disappeared. I'd never seen them until I looked in that drawer after she'd gone. They looked expensive.'

'I think they were,' Luke said gently. 'They were from Harrods. She liked red, I'm guessing. Her walls, her curtains, the undie set...'

'It's clear Alan didn't buy them for her.' Hattie smiled. 'He didn't like spending anything. He always said they were saving for a house, which I think upset me more than anything. And yes, she loved red. Her hair was red, completely natural. You know, Alan was really taking her away from me – or so he thought anyway.' She stood to pour the water into the teapot, and Luke took out a small receipt book.

'I'm leaving you with a receipt for the diary. As soon as I get back to the office I'm going to photocopy every single page, even the pages with nothing on them, because as soon as the police find out I have this book, they're going to kick off, so I shall simply hand it over with a smile. It's fine for you to show them the receipt, that covers you, and it's fine for them to know there is a diary. As far as I'm concerned, if they'd done their job properly when you reported her missing, this diary would be in their evidence files now. They can have it when I've finished with it. I haven't touched it with my bare hands, so my fingerprints won't cloud any issues, unlike the young PC who picked it up, then dismissed it as not worth bothering with.' Luke dropped the diary into his briefcase and took off the gloves.

Hattie stirred the tea, and poured milk into their cups. She tipped the teapot, and Luke held his breath. No spillage. What sort of a teapot poured perfectly with no spillage? He took the cup from her, and wrapped his hands around it, deep in thought.

'Did you have any theory of your own about what happened to Evelyn?'

Hattie shook her head. 'Not really. She gave me no clue she was thinking of leaving. We were remarkably close, always, and she was a good girl. Art, creativity, was her life, I encouraged it, and we discussed everything. I started to worry about where she was when she was two hours late, we were that close. As the days and weeks went by, and I saw that even Alan, quiet Alan, was concerned, I knew that wherever she was, she was unable to contact me. I never believed she was dead, I couldn't think that. Even up to those bones being found, I didn't believe she was dead. I expected to see her walk through the door one day and say "hello, Mum". I wove a story in my head that had her having fallen in love with someone unsuitable, maybe a married man, and the only way she could be with him was in total secrecy. I never thought she was dead. I can't say that often enough.'

'When do you get the DNA result?'

'Some time today. DI Heaton said he would come to see me.'

'Okay, when he does, you can tell him then that I have the diary.'

Hattie nodded. 'I'll tell him before he leaves. That'll give you a bit extra time. You're a good lad, Luke. I'm glad it was you I bullied into taking me on.'

Luke laughed. 'You're welcome. I'm used to being bullied by the older generation, believe me.'

Tessa pulled up outside a small house in Bakewell, and checked her watch. Ten minutes early. She sat for a while, then picked up her briefcase from the footwell before opening the driver door. Thursday had been the first day she could see both clients on the same day, and both women had been agreeable to her request that she do that. Denise Jordan was her first appointment at ten, and the arrangement Tessa had made was that she would see Lorna Thompson as soon as she finished with her first client. She had deliberately kept it from the two ladies that their cases were in any way connected – time enough for that when she could confirm facts.

She smiled at the thought that Denise Jordan was her first civilian case, and Tessa would be working without the protection of a police force covering her back. She walked slowly up the path, gathering her thoughts and her courage, and knocked on the door.

It was opened almost instantly, and Denise waved her through, before leading her into the lounge. The overall impression was green, and yet it wasn't. Accessories were cream and lifted the green on the wall to a pale one. It was a room in which to relax, that much was clear, and Tessa sat in one of the armchairs.

Aware of needing to put her client at ease, Tessa accepted the offer of a coffee, and while she was waiting removed her notebook and diary from her briefcase.

Denise placed the drinks on the coffee table, and sat facing Tessa, holding two pieces of paper. She handed them over. 'These are the notes that have arrived. They were hand-delivered, but I don't have CCTV or anything, so I don't know who brought them. I didn't want to take them to the police because my ex is a policeman with the Derbyshire force, and I don't want him to know about them. He's trying to get custody of our son, Alex, and he'd use this to help him.'

Tessa nodded, to show she understood. Time to find out who this officer was later. She slipped on her nitrile gloves, took the notes and opened them.

The first one was short and sweet. *Never go out on your own. I'll be waiting.* The second one wasn't so ominous but equally as scary. *You are beautiful. You won't be soon.*

Tessa looked at Denise. 'And these are the only two you've had? No phone calls, no texts?'

'There was another one, the first one, but I threw it away. I thought it was somebody being stupid. It said *Can't get you out of my head.* It was only when the second one arrived I began to feel uneasy, and then the third one had me ringing Connection. And before you ask, I can't think at all who could be sending them. I rarely go out to meet anybody, it's not that long since my marriage fell apart, and to be honest it's nice to have my home to myself, where I can relax with Alex who is so much more laid back now he's not seeing the constant battles between his parents – no, I can't begin to imagine who could be sending this rubbish, but it's a bit scary.'

'I need to take these away with me,' Tessa said. 'They're handwritten, which is always a help when we find the perpetrator, because we can do comparison tests, but there are a couple of other tests we can do. Has anyone but you touched these?'

Denise shook her head. 'No. Alex is only nine, I would prefer he knew nothing about this. And really I have nobody close I can tell.'

'That's good. It will be necessary to take your fingerprints to eliminate them from any others that may be on the paper.' Tessa reached into her bag and produced a small handheld fingerprint machine. The formalities were speedily dealt with and the machine returned safely to her bag. 'Now we come to your safety. Don't venture out on your own. If you can have groceries delivered, then do so. If another note arrives, I need to know immediately.' She handed her business card to the pretty, dark-haired woman facing her. 'These are my office and mobile numbers. If you feel you are in danger, always ring 999. If it's anything else, ring me. I'm going back to the office to begin work on this, but I'll ring you if I have any further queries. Is that okay?'

Tessa took the contract out of her briefcase and pushed it across the coffee table. 'I need your signature and deposit today. Full payment is when we have completed to your satisfaction.'

Denise nodded and signed without reading anything, then handed over a cheque. 'I didn't need to wade through the contract. You come highly recommended.'

. . .

Lorna Thompson could have been the twin of Denise Jordan. Pretty, shoulder-length dark brown hair, and troubled brown eyes.

Tessa followed her through into the kitchen and they sat at the table. She remembered the contract this time, and they sorted out that little detail at the beginning of the conversation.

'Tell me what's been happening,' Tessa said, hoping a smile would put the nervous woman at her ease.

'I've had some notes delivered,' Lorna said. She stepped to a drawer and took them out. 'There's three. They came over a period of about three weeks, and I don't know what to do.'

The notes were identical to the ones Tessa already had in an evidence bag in her briefcase. 'I need to take these. If any more arrive can I ask that you ring me before you open them? We can get DNA evidence from envelopes and possibly fingerprints from the note itself.'

Once again she repeated the ritual of taking Lorna's prints, and followed that action by placing the second set of notes into evidence bags. Once all that was out of the way she returned to the conversation.

Tessa gleaned from Lorna that she was single – she had split from her long-term partner six months earlier and definitely hadn't met anybody else. There was a pattern emerging and Tessa felt uneasy about it.

She drove away from Lorna's home wondering if other single women had been targeted but had simply screwed up the notes – was it a joke, or was it a real threat? Was it only Bakewell, or was the net cast much further afield? She put her foot down and headed back to Eyam, knowing she needed a discussion with one or more of her colleagues, and recognising life wasn't so simple now for checking for fingerprints and DNA as it had been three months earlier when her ID card had said DI Tessa Marsden of the Derbyshire Police.

10

Luke walked into the office to see the little black cat happily ensconced on Cheryl's knee.

'He's wearing a collar...'

'Beth bought it. It seems this little feller didn't want to leave us and go out into that nasty cold weather, so he now has a litter tray and feeding bowls. She says you're responsible for food. Oh, and she also said what's his name.'

Luke picked him up and looked at him. 'You need a name? Okay, let's think about this. You're a smart-looking cat, being mainly black, and that bit of white under your chin is a bit like a bow tie, so let's find a name that befits your obvious status in life. We'll call you... Oliver!'

The cat said nothing, climbed up Luke and sat on his shoulder.

'He'll be spoilt rotten,' Cheryl mused. 'Everybody's taken to him.'

'We'll wait a week in case anybody claims him, but according to Maria he's been checked out for ownership before, which tends to mean he's probably been abandoned, or simply didn't like where he was living.'

'Maria?'

'She works in the vets.'

'The nice-looking lass with the blonde hair?'

Luke walked towards the lift, Oliver still perched on his shoulder. 'I'll show him round upstairs.'

'Nice swerve, Luke Taylor,' Cheryl called. 'And her name's Maria London, in case you're interested.'

It took Luke a little over half an hour to photocopy the diary, and he couldn't help but notice the quality of it. The paper had been protected because it hadn't been opened for twenty-five years, and the weight of each page was considerable. Bought from a high-end stationery shop, he suspected. He finished the last page, and then saw attached to the end cover was a built in envelope for saving items. He eased it open and there was a tiny piece of paper in the bottom.

He used a biro to pull it out. It was lined, clearly torn from a notebook, and it said *I love you, M xxx*

This time using two biros he placed it carefully, if a little awkwardly, on the machine without touching it, and took the final copy of the book. He left it until he had gathered up all the pages, then he and Oliver went to find Cheryl.

'You have any tweezers by any chance?'

Cheryl picked up her bag. 'I do. You plucking your eyebrows?'

Luke laughed. 'No, something much more simple. I want to pick up a piece of paper without touching it.'

She rummaged in her make-up bag and handed him the requisite tool. 'And don't forget where they belong.'

Luke smiled, and he and Oliver headed back to the machine. He wedged open the envelope on the hardback with his biros, then carefully picked up the paper, sliding it down into the bottom corner. He hoped whoever came to claim the diary would think he hadn't seen it. They were more likely to say things if they thought he didn't know what they were talking about.

His gloved hands closed the book, and he slipped it inside a plastic folder, ready to hand over when someone requested it. He took the folder and the tweezers to Cheryl. 'The police are going to turn up here at some point and ask for this,' he said. 'Let's look efficient and have it locked in the safe.'

She nodded. 'No problem, boss. I presume I can put my tweezers back in my make-up bag though.'

She reached down for her bag, as the phone rang. She listened carefully, then said, 'I'm putting you through now, Mrs Pearson. Please hold.'

'For you, Luke. I'll put it through to Fred's office to save you galloping upstairs.'

'Hattie?'

'Luke, DI Heaton's left. I've told him you have the diary, so he's calling to collect it. Oh, Luke...' Her voice broke.

'It is Evelyn?' he asked gently.

'It is. I finally have some answers. I'm going to have a damn good cry now, and then wait for the Forensics team to arrive. He's getting them out here to go through Evelyn's rooms. Perhaps when that's been done I can think about sorting them out, but we'll see. It feels a bit double-edged, Luke, knowing it is her, but all hope of her returning is gone.'

'If you need to talk, Hattie, ring anytime. Go and have your cry, it will help.' He gently replaced the receiver and sighed. His feelings were extremely mixed now they had concrete proof of the identity of the bones, and he guessed it would be a bad night for his elderly client.

. . .

Luke was reading through the lyrics of 'Common People' when Cheryl rang to say DI Heaton needed to see him. 'Okay, Cheryl. Send him up.' He slipped the printout into his desk drawer, and smiled at Carl as he walked through the door.

'Carl. Welcome. Coffee?'

Carl nodded. 'Please. You okay now, Luke?'

'I'm good, thanks. I seem to get less aches and pains every day, and no longer on any sort of painkillers, so that's a big improvement.' Luke poured them both a drink, and handed Carl his in a Connection mug. 'Is this a professional visit, or are you here just to see us? Kat okay?'

Kat, silent partner at Connection, and pregnant wife of Carl, had removed herself from the business at Christmas due to seemingly non-stop pregnancy sickness.

'She's fine, vomiting more or less under control unless she eats eggs.' He smiled. 'I'm here sort of professionally. I've collected the diary. I presume you've looked through it?'

'In a random sort of way. I've photocopied it. I used gloves, so none of my fingerprints are on it. However, no doubt Mrs Pearson has told you it was handled by a member of the police force at the time Evelyn disappeared?'

'She has. And you haven't looked through it in any depth?'

'A glance as I opened each page to place it on the machine bed. Evelyn didn't seem to be much of a diary keeper, but I'll be looking more closely at it tonight. I'll take it home with me.'

Carl laughed. 'Nothing on telly then?'

'Nothing that's likely to interest me,' Luke responded. 'Are Forensics still at Mrs Pearson's home?'

'They are. Bagging up clothes and stuff when I left.'

'Huh! I don't want to come across as sarcastic, but it's a pity they didn't do that twenty-five years ago.'

'Sarcasm doesn't come into it. You're quite right. So the diary was the only thing you brought away with you?'

'It was. I did go through both of Evelyn's rooms, though, and took some photographs. You do know we've been employed by Mrs Pearson to find out what happened?'

'I do, which is really why I'm here. This will be investigated fully, Luke, no corners cut, and we'll be looking back as far as we need to go. We won't let it drop.'

'I'm sorry that Mrs Pearson doesn't trust you. I don't mean you personally, I mean the police. You let her down when her daughter disappeared, and she's not giving you a second chance. She wants answers this time, and she's decided we're more likely to get them than you are. I don't know whether she's correct in thinking that, but it's what our client feels, so we'll comply with what she says.'

'You'll keep me informed?'

'Of course, after I've kept Mrs Pearson fully informed. She's really pissed off with the police, you know.'

Carl sighed. 'I know. My reassurances fell on deaf ears, I'm afraid. After all this time it's possible the killer is dead also, but one way or another she'll know who did it.'

Luke took out the lyrics to 'Common People', and read them slowly, taking in the words, digesting what the five songwriters in the group had tried to convey. He knew the song, had heard it many times, but had never really listened to it. It was obvious it was about lovers from different backgrounds, but he felt it was a reversal to the lyrics with Evelyn Pearson. She wasn't the rich female as the song lyrics suggested, she was the poorer half of the equation mixing with somebody much more affluent. Somebody who could afford lingerie sets from Harrods... an older man?

Luke put the lyrics to one side and gathered together the diary sheets. I love you. M xxx. Was M the rich half of the relationship? Could Alan have been the unwitting cover for them? Maybe the diary sheets themselves would give Luke further clues, but failing that he could see him having to go on a trip to London, armed only with photographs of the lingerie still on the hanger and the set's tag. He held out little hope of getting a result from Harrods, but failure to try meant he definitely wouldn't.

The first entry in the diary was on New Year's Day, and Evelyn had simply inscribed *New Year's Day, and I have a headache.* Luke smiled. If he kept a diary, that would have been his entry for the current year. January the second revealed Evelyn felt a bit better and had enjoyed a quiet day back at work after the Christmas break. There were no entries until the fifth of January, when Evelyn revealed it was *Mum's birthday – 49! Next year a biggie!*

This small statement troubled Luke, knowing that although Hattie reached beyond that landmark age, Evelyn didn't even get to share it with her.

He had put together an Excel sheet that he had printed off, listing the dates from first of January through to the day Evelyn disappeared, the twenty-first of August. He wanted to be able to write thoughts as they occurred to him while he was reading through the diary, and he scribbled Hattie's date of birth down in the column dedicated to the fifth. Once again he grinned. The fifth column. *My God*, he thought, *it feels good to be back at work and letting my thoughts roam.*

He then added stars to the dates she had actually made entries, the first, second and fifth. *Okay, good start, Luke,* he pondered, *now find something that's even vaguely useful.*

January had intermittent entries. Alan was mentioned a couple of times; they had gone to the cinema to see *Pulp Fiction* and *Forrest Gump*. She gave *Pulp Fiction* three stars and *Forrest Gump* five, adding *brilliant* after those stars. Luke realised he had never seen *Pulp Fiction*, and decided it was something to do, in case it told him anything. The word pulp seemed to have cropped up twice, and yet neither suggested any clue as to why they were in the life of Evelyn Pearson.

February the fourth was the day they had seen *Pulp Fiction*, and inspired a longer entry than previously written by Evelyn. It said *Went with Alan to see Pulp Fiction at UCI, Crystal Peaks. Went for meal after. Met his friend and girlfriend. Mmmm.*

11

Luke stared at the entry. A friend of Alan's? And what did mmmm mean? Did she mean the meal was good, or had cupid already played his part and she was saying mmmm with reference to Alan's friend? Or Alan's friend's wife? Was mmmm her own code for his or her name?

He reached for the phone to ring Hattie – he recognised she would be the starting point for tracking down Alan – and was quite startled as it rang at the same time as Luke touched it.

'Hello?' he said, not really sure what to say.

'Luke, Mrs Pearson is here. She's got something for you.'

'Brilliant! I was about to ring her. Tell her I'll meet her at the lift door.'

Hattie clasped her hands around the mug, and sipped at the tea. 'I prefer tea to coffee.'

'I'll remember,' Luke said, as he pushed the plate of biscuits towards her. 'Help yourself, we like to feed our clients.'

'I've brought you something.' She carefully put the mug on

the coaster, reached into her bag, and took out a carrier bag which she pushed across to Luke.

He opened it carefully, wondering if he should be wearing nitrile gloves. Inside was the red silk lingerie set.

His brain kicked into gear as he realised what it was. 'The forensics team didn't take it?'

'The forensics team didn't see it.'

'Hattie! You can't do that!'

'I can and I did. It was there twenty-five years ago when they could have done something with it. I doubt they can get any information from it now, but I reckon you can. You see things from a different angle, I know you do.'

He stared at her and slid the set back into the carrier bag before placing it in his drawer. 'I was within seconds of ringing you when Cheryl rang through to say you were downstairs. Guess what I needed to know.'

She thought for a moment. 'Alan. You want to know where he lives.'

'More than that. I don't even know his surname.'

'Alan Egerton. As far as I know, he lives in Calver, but I don't have an address. He was married within about eighteen months of Evelyn's disappearance. He did come and tell me, but I've no idea who he married. I wasn't interested. I never had him down for doing anything to hurt Evelyn, he was too dopey and soft.'

Luke gave a brief nod. 'Thank you. It's a start. If I track him down, I'll let you know.'

She smiled. 'Oh, you'll track him down. And when you've managed to get some information about that Harrods set, you can pass it on to the police. I'm not withholding anything from them, it's simply going via you first.'

. . .

Tessa could hear Luke talking in the other room, and the fact that she could hear him talking told her exactly who his client was. He had had to raise his voice a notch to accommodate the slight loss of hearing in the ears of a seventy-plus woman – and that had to be Hattie Pearson. *Good detective work, Tessa,* she thought, *you've not lost your touch.*

She spread out the notes she had picked up from the two Bakewell clients, and stared at them. All five messages had been written by the same person, and the fact that they were handwritten gave her cause for concern more than if they had been assembled by bits of words cut from newspapers and magazines. It meant the person making the veiled threats didn't really care. Catch me or don't catch me, I shall follow through. Tessa shivered.

She picked up the phone and dialled quickly. It only rang once before she heard the words 'Hi, lovely Tessa.' They had a brief conversation and Tessa disconnected. She gathered up the notes, careful to keep them in their separate evidence bags, and spoke to Cheryl on her way out. 'I'm going to Chesterfield, then to Bakewell, probably to see Denise Jordan, but if she's not in I'll go to Lorna Thompson's house. One of them will be in, hopefully.'

Cheryl wrote as Tessa spoke, then looked up. 'And Chesterfield?'

'Police headquarters. The coffee shop nearby, anyway. It's a Costa.'

Cheryl nodded. 'Take care. You calling back here or going straight home? It is nearly three now.'

'I'll see. Either way, I'll let you know. That okay?'

'It is. If ever they come to arrest you for using police resources, I'll know where they can find you.' She kept her face straight as she spoke.

'Smart arse,' Tessa said with a grin, as she walked out of the door.

The coffee shop was busy, and Tessa spotted Greg's waving hand as she entered. She headed over towards the corner table, and leaned across to kiss his cheek. 'Mr Overton.' She smiled. 'It's so good to see you.'

'Cut the flannel, Marsden. I ordered you a latte. That okay?'

'Perfect, Greg. Thank you.' She shrugged off her coat and placed it on top of Greg's, effectively stopping anyone from sitting on the third chair at their table. She reached down into her bag and took out a brown envelope containing the two evidence bags.

'They're notes that have been sent to two clients we now represent. My clients have touched them, and I've already taken their prints so we can eliminate them from whatever you find. I used gloves, obviously, so in theory there should only be two sets of prints on them, the recipients and the plank who sent them.'

'Plank?'

'No self-respecting potential rapist or killer would write their own notes. They'd either type them on a computer, or cut words out of a newspaper, but oh no. Our plank has to write them. I'm hoping this will soon be sorted, with your help.'

'I'll have answers by tonight. I'll drop them off at Connection afterwards, don't want to leave them on the premises. That okay?'

'That's fine. It's a secure letterbox. Did you hear about our body in the outhouse?'

He laughed. 'I did indeed. I also said Connection would solve it before we did. Am I right?'

'Probably. Luke has taken it on, with me as back-up if he needs an extra right-hand man at any point.'

They chatted for the time it took them to finish their coffees, then Greg stood. 'I'll go look at these. Take care, Tessa. If I find anything that I need you to know about before tomorrow morning, I'll ring.'

'Thanks, Greg. You're a star.'

Greg left first after returning the kiss on the cheek, and waved from the door. Tessa sat for a moment remembering the huge bunch of flowers he had sent following the death of her work, and life, partner, Hannah, and she angrily brushed a tear away. She counted to ten, recited 'Mary had a Little Lamb' inside her head, and stood up to put on her coat and replace her bag on her shoulder. He was a good friend, and she knew he would find some answers for her, even if they were negative ones. Anything would help.

Tessa parked outside Denise Jordan's home and sat for a moment. Denise had shown a clear reaction of fear when she had mentioned her husband's name, and Tessa knew that had to be the starting point. She needed to know who he was, and why they had split up.

The front door of the house opened as she walked up the path.

'I thought it was your car,' Denise said with a smile. 'Come in and meet Alex.'

Alex proved to be a nine-year-old boy who grinned as his mother introduced them. 'You're Mum's friend?'

'I am,' Tessa agreed. 'You're Mum's son?'

He laughed. 'I am.'

'Good. Alex, I need to talk to your mum for a bit, so we'll be in the kitchen. Okay?'

He nodded, and turned his head back to the television screen. 'Okay. Mum'll put the kettle on, she always does.'

Tessa sat at the table, and as Alex had prophesied, Denise switched on the kettle.

'I apologise for that precocious child,' Denise said as Tessa followed her down the hallway and into the kitchen. 'He's been brilliant since his dad left, so supportive, so caring. When he came home from school the night I managed to get rid of his father, I explained everything to him. He said, "I'm glad he's gone".'

'That's really what I'm here about,' Tessa said. 'Your husband. I need to know more about him, even if it's only to rule him out. And to explain something to you that you don't know about. I'll wait while we have our drinks, then we'll talk.'

They clasped their hands around their mugs and faced each other. 'I need to know his name,' Tessa began.

'Sergeant Ben Jordan. He's based at Chesterfield.'

Tessa's mind flew instantly to the big sergeant, the one whose sarcasm was well known, who was universally disliked at work, and who, with a personality transplant, would have risen much higher than the level of sergeant.

'I know him.'

'Then you probably realise why he no longer lives here. I put up with him for the sake of Alex, until one day I realised to my horror how much Alex disliked him. That was the end for Ben, as far as I was concerned. I managed to get him out by simply changing the locks, leaving his clothes in the shed, and quivering in the kitchen until he drove away. I was so lucky in that this house is mine, I inherited it from my nan, so his name is nowhere on it. He'll never forgive me, he's now living in a tiny flat, but one thing I'm sure of, the handwriting on those notes isn't his. We're divorced, and he's trying for custody of Alex, but he'll not get it. Alex's school is here, his friends are here, and I'm here. I provide for my son, which is more than his father does, so I'm not worried the court hearing will go against me, it's the stress of the whole thing that's wearing me out.'

'Was it only his nastiness, or was violence involved?'

'Violence at times, but it's words that hurt. He's a horrible person. And now it seems I've acquired another one without knowing how.'

'You've obviously given it some thought. Nobody else would do this to you that you can think of?'

Denise shook her head. 'No. Most of my friends have seen how Ben was, and have been really supportive.'

'Okay. Here's what I need, and then I'll tell you why I need it. I want you to get together a list of your friends, initially only their names, and by this I mean friends who you send birthday and Christmas cards to, friends who would ring for a chat, that type of friend. Then I want you to send me a screenshot of Facebook friends. I know there will be a crossover of some of the names, but you will have Facebook friends you've never met...'

Denise laughed. 'I only put my Christmas book away this morning. Hang on, I'll fish it out again.' She disappeared into the lounge and returned with a brightly coloured hardback journal.

'It will be easier for you to photograph the pages,' she said. 'The birthday card list is at the back of the book.'

Tessa felt in awe of such organisation. She took five pictures, then waited as Denise did the Facebook screenshots.

'I'm not much of a presence on Facebook,' she explained. 'It says I've only got forty-five friends, so that's it, all sent now. What will you do with this information?'

Tessa sat back after checking she had everything through on her phone. 'There's something I have to tell you. You aren't the only one to have received these notes. There is another lady in Bakewell who has also received them. I can't tell you her name yet as she too is a client, but I'll ask her permission when I go to get the same information from her as I've got from you. Then I'll compare both sets of lists to see if you share any contacts. Is it okay if I use your name when I go to see her?'

The shock was apparent on Denise's face. 'Somebody else? Of course you can tell her. Do whatever it takes to catch the bastard.'

12

Lorna Thompson was about to go out, so Tessa quickly explained what it was she needed, and asked her if she could do the lists once she was back from her doctor's appointment and email them to her as soon as possible.

News of a second set of notes caused her eyes to open wide. 'Really! Do I know the other lady? Is she from Bakewell?'

'She is. Her name is Denise Jordan. She has given me permission to tell you her name.'

Lorna smiled, recognising the name. 'Yes, I know Denise. She comes to the book club at the library. Maybe the three of us should meet next time, to save you having to do two visits.'

'It's okay for me to share your name with her?'

'It is. Anything to make this go away.'

Tessa checked the clock in her car and decided to go via Connection – it was almost six and she felt sure Greg would have delivered the envelope by now.

The shutter was down, the door locked, and she solved both issues immediately, hoping Greg had arrived before the shutters were lowered. He had. The envelope was in the mesh letterbox on the inside of the door, and she removed it. There was a sliver of light showing from Beth's office, and Tessa pushed open the door to switch it off.

Beth looked up and clutched at her throat. 'Good lord, Tessa, you frightened me to death.'

Tessa doubled up in laughter. 'I'm so sorry. I thought you'd left your light on. I came in to switch it off. With the shutters being down I assumed everybody had gone home.'

'No, I got involved with something, and I'm on a conference call at seven, so I thought I'd hang on here. It's easier when I've got all the information in this office and not at home. There's an envelope in the letterbox for you.'

Tessa waved it. 'Got it. It's why I called back here. I've... erm... had some fingerprints checked.'

'Sit down. Drink?'

'Just water, please.' She sat down opposite Beth, and waited while Beth produced a bottle of water and a coffee.

'Okay, let's talk fingerprints.'

'I have the equipment for lifting them, and I have a snazzy little machine that can take them on the go, so to speak, but what I no longer have is access to the database. I called in a favour...'

Beth took a sip of her coffee. 'I've been somewhat remiss in mentioning some things, it seems.' She tried to hide her smile. 'You're a smart cookie, Tessa. You knew we always seemed to be one step in front with cases in the past, and it was mainly down to one woman, my nan, the great Doris Lester. Now she may be far away but in real terms it's only a mouse click. So if you have prints to be checked in future, that mouse click can now come from my computer.'

'Really?' Tessa's eyes twinkled. 'Should I be making a citizen's arrest at this point?'

'You could try. Remember the black belt first though. And you'd never be able to prove anything. If I can access police files, I can certainly hide the fact that I've done it. You want to talk about the case?'

'It's a strange one, a little unsettling.' She opened the envelope and removed the returned notes. 'They're handwritten.' She pushed the evidence bags across to Beth, and opened the results sheet from Greg. She sighed. 'No prints apart from the ones left by the ladies. It was a long shot. Back to the drawing board, I guess.'

'They have families?'

Lorna Thompson doesn't. She split from her partner six months ago, but I get the impression it was amicable. They'd reached the end of the line. I'll look more into him now we have the fingerprint issue out of the way. Denise Jordan is a little more difficult. She's divorced from her husband, has a nine-year-old son called Alex, but the husband is a sergeant in the police – based at Chesterfield. Horrible feller. I'll have to talk to him, but I expect to get absolutely nothing from it.'

Beth pulled the evidence bags towards her again and stared at them. 'This handwriting... it's feminine. Rounded. When are you seeing them again?'

'Tomorrow. I've left Lorna producing a list of close friends and a list of Facebook friends. She's emailing them over later. I already have Denise's lists. I'm hoping to bring the two ladies together tomorrow, for a joint discussion. We'll see then if anything is relevant to both of them, and go from there. So far the notes have been hand-delivered, so it might be worth fixing cameras to cover their front doors.' She glanced at her watch. 'I'm going home now, it's not far off seven and you've probably got stuff to get ready. I'm assuming it's not only fingerprints you can access? You could look up certain people more in-depth than a casual internet search?'

Beth smiled. 'With Doris Lester for my teacher, you bet your sweet life I can.'

Tessa lowered the shutters and smiled. It really did feel strange working as a private investigator without the might of a police force behind her, but it seemed anything and any one was available to her simply by switching on a computer. IT lessons at school had never said anything about this...

The roads were turning icy as she drove home, and she breathed a sigh of relief as she went through her front door. She clicked on the heating and headed for the kitchen. Time to eat, and to switch off for the day.

When the phone rang it was Greg. She was in the middle of eating a chicken leg with her fingers, and her voice came out with some difficulty.

'You eating, Tessa?'

'Chicken leg,' she tried to say.

'Okay. The only prints were matches to those you took of the two ladies, nothing else. The envelopes are self-seal, so no saliva. Whoever has written these is forensic savvy. They must have used gloves, so I'm really sorry I couldn't help.'

'No problem.' Her tongue was working to get a piece of chicken out of her tooth. 'I can speak better now. Thank you for your help anyway, Greg. They've all been hand-delivered, so we're looking at putting small cameras in, trained on their front doors. The two women are meeting up tomorrow hopefully, and I'm going to try to get them chatting, see if anything, any little clue, is thrown up without them realising it.'

Greg laughed. 'I don't doubt you'll sort it. Enjoy the rest of your meal, super-sleuth Marsden. Take care.'

. . .

Beth's conference call lasted beyond eight, and before she locked up for the night she left a note for Cheryl.

Don't send out search parties, I won't be in till later. Knackered.

She lowered the shutters and sank into her car, resting her head on the back of her seat for a moment. The discussion had generated more work, and she recognised it meant taking on extra staff. In her head she moved her office furniture around, and knew she could fit in another desk – the decision now was whether to split the room by a stud wall, or put in a ready-made room divider. She picked up her phone and five minutes later had her answer. If she could move out for three days, the office would be made into two rooms, job done.

They would start on Monday, Stefan assured her, and it would be completed by Wednesday evening, unless they found any more bodies.

She smiled to herself as she pulled away, and decided to put feelers out the following day, for the help she needed. She would work from home Monday to Wednesday while the work was ongoing, and begin interviews on the Thursday. Exciting times, she decided, very exciting. She felt she knew who she wanted... could he be persuaded?

She drove up the hill towards Little Mouse Cottage and was surprised to see lights on. She was sure Joel had said he would be home late, he was going out for a meal with clients.

'Hi,' she called, 'you home?' She closed the door behind her.

Joel walked out of the kitchen holding a glass of wine. He passed it to her then took her by the hand and led her into the dining room.

The table was beautifully laid, the candles lending a romantic touch to the ambience.

'Have I missed something? Is it an anniversary I don't know anything about?'

'No, it's in celebration of my client being ill and not being able to attend our meeting and me getting an afternoon finish. Sit down, I'll bring out the starters.'

It was only as they were tucking into their Marks and Spencer version of tiramisu that Joel revealed the real reason behind the meal.

'I want to marry you.'

'I know. I said yes.'

'I mean I want to marry you soon. I don't want to wait until we can go visit Nan and Alistair in France, then have to make all the arrangements long distance. Why can't we do it soon, in Eyam or Bradwell church?'

'Yes,' she said.

'Yes? Yes what?'

'Yes I want to marry you soon, and I'd like it to be in Eyam church with the woman who saved my life officiating. Can we do that?'

Joel stood and walked around the table towards her. He slowly pulled her to her feet, took her in his arms and kissed her.

'My God, thank you,' he said. 'I've been dreading this conversation all day, fearing you would want to wait for France.'

'Nan can come here. Beginning of April okay?'

'Miss Efficiency. Beginning of April is good if we can't have it earlier than that. I love you so much, Beth, I want everybody else to see it and know it.'

'Oh, I think they do,' she said. 'I think they do.'

13

His postbag felt extra heavy thanks to the parcel to be delivered to Mrs Khan, and he shuffled the bag further onto his shoulder. Dave Shaw would be glad when today was over; he'd had a blazing row with his wife, and he felt he needed to put things right before everything went completely wrong. He glanced at his watch and saw it was a little before seven, so he was on course to finish early and his footsteps quickened as he walked up to the front door of Lorna Thompson's house. He lifted the flap of the letterbox, and the door swung inwards.

He hesitated. 'Lorna. You okay?' His voice sounded loud as it reverberated around the hallway. 'Lorna?'

There was no response so he pressed the doorbell, then stepped inside. Again he called her name, this woman he had known for years, a friend of his wife's from the book club the two women attended.

He felt awkward, so moved no further than the hall and took out his phone. He rang his wife, and asked her to ring Lorna, explaining the situation. Seconds later he heard the ringtone of a mobile phone in what he presumed to be the lounge. He opened the door.

. . .

Carl Heaton took in the scene, and felt sick. Now he knew exactly why the postman was sitting on the garden wall, dithering in the early-morning temperatures of a January day. So much blood. He stepped back out of the room and hoped the Forensics team wouldn't be much longer.

Joining Dave on the wall, Carl took out his notebook. He noted down his details, then waited for the postman to tell him what he knew.

'She's dead, isn't she? Lorna...'

'She is. You know her?'

'I more or less know everybody in Bakewell. I've been working this round for about twenty years. But I know her anyway, she's a friend of the wife. They go to a book club at the local library. That's where she works, Lorna. When you check Lorna's phone, it'll show a missed call from Sharon. When I got no answer from Lorna, I didn't want to go checking the house, so I rang the wife, and she rang Lorna. I heard it ringing, so followed the sound, and...'

He shivered and it wasn't only from the cold. 'I didn't go beyond the doorway of the room, and I had to turn the knob to go in. I backed out at speed, I can tell you. She was a lovely woman, who would do this to her?'

'We'll find out.' Carl put away his notebook as the Forensics team arrived. 'Can you hang on for half an hour, then I can let you carry on with your round?'

The house was already encircled by crime scene tape, with neighbours in its semi-detached partner house looking out of bedroom windows at what was unfolding before them.

Rory Thomas, the pathologist, nodded briefly at Carl, and the two men entered the house.

'It's bad,' Carl said, warning the young man who he felt

couldn't have seen that many violent deaths – he didn't look old enough.

Rory's gloved hand opened the door and he paused on the threshold of the room, taking in the scene before him. There was blood, a lot of it, and he carefully manoeuvred his way to the body. It was clear her throat had been cut, but he suspected as soon as they removed her clothes he would find multiple stab wounds in her body.

'She was killed last night,' he said. 'I'll know more when I get her back to the autopsy suite, but a rough guess is between ten and midnight. Other than that I can't tell you anything yet.'

'Thanks. Let me know when you're doing the post-mortem and I'll be there. I'll go and send our postman off to finish his round, he needs to warm up, I think.'

Dave Shaw had left the dubious comfort of the garden wall to stand outside the crime scene tape. A woman had her arms around him, but stepped back as she saw Carl approaching.

'My wife, Sharon,' he said, by way of explanation.

Carl shook her hand. 'Good to meet you, Sharon. I understand you know the deceased.'

Sharon nodded. 'I do. We've been friends for years, but not close friends. She didn't really have any close friends, her partner discouraged it.'

'Partner?'

'Ex-partner. They split about six months ago, amicably. It had run its course. I think he moved to London, he got a new job, and she didn't want to leave here so off he went. She wasn't upset by it, they'd drifted apart anyway.'

'You have his name?'

'Ian Ancaster. No idea where he is, though, or what he does.'

Carl added the name to his notes. 'Thank you. This is helpful. Dave, if you're okay to do so, you can carry on now.'

'I'm off home,' Dave said. 'Somebody will be here in the next couple of minutes to take this,' he patted his bag, 'and I'm going home for a stiff whisky.'

Carl looked up as his office door opened. DC Nigel Glossop stood in the doorway, a printout in his hand.

'Thought you'd want to see this, boss. I'm going through the victim's laptop, and this is the last email she sent. It went last night shortly after eight, to a Tessa Marsden. I'm presuming it's our Tessa Marsden. The last part of the email address is @connection.co.uk.'

'Thanks, Nigel.' He took the printout from the DC, and waited until the door had closed before placing it on his desk to read it.

Two minutes later he picked up his phone.

'Hi, Carl. You okay?' Tessa collected the printout of the email sent by Lorna from the printer tray, and walked back to her desk.

'I'm good, thanks. I may have some information for you.'

'Oh?'

'You have a client called Lorna Thompson?'

Tessa hesitated. 'Maybe.'

He gave a short bark of laughter. 'God, you don't change, do you. Let's presume Lorna is your client, shall we? I actually know you do, because in front of me on my desk is a copy of an email she sent to you last night.'

Tessa waited. The same email was in front of her.

'I was called out at some ungodly hour this morning to a

report of a suspicious death. A postman found her. I'm sorry, Tessa, she's dead.'

'And it was suspicious?'

'Nothing merely suspicious about it. It was definitely murder. No details yet, but there was a lot of blood, her throat had been cut and her pyjamas were soaked in blood.'

'My God, Carl. We need to talk. But first I need to contact another client. Do you want to come here, or shall I come to you?'

'Tess, I'm sorry to be blunt about this, but you're now a civilian, you're the last person to have seen Lorna Thompson alive, and I need to formally interview you. Can you be here for ten?'

'Let me make sure I have this right,' Cheryl said, 'you're off to Chesterfield to be interviewed formally as a suspect in a murder that's happened overnight. A murder of one of our clients?'

Tessa nodded. 'You said we had to notify you wherever we went, so I'm telling you.'

Cheryl stood. 'You're going to no formal interview without me being there. Luke's in, he'll cover on reception while we're gone.'

Tessa smiled. 'I don't think I'll need legal representation...'

'And there speaks somebody who's never been on the receiving end of a police interview, only dished them out. You're not going on your own, Tessa. I've done this dozens of times, trust me to stop you putting your foot in it.'

Luke laughed at the explanation of why he was needed on reception, despite the calamity of the death of a client, and he moved downstairs with alacrity, waving them off as Tessa's car disappeared into the distance.

Telling Beth when she arrived was just as funny, but it was only as the day wore on that they became concerned.

Tessa and Cheryl arrived back in the office shortly after two, carrying designer label bags.

'We went for lunch in Debenhams,' Tessa explained, 'and accidentally found our credit cards. Anyway, I haven't been arrested, I've convinced them of my innocence, so now I'm back to get to work on solving who did this to Lorna. I've had to tell them the story, so they now also know about Denise Jordan, and I've left them the notes to check for fingerprints. I didn't tell them it had already been done by them, I let them think we'd done it to check for any prints other than our clients.'

'Has a check been done on Denise Jordan?'

'Yes, she's fine. She wasn't too happy at police turning up on her doorstep apparently, but when they'd finished explaining she texted me to ask me to ring her. I'm going to do that now.'

Tessa changed her mind. Suddenly she knew she needed to see Denise, a phone call was too impersonal, and maybe by looking at Lorna's email it would trigger a memory, anything to put them on the right track. She had explained to Carl what the email with the list of friend's names was about, but hadn't told him she already had it captured in photos on her phone. It was time to put some work into those names, and that would have to start with showing them to Denise.

Denise was clearly upset. 'As you can see, I now have a policeman outside, who will be there for some time – until they catch this lunatic anyway. I'm really scared – and don't forget I have Alex to worry about on top of everything else. They said she was stabbed...'

'She was. The postman found her, apparently, and they took her laptop into headquarters for forensic examination. That's how they found my connection to her – she'd emailed a list of her friends to me last night.'

Denise handed her a coffee, and they sat for a moment, enjoying its warmth.

'Do you think you can look through the list of Lorna's friends for me? Tell me if anything stands out?'

'Of course. Let's get this bastard caught. I can't live my life in fear, I thought that had stopped when I divorced Ben.'

Tessa took the list out of her bag and pushed it across the kitchen table, along with a yellow highlighter. 'Take your time. Highlight anybody you know. I'll keep quiet while you go through it.'

Maria ran across the road, hands in her overall pockets to stop anything jumping out as she ran, and reached the door of Connection safely. She pressed the entry button and waited for it to be released.

Cheryl smiled at the pretty young girl. 'Hi, Maria. Can I help?'

'I've brought an address for Luke so he knows where we're going on Saturday for the school reunion thing. The times and stuff....' Her voice filtered away.

'I'll tell him you're coming up. The lift is there, press one and his office is almost opposite the lift. His name is on the door anyway.'

'Oh!' She looked around almost in panic. 'Is it okay? He's not busy?'

'He might be playing Solitaire, or he might be studying for

another certificate, but either way he'll stop for you.' She smiled and pressed Luke's extension. 'Visitor for you,' she said, and disconnected.

Maria walked towards the lift, and disappeared.

Thirty minutes later the lift door reopened on the ground floor and Maria and Luke exited, laughing. 'Won't be a minute,' he said to Cheryl as he escorted Maria outside.

Cheryl watched as they walked and half ran across the busy road, and then saw him kiss her cheek as she re-entered the door of the vets.

Yes, she thought, *exactly what that young man needs.*

The phone rang, and she heard the Yorkshire tones of Fred. 'Letting you know I've finished the two appointments I had for this afternoon, surveillance jobs, and I have deposits in my briefcase. I'll bring them on Monday. Also, I'm out tonight. The Great Hucklow surveillance is on, so I fitted a couple of cameras inside the house this morning I hope will work. I'm going to be outside with this super-duper camera trained on any arrivals. Our client is taking her mother to the theatre in Sheffield, and staying in one of the theatreland hotels overnight, so we'll see what hubby gets up to.'

'Take care, Fred. And I stay up till about eleven, so if you've been successful before that will you let me know you're safe?'

'I will.' He laughed. He liked this crazy woman who thought she was his mother. 'Don't worry, I'll be safe.'

14

Fred parked his car quarter of a mile away from the Barker home and walked up towards the house. His daytime few minutes spent taking in the cold Derbyshire air had been partly spent deciding on the best surveillance point, so he knew exactly where he was going. The gorse bushes behind the dry stone wall directly opposite the house provided ample cover, and he removed a loose stone to sit the camera in position, trained on the door.

He checked his phone to make sure the cameras inside the house were working, and he could see Tony Barker in the bedroom, a towel around his waist. The one in the lounge was a static picture.

The only car on the drive was the midnight-blue Jaguar, so Fred guessed Tony's companion for the night still hadn't arrived. Fred shuffled around to gain a little more comfort, hoping it would soon be over. Surveillance in the depths of winter was no picnic.

.   .   .

A small white Fiat 500 arrived thirty minutes later and Fred breathed a sigh of relief. He was stiff, and needed to move but couldn't risk it.

The Fiat pulled on to the drive, parking to the right of the Jaguar, and Vanessa Noone climbed out of the driving seat. She glanced around before closing the car door, but by then Fred had already taken three photographs.

She straightened her skirt, flicked back her hair, and went towards the front door. Fred took several more photographs of the cars and then returned the camera to its case before putting it around his neck.

He replaced the stone he had removed, and still keeping behind the wall headed back down the road towards his car.

The heater was put on immediately, and while he was waiting for it to warm up he took out his phone. The bedroom camera was static, its motion sensor not having been activated, but the lounge camera revealed two naked bodies on the rug in front of a glowing fire, and Fred laughed quietly. The motion sensors were fully working. He took a couple of screenshots, but knew the cameras were filming anyway, then put the car into gear and drove home.

Fred rang Cheryl, trying desperately to keep the laughter out of his voice. She listened to his report, waited until he had finished and then said, 'You've had a good night then?'

'Cheryl Dodd, you're wicked. It was a successful night, and by the time I've seen Amy on Monday this one will be wrapped up. She'll have all the ammunition she needs, so I'll get Luke to show me the billing routine and that will be it. Shame really, I like Amy. Strong woman. I think Tony Barker will find that out in the weeks and months to come. This will wreck an entire family, though, but you can hardly ignore your husband sleeping with your sister.'

'You're right, of course. You got warm now? I kept thinking of you out in the cold, you must have been frozen.'

'It was a bit parky. I was glad to get back in the car with the heater on. I left a stew in the oven, so I'm going to have that now, and get properly warm. Mark me down as not working Saturday or Sunday, will you?'

'I will, but I bet you go in the office. Luke's going in to feed Oliver and change the cat litter tomorrow morning, and I said I'd pop down tomorrow night and feed him. He's such a lovely cat, it's like he knew we would look after him.'

'I've got one, a cat. She's pretty old now, fourteen I think, but you wouldn't know it. Mad as a hatter. Loves her toys, comes and goes as she pleases, brings me mice and birds and leaves them on the mat outside the front door... she's called Angel. If ever a cat had the wrong name, it's her.'

They said goodnight, and Fred went into the kitchen. He ladled himself a bowl of stew, went to the cupboard for the Henderson's relish, and looked in disgust at the small amount left in the bottle. He wrote *relish* on his shopping list, knowing if he didn't do it immediately, it would be forgotten, then loaded up a tray with the bowl, and some crusty bread.

He watched half an episode of *Dalziel and Pascoe*, then switched everything off and went to bed. Angel went through the cat flap, and out to meet her friends.

Beth and Joel discussed wedding plans over their meal, and after they had cleared away Beth rang Kat, who confirmed that Saturday, the fourth of April would be a beautiful day for a wedding and she would be delighted to officiate, whether she could still fit into her clergy clothes or not.

'I need to go shopping,' Beth declared with a smile, after putting down the phone.

'Immediately?'

'No, tomorrow will be soon enough.'

'Oh good. I really didn't fancy going out tonight. What sort of shopping?'

'Wedding dress, bridesmaid dresses, flowers, venue for a reception... you want me to go on or shall I turn on the TV?'

Joel picked up the remote control, scrolled through the planner and clicked on *Dalziel and Pascoe*.

Luke spent some time on the internet checking out train times, then booked a ticket for the Monday 6am departure, leaving from Chesterfield, and arriving in London mid-morning. He couldn't remember the last time he'd been on a train, and felt a degree of excitement at the change in routine promised for Monday. He needed to go to Harrods, but driving in the capital filled him with dread. Add that to arm discomfort after such a long journey, and he knew it was a no-brainer taking the train. He closed down his laptop and went through to the lounge where his mum and nan were watching television.

'Girls in bed?' he asked.

'They've got new library books,' was his mum's reply.

He leaned over the back of the sofa and kissed her. 'I'm off to London on Monday. I won't require feeding.'

'That's okay. We'll have yours. It's curry.'

'You've done that to annoy me, haven't you.' Luke sat down by her side. 'What's on TV?'

'*Dalziel and Pascoe.*'

'Good. I like a good murder.'

Within ten minutes he was asleep, his arm finally comfortable.

. . .

Tessa was determined not to work. She ordered in a pizza, opened a bottle of red wine, and having spotted that a *Dalziel and Pascoe* was on TV, settled down to watch it.

Her mind kept drifting to the list of Lorna's friends with the yellow highlighters through them, and still she resisted getting out the list.

Until shortly after ten.

She pulled the coffee table towards her and took the list from her bag. She stared at it for a moment, then rang Denise.

'I'm checking you're okay.'

'Hi, Tessa, I'm fine. My mum has been and collected Alex until it's safe here, but I'm staying put. The police car's still outside, so I feel okay, but my head is spinning, wondering what's happening to me. At first, you know, I wondered if it was something to do with Ben, but sending silly little notes isn't the way he does things. He'd come barging in, openly threatening. This is somebody I must have upset at some time, but I'm blowed if I know who it is or what I did. And where does Lorna Thompson fit in? The only way our paths cross is through the library, the book club is run by her and I'm a member of it, but I use the library a lot anyway. I didn't know her surname, her badge only says Lorna. She was lovely, really helpful, nothing too much trouble especially with the children in their section.'

'But it is a connection...' Tessa breathed out slowly. 'When does the book club meet?'

'The third Monday of every month, so this coming Monday is the next meeting.'

They said goodnight and disconnected.

Brilliant, Tessa thought with a sigh. Unless you wanted to actually visit Bakewell market, Monday was never a good day to go to the small Derbyshire town, it was always heaving with visitors.

Tessa gave in to temptation and picked up the list of Lorna's friends, both from her personal list and also from her Facebook connections. There were six names highlighted in yellow that Denise had recognised, but only one had a double thickness of highlighter pen and a biro box around it, with the words *Ben's cousin* arrowed to it. Grace Jordan. The name was on Lorna's list of personal friends, not on her Facebook friends list, and Tessa sat back to ease her neck pain, deep in thought. Grace Jordan. Possibly one to check out.

Tessa packed everything away, and went upstairs to bed. Her mind refused to close down, and it was the early hours of the morning before she fell asleep. She simply couldn't get rid of the names on the lists from her mind.

And so Friday drew to a close. Things were changing once again with the addition of a new office at Connection, Beth needed to recruit an assistant, Fred considered his first job satisfyingly finished and well executed, and Luke was slightly worried about his trip to London after the weekend. He was, however, looking forward with a great deal of pleasure to his night out on Saturday night, and to getting to know Maria better.

Cheryl fell asleep quickly, feeling grateful for the opportunity that had appeared – the right job at the right time, with the right people. She knew Keith would have approved – he had hated her having to travel into Sheffield city centre every day, he would have loved the fact that she could walk down into the village to go to work. She slept deeply.

The rain fell heavily through the night and Saturday brought with it a grey sombre atmosphere that held the promise of more rain to come. Hattie Pearson took the tablets that kept her alive, and clicked on the kettle. The text the previous night from Luke confirming he was going to Harrods on Monday had filled her with such a strange feeling, that she almost felt overwhelmed by it. She poured cornflakes into a bowl, chopped up a banana and added far too much milk, but she liked milk. She sat at the kitchen table, her eyes moist. He was a good lad, her Luke, and she knew he would deliver what she wanted delivering, because he listened to her.

Saturday was a day of hope, of change for everyone.

15

SATURDAY 18TH JANUARY 2020

Oliver was waiting patiently for his breakfast, and Luke quickly fed him before clicking on the kettle for his own sustenance. Both he and the cat headed up in the lift to his office, leaving the downstairs in darkness with the shutters down.

It made him smile at how quickly the cat had settled in, almost as if Oliver had decided that this was it, his home for the foreseeable future, and here he would stay. Luke opened up his laptop and Oliver jumped on the desk. He walked around the surface, carefully tip-toeing over pens and other items, before heading to investigate the keyboard.

'Get down, Oliver.' Luke laughed. 'You can't possibly work this. Go and do cat things, like catching mice. Don't bring any birds, I can't handle that.'

Oliver stepped down onto Luke's knee, kneaded with his front paws and settled in for the duration. Luke gave a sigh, rubbed his legs where the claws had dug in, and switched his mind onto the job he was supposed to be doing.

Luke brought up the file headed Harriet Pearson and read through everything written in it so far. He then unlocked his desk drawer and took out the lingerie set. Although he was no underwear expert, to him it seemed it could have been bought yesterday, so pristine was its appearance. He folded it carefully and slid it into a plastic bag, then pressed the seal closed. Placing that inside a large brown envelope, Luke put it into his briefcase. Now he was ready for Monday morning.

Oliver hadn't moved, so Luke gently lifted him and placed him on the floor. 'Come on, let's have you outside for a bit, and I'll come back later and let you in.' They returned to the ground floor via the lift, and Luke led him through to the kitchen and out the back door, watching as the cat disappeared into the long grass and overgrown shrubbery of what had so recently been revealed as the back garden of the office. Maybe they needed a gardener, once this blessed winter was over.

Luke returned to his office, and typed Alan Egerton into Google without Oliver's feline help. He found someone with that name and of the right age living in Calver, confirming what Hattie had told him, so he made a note of the address, closed his laptop, and headed downstairs. After double-checking all was locked up, he slipped on his jacket and pressed the button to raise the shutters.

Tessa decided to go into the office. She needed to write up everything so far, and she didn't need to be in the house with memories.

To her surprise the shutters rose as she pulled up outside the shop. Her smile was automatic as she realised it was Luke operating the equipment.

'You finished for the day?'

'You starting yours?'

'Clever monkey. I thought I'd come in and spend some time writing up the casefiles, while it was quiet.'

'I'm off to Calver. I think I've managed to track down Alan Egerton, who was Evelyn Pearson's boyfriend when she went missing. I can't get his phone number, so I'm going on the off-chance he'll be in.'

'Want some company?'

They pulled up outside the address Luke had scribbled on a Post-it note, and looked around for a moment.

'This is nice,' Tessa remarked. 'He must have done well.'

'Hattie said he was careful with money, even back then.'

'It's paid off,' Tessa said as she opened the passenger door. 'I'll leave you to do the talking unless my police head takes over and I think of something you've forgotten. Okay?'

'That's fine. My gut feeling says he knows nothing, but that's from listening to Hattie. However, I also suspect he may have had a friend whose name began with M. I'm more interested in him.'

Luke locked the car and they walked up the small front path, carefully crazy-paved, with flower borders planted with winter pansies either side. The small lawns either side beyond the borders were cut, and for a brief moment Luke thought about the jungle effect of their garden behind the office.

A young woman answered their knock, and when Luke asked if Alan Egerton lived there, she called him to the door. 'Dad, somebody to see you.'

Alan Egerton looked at them with some suspicion. Saturday was his day of rest, and he didn't really want, or expect visitors in his ordered life.

'Can I help you?'

'Luke Taylor, Connection Investigation Agency.' Luke held out his ID card.

'And I'm Tessa Marsden.' Tessa showed her ID.

He carefully inspected both of them. 'I've heard of you. What can I do for you?'

'We'd like to talk to you about someone you knew a long time ago, Evelyn Pearson.'

'Evelyn? Good Lord. That's a name from the past. I haven't seen her for about twenty-five years,' and he made to close the door.

Luke held out his hand to stop it, and said, 'Can we come in for a few minutes, sir? We have a couple of questions, that's all, and then we'll leave you to your Saturday.'

Egerton looked unsure, but then held open the door. 'I can spare you five minutes.'

He led them through to a lounge, a cold room that didn't merit heating being on during the day when it wasn't being used. Tessa shivered and sat down. Luke sat beside her, and opened his briefcase. He placed a recorder on the coffee table.

'I hope you don't mind, it saves taking notes.'

'Erm... no, I don't suppose so. What is this about?'

'We have been employed by Harriet Pearson to find who killed her daughter.'

'Killed?' Egerton looked shocked.

'The body of Evelyn was found a couple of days ago, and it appeared it had been in the place she was found for around twenty-five years, so it's quite possible you would have been the last person to see her alive. I believe the police will eventually get around to interviewing you, so you need to be aware of that. It is their investigation, as it appears she was murdered. Mrs Pearson wants us to look into the case as she says the police did nothing when she reported Evelyn as missing. I'm afraid she doesn't have a deal of confidence in the police.'

'And quite rightly so,' Alan Egerton said. 'Honestly, at the time, they thought she had run off. She wasn't a teenager, she was twenty-five, we were planning our wedding... she had no reason to run off. The police officers we saw all seemed to be about sixteen, they were only kids, and we both said many times that they simply weren't taking it seriously. You said she was killed. How?'

'We're not sure yet of the cause of death, but her body was found in a small outhouse we were renovating for storage round the back of our offices in Eyam. We're across the road from the Co-op. Do you know it?'

He nodded slowly. 'I do. And so you know, I wasn't the last person to see her. I hadn't seen her for nearly a week before she disappeared. I kept calling round to her mum's to see if she was there, and she was getting a bit more frantic every time I called, but neither of us had seen her. In the end I reached the conclusion that she'd chosen to disappear rather than spend the rest of her life with me, boring old Alan. When that's said to you often enough, you start to believe it, you know. She'd been in that outhouse all the time then?'

'It seems so. Obviously, when our builders found the bones, the police were called in immediately, and they've started their investigation, but Mrs Pearson came to us once she heard a body had been found, to see what we knew as it was on our premises. We knew nothing, but we passed what she could tell us onto the police, and they have now formally identified the bones as those of Evelyn Pearson.'

Egerton gave a huge sigh. It was clear his frostiness was melting, the more information he was absorbing. 'She was a lovely girl, What an awful end to her life.'

'She kept a diary of sorts. Did you know?'

'Kind of. I'd seen it, but she didn't seem to write much in it. Somebody bought it her for Christmas, and the idea was she would organise the wedding and keep notes of the stuff she needed to do and remember in that diary, but I must admit I didn't have anything to cancel because she hadn't even started on the organisation.'

'Can I take you back to one of the entries on the fourth of February, nineteen ninety-five? You went to the cinema with Evelyn to see *Pulp Fiction*, at the cinema that isn't there now, UCI at Crystal Peaks. Do you remember?'

'I do. I only took her because she wanted to see it, it wasn't really my sort of thing.'

'You went for a meal after.'

'We did. One of the eating places in Crystal Peaks, but I'm sorry, I can't remember which one.'

'It doesn't matter. Do you remember you met with your friend and his girlfriend?'

'I do. It sort of rescued the night, the film had been such a disappointment to me.'

'Would you mind telling me their names, please? We have to check all leads.'

'Yes, his name is Martin Synyer. That's S-Y-N-Y-E-R, strange spelling, but it's pronounced senior. He lives, as far as I know, in Alport. Huge place, but I believe it belonged to his latest wife. Not heard from him in years, although I did see him from a distance a month or so ago, shortly before Christmas. We went to Chatsworth for the Christmas fair, and he was there. We waved, so it was definitely him, but we weren't close enough to speak. To be perfectly honest I distanced myself from him after Evelyn went missing. He was quite nasty about it, said she'd probably gone off with somebody with a personality, or words to that effect, and I know he was drunk when he said it, but it wasn't necessary. Evelyn and I loved each other.'

'Was he with the same person he was with when you went for that meal?'

'Definitely not. I can't remember her name, but they split up a couple of weeks after that night, and the one he was with at Chatsworth looked half his age.'

Luke switched off the recorder, and opened his notebook. 'Can I have your phone number, please, Mr Egerton, and thank you for your help. I don't think I'll need to contact you again, but if I do, it can be over the phone.'

Alan said his own number, and apologised for not knowing more of the whereabouts of Martin Synyer. The two Connection colleagues left the cold room and headed out towards the car, eager to get the heater set to maximum.

They had only been travelling for a minute when Tessa spoke. 'Pull up as soon as you can away from view of his house. I want to show you something, and I don't want him thinking he's been helpful in any way. He'll dine out on it for years to come.'

'You're all heart, Tessa Marsden. This is probably the most exciting thing that's happened to him in years.' Luke put on his indicator and pulled into a layby. He left on the engine, they needed to get warm.

'What is it?'

Tessa delved into her handbag and pulled out the email from Lorna with the friends lists on it. 'Look at the personal list.'

Halfway down was the name Martin Synyer. Highlighted in yellow by Denise Jordan.

16

Tessa opened the shutters and they went inside.

She made them a coffee and they sat in Luke's office, staring at each other.

'Coincidence?' Luke asked.

'Don't believe in it.'

'Me neither. Two dead bodies, albeit twenty-five years apart, and the same name linking both of them.'

Tessa took out her phone and rang Denise. It went through to voicemail, so she left a message asking her to call back. She frowned. 'I hope she's not doing something stupid like going out.'

'You know what I've come to realise, Tess, is that people always think it can never happen to them. Working here has certainly put an old head on my shoulders, if you know what I mean. Last year, with the Clark case, that certainly aged me, made me stop and think about everything, and daft as it sounds, when you offered to go with me today, it lifted me. I wasn't aware I was feeling worried or anything, until you said *want some company.*'

She nodded. 'It's why I tried never to send my officers anywhere on their own. People can change at the click of a finger, and violence always seems to be just below the surface. That, however, wasn't why I offered to go with you today. I think I needed the company, not you. I'm glad I did, though, because neither of us, working on independent cases, would have picked up on this at this stage. Now we have to work out what happens next. We have to find this Synyer chap, see exactly what the connection is.'

'You think we should go round and see your lady? Denise, is it?'

'It is. There's a police car out front, so she should be okay. I feel a bit uncomfortable because she hasn't answered her phone.'

Luke stood. 'Come on, I don't need to be home till about five, so we've plenty of time to find her.'

'You going out?'

'You know I am, so don't play the little innocent. I know damn well Cheryl will have told you I'm going out with Maria across the road. And before you say anything, it's not a date, not really, it's a school reunion.'

Tessa laughed. 'We'll see, shall we. Your car or mine?'

'I'll drive as long as you don't interrogate me.'

'Agreed.'

The police car was still out front at the house in Bakewell, and Tessa and Luke approached it with some relief.

Tessa showed her ID, and asked if Denise had gone out.

The officer in the driver's side said they hadn't seen her since ten when she had brought them a cup of tea.

'And you haven't checked she's okay?' Luke said.

'You think she isn't?' A look of alarm flashed across the officer's face.

'She's not answering her phone,' Tessa said, her voice sharp. She turned and walked up the path with Luke following.

Tessa rang the doorbell, tapping her foot impatiently.

'I'll check the back garden,' Luke said, and headed round the corner of the house. There was nobody in the garden, but the gate at the bottom end, which led onto a playing field that looked as though it belonged to the school, was open.

He walked towards the kitchen door, and opened it with his coat sleeve over his hand.

The slumped-over body was behind the door, and he had to push hard to step inside. He felt her neck but knew she was gone. Everything was red; so much blood congealing on the black and white kitchen floor. She couldn't possibly have survived such a huge blood loss.

He stepped back outside and yelled for Tessa. Seconds later she was with him.

Carl Heaton watched as the two of them drove away. Luke had that ashen-faced look of somebody who hadn't seen too many dead bodies, certainly not with a blood splatter as wide as this one, and Tessa had clearly been knocked sideways by the loss of a second client.

He had sent them away, requesting that they attend the following day to give their statements, but he felt something was being held back. Tessa knew something, and he guessed she hadn't had time to check it out. He also guessed she would have done so by the following morning.

The forensic team were busy but almost finished by the time Carl returned to the kitchen. The two officers who had been on guard duty had already explained they had checked everything was okay when they had returned their cups at approximately quarter past ten, and had asked the deceased about the garden gate. She had told them it led into the school playing field, but it hadn't been opened in years because she didn't need access to a schoolful of kids, having one of her own was enough. They both said she had laughed about it, but had also explained it had a padlock on it that didn't have a key, so it had been left as it was for quite a few years.

Carl walked down towards it and saw that the privet hedge to the right of it was damaged. The padlock had disappeared, and he guessed it was in an evidence bag somewhere. He hoped it was. The gate had been pushed against the overgrown grass behind it, and it was open sufficiently that a person could get through it; not easily, but it was possible, as had been proved.

He stood by the cabbage patch and looked around him, trying to work out what had happened. If Denise Jordan had seen someone forcing that gate she would have yelled like hell out of the front door for the two policeman to come to her aid.

That hadn't happened, so when the killer came through the garden gate, Denise must have been in the lounge at the front of the house. Had she heard a noise in the kitchen? The sound of the back door opening? Something had taken her through to meet her killer, and Carl was itching to get into that kitchen and take it all in – the shape of the room, what she would see coming in from the hallway, where the killer was positioned when she arrived in the kitchen.

Luke watched as the technicians wheeled a trolley around the side of the house. They must have decided it was the easiest way of transporting the victim to the mortuary vehicle waiting outside on the road. The four steps up to the front door would have been difficult to navigate.

Two minutes later they disappeared with their cargo, and he walked across the lawn and into the kitchen. He balanced carefully on the plates laid down on the floor, and stopped by the table before doing a three-hundred-and-sixty-degree turn. With the kitchen door leading from the hallway open, it left a space behind it. Certainly big enough in which a man or woman could stand, knife in hand, waiting for their intended victim to check out a noise caused either deliberately or accidentally by him or her.

He almost felt himself lost in the scene he was envisaging. He knew he was right. As a result of their incompetency in not positioning an officer at both doors, this woman had lost her life, her son had lost his mother, and her mother had lost her daughter. A destroyed family because they had got it wrong.

As they had got it wrong twenty-five years earlier with the Evelyn Pearson case...

Luke didn't speak on the way back to the office. He pulled up outside to let Tessa get out, and she turned to him.

'You're okay?'

'No.'

She touched his hand. 'I know it's hard, I saw my Hannah. All you can think is so much blood, so much redness, and what you have seen will never leave you. But what you have to think is that we are here to help find out what happened, to bring this killer to justice, and by telling the police everything we know we can help them. Tomorrow.'

Luke stared out of the windscreen, taking in everything Tessa was saying to him. 'You're not going out tracking down this Synyer bloke, are you?'

She didn't answer.

Luke glanced at the clock and saw it was almost four. 'Tess, will you leave it until tomorrow? We don't have to be at the police station until twelve, so we can go find Synyer before we go there. At least we'll have something to pass on to them. Please, Tess.'

His use of her name as Tess sealed it. 'Okay, I give in. I'll do an internet search, find out what I can about him, and then tomorrow we'll go talk to him.'

'Promise?'

Tessa held out her little pinky finger, and linked it with his. 'Pinky promise. I'm going home now, this afternoon has knocked me for six so I'll get my PJs on and settle down with a laptop and a glass of wine. Enjoy your evening, Luke, and go steady if you're drinking. We could have a busy day tomorrow.'

'I'm picking Maria up from her home, so no drinking at all. It won't be a late night, my brain is buzzing.'

And it wasn't a late night. Maria walked down to his car, and climbed into the passenger seat. 'You look absolutely stunning,' he said.

'Right words,' she said with a smile. 'You've scrubbed up nicely yourself.'

'How soon can we leave?'

She laughed. 'We haven't got there yet. Didn't you want to go?'

'I wanted to see you...'

'Why, thank you, kind sir. Look, let's compromise. If it's really rubbish, and we don't like or know anybody who's there, we'll stay five minutes, then go and get some fish and chips and head back to mine. They're playing Uno tonight, so it'll be a riot, but you'll be welcome.'

'That might be what I need, I've had a funny old day.'

'Want to talk about it?'

He shook his head. 'Not tonight. Maybe one day.'

Luke and Maria arrived at the Drovers Arms shortly after seven and walked through the door to be met by flashing lights, and a cacophony of music blast and loud voices. The buffet was scheduled to open at eight, and they walked down past the table already laid out with cling-filmed plates, looked at each other and said simultaneously, 'Fish and chips?'

They finished the Cokes Luke had bought as they had entered the room, placed the empty glasses back on the bar and crept out without having actually spoken to anybody other than each other.

Their laughter filled the car as Luke turned on the ignition. 'Fish and chips it is, then. But can I take you out again, and buy you a proper meal next time?'

'You certainly can. Tuesday?'

'Tuesday is fine. I'm glad you didn't say Monday, I'm in London all day.'

'And Luke... I do realise you have a job that could mean cancellation of plans at any time. All you need to do is ring me.'

He leaned across to kiss her cheek but she turned her head towards him.

Two minutes later, Luke shook his head as if to clear his brain.

'Let's go get these fish and chips. You're driving me crazy. And before you say anything else about cancelling, I will definitely be picking you up on Tuesday, I shall make the booking tomorrow and ring you to let you know where we're going, and we'll start things properly.'

She laughed. 'That will be lovely. Let's go play Uno, and I'll introduce you to my family. I think Mum has kinda clicked on to the fact that I really like you, so let's get the introductions over with and they'll leave me alone.' She looked at him. 'I do, you know. Really like you, I mean.'

He kissed her again, and didn't even aim for her cheek. 'And I really like you.'

17

Luke was in the office by nine, surprised to see that Tessa was already there. He looked around her door and asked if she wanted a coffee. She appeared to be busy putting cards into envelopes.

'Yes please, Romeo. How was Juliet?'

'Juliet is fine. What are you doing?'

'I've had some cards made advising my personal friends of the changes in my life. Really, I'm letting them know I am a partner in Connection, which will probably bring in extra business. My years in the police have given me lots of people I keep in touch with, so I thought this was a good idea.'

He picked up one of the cards and read it. 'Smart lady. All the villains you've palled up with will be happy to come to us for help now.'

'Not all of them were villains,' she said. 'Most of them were victims who I had to keep in touch with until the case had been to court, and you strike up relationships. Then they become Christmas card acquaintances, then they'll ring for a bit of advice...'

He nodded. 'I'll get the coffees.'

'Good. You can tell me all about last night, and then we'll talk about Martin Synyer.'

'You played Uno?'

Luke nodded. 'We did, and had fish and chips. Honestly, Tessa, if you'd seen that buffet at the Drover's Arms... we went to the chippie, then back to hers for a family Uno night. I never stopped laughing from the minute we walked through the door. I went home about half ten because I knew I needed to get up fairly early, but it was a brilliant night.'

'You're seeing her again?'

'Tuesday. I'm taking her for a proper meal. We stayed at the Drovers for long enough to drink a Coke, then sidled out of the door. We didn't speak to anybody, simply got in the car and exited the scene, so to speak. So what did you do?'

'I found our Martin. He's a wealthy man, I suspect. He inherited a company that makes specialist tools for the medical world. His father started the business, and when he died Martin got the lot as he was an only child. He was born in sixty-nine, making him a year older than Evelyn, and he's been married to his current wife, wife number three, for twelve years. If that girl wasn't his wife who Alan Egerton saw at Chatsworth, it seems he could be heading for wife number four.'

'Of course!' Luke said. 'As you go down into Sheffield and you turn left at the Moor roundabout, there's a massive place on the right called Synyer Medical. I never really knew what it was, but I'm assuming that's his place of work.'

Tessa nodded. 'It is. His father had it built when the company expanded, they needed much more room than their original premises. I've put all of this into my report, was up till about eleven researching him. The upshot of it all is I don't like him. He now lives with wife number three who is called Phyllis.

She was Phyllis Ashford before she married him. Of the Ashford Hotel chain.'

'Serious money then.'

'Very serious. She's a fair bit younger than him, twelve years or so, so I do wonder if he needed an influx of money, but perhaps I'm prejudging. Maybe he loves her.'

'So where do they live?'

'A little way outside Alport.'

'Wow. Really serious money then. I take it it's a big house?'

Tessa swung her laptop screen around. The house was what could be loosely termed a mansion. The grounds were gated and surrounded by fencing and shrubs, with lawns bordered by well-established trees. Tessa zoomed out a little and it was clear the neighbourhood didn't include neighbours. It was secluded, and beautiful.

'She lived here before she married him, so I'll ask Beth to do a bit of digging to see who owns it now. Is it her, or is it a joint arrangement?'

'Are we going to turn up, or should we ring to make an appointment. Don't forget I can't do tomorrow, so it'll have to be today.'

She laughed. 'How come I don't get to jaunt off to London? And you're going to Harrods.' She glanced at her screen to check the time. 'I'll ring now, and tell him we're coming to see him. Let's start the pot boiling.'

The phone rang for several rings and was answered by a woman. 'Phyllis Synyer. How can I help you?'

'I'd like to speak to Mr Martin Synyer, please. My name is Tessa Marsden, and I'm with the Connection Investigation Agency in Eyam.'

'He's having breakfast. Ring back later, please.' The receiver was replaced, and Tessa looked at her phone with some astonishment.

'Silly stuck up cow,' she muttered and immediately rang the number again. The call was answered after three rings, and Tessa spoke before Phyllis could.

'Is this later? I'd like to speak to him now, please. It will take one minute, and then he can go back to his eggs Benedict or whatever he's having.'

The next voice on the line was even grumpier than the first one. 'What do you want? I'm busy.'

'It's a courtesy call, Mr Synyer. I am a partner in the Connection Investigation Agency, and I would like to see you this morning, along with another of our partners. Would eleven be okay?'

'No, it bloody wouldn't. It's Sunday!'

'I know. Crime doesn't stop because it's the seventh day, Mr Synyer.'

'Crime? What the fuck are you talking about?'

'Please don't swear, Mr Synyer. We need to speak to you with reference to the death twenty-five years ago of Evelyn Pearson.'

There was a momentary pause, but a pause it definitely was. 'I don't know anyone of that name.'

'I know you don't, she's been dead twenty-five years. But you did, didn't you. Your name has also cropped up in two recent murders, both women dying within the last few days. I suspect it will be to your advantage to speak to us today before we pass your name on to the police. They won't give you the courtesy of speaking to you in your own home, trust me. And this way you can alert your solicitor before you're taken in for questioning. Now, will you have finished your breakfast by eleven?'

Again there was hesitation. 'I'll give you fifteen minutes at eleven. That's all.'

'I don't think you understand, Mr Synyer. We'll possibly

need longer than that, depending on whether we believe you or not. See you at eleven.'

She disconnected, and breathed out.

'Awesome,' Luke said. 'We should have recorded that, and made it part of a training manual in how to deal with dickheads. Cheryl's going to be so pissed off she missed it.'

Tessa pushed her empty cup towards Luke. 'Shall we have a refill? We don't need to go anywhere yet, and I've got croissants in my bag.'

Luke and Tessa travelled to Alport in Tessa's car, and Tessa held up her ID towards a camera high up on the gate post. The gates opened slowly and she drove through. She parked outside the front door, and Luke rattled the lion's head knocker while she retrieved her briefcase and locked the car.

Phyllis Synyer admitted them, then left them standing in the hall while she went to get her husband. She was a tall woman with hair that was more grey than black, and as they watched her move away it was clear she was favouring her right leg, limping in an almost ungainly fashion. She appeared much older than her forty-one years, and Tessa felt surprised by that. She wondered if their ponderings about marrying for money could possibly be correct and she was about to say something to Luke when Martin Synyer arrived in the hallway. He was about the same height as his wife, smartly dressed in jeans and a designer jumper, his dark blonde hair falling fashionably forward onto his forehead. His eyes, however, were hooded as he stared at them, and angry.

'What do you want,' he demanded.

'To sit down with you and talk about Evelyn Pearson.'

He hesitated, then said, 'Follow me.'

He took them into a study, where he sat behind a desk, and

they took chairs facing him. Tessa placed the recorder on the desk and switched it on. He looked at it with some suspicion. 'What's that for?'

'Saves us taking notes,' Luke said. 'I'll email you a transcript if you need one.'

Synyer ignored Luke, and concentrated on Tessa. 'I remember little about Evelyn Pearson. Why you should need to speak to me, I have no idea. This is upsetting for my wife, as you can imagine.'

'Did your wife go with you to Chatsworth a few weeks ago, Mr Synyer?' Tessa kept her voice smooth.

'I didn't go to Chatsworth this year.'

'Not *this* year. December. Our witness saw you there.'

'I said I didn't go.'

'I know what you said, Mr Synyer. I also know you did go.'

'Bloody Egerton,' he muttered.

'Okay, now we've established you did go, I take it your wife doesn't know you went? We're trying to build a picture here, Mr Synyer.'

'I went with a friend.'

'A friend? Does she have a name?'

'No.'

'Then let's hope she's got one by the time the police arrive to take you in for questioning.'

Tessa pursued it no further, but looked down at her notes.

'When you met Evelyn, she was the girlfriend of your friend Alan Egerton. Is that right?'

'She was. Too good for him, the wimp.'

'You became... friendly... with her?'

'I had a girlfriend of my own.'

'Mr Synyer, your lifestyle suggests to me that fidelity isn't all that relevant to you. Isn't your wife your third one?'

'You've done your homework, I see.'

'The clue's in my job title,' Tessa said, allowing a touch of sarcasm to creep in.

'So did you intend Evelyn Pearson being Mrs Synyer the first?' Luke interrupted, aware that Tessa was getting to a point where it would have pleased her enormously to slap handcuffs on him and arrest him.

'No. I took her out a couple of times, but that was all.'

'While she was still with Alan?'

'Yes. She was about to finish with him when she disappeared. He didn't know we'd seen each other.'

'She was finishing with him so she could go public with you?'

He shrugged. 'If you say so.'

'No,' Luke persisted. 'I don't say so. I'm asking the question. Did she intend being with you? We do have her diary...'

'Then you'll probably know, won't you.' His voice had regained its sullenness.

'You bought her gifts?'

'Occasionally.'

'High-end gifts?'

'Of course. She was a beautiful girl.' Synyer's replies were stiff, non-committal.

Luke saw his planned trip to London vanishing before his eyes. 'Such as?'

'Oh, for fuck's sake. I bought her a lingerie set in red silk and a small teddy bear from Harrods one time, and a pin with our two initials on it that I had made specially for her. I can't remember much else. We weren't together for that long, you know. I didn't meet her until February or March of that year, and she disappeared in the August. Is all this enough to hang me?'

'It could be,' Tessa said. 'We will be notifying our colleagues in the police. I didn't use that as a threat, we keep them fully informed of everything we discover. Now, we need to talk about Denise Jordan and Lorna Thompson.'

His face blanched. 'Why?'

'You know them?'

There was hesitation. 'Yes. The woman I was at Chatsworth with – that was Lorna Thompson.'

18

Luke and Tessa didn't see Phyllis Synyer again; Martin had escorted them to the door, eager to get them out of his house and to come up with a sensible idea to tell his wife the reason they had visited on a Sunday morning.

Luke cancelled his train ticket for the following day, then leaned back. 'I'd have brought you a Harrods carrier bag, you know,' he said.

Tessa squeezed his arm. 'I know you would. You're a lovely man, Luke. I hope you would have thought to have put some Baccarat Rouge 540 perfume inside it, naturally.'

'Of course I would, once I'd organised the bank loan. Right, let's go and get these statements done for Carl, and we can knock off.'

Oliver was waiting outside the front door of the Connection premises for them when Tessa pulled her car into the kerb.

'Really settled with us, hasn't he?' Luke said.

'Yes. We need to get him chipped, and have a health check done on him. I was wondering about having a cat flap put in, talking to Stefan about it. He's here tomorrow to sort out that extra space in Beth's office. I was speaking to her last night, she thinks she's found her new assistant. It's handy, I suppose, being in recruitment when you're looking for an employee yourself. Whoever it is lives in Tideswell, so easily commutable unless it snows.'

'Good. Beth always looks slightly frazzled, as if she's taken too much on, which she probably has. And now she's got a wedding to plan on top of her work life.'

They let themselves in, surprised to find Fred already there, immersed in his laptop.

'Hi, Fred, it's Sunday,' Tessa said. 'Your coffee pot on?'

'It is. And I might feel inclined to say it's Sunday to you two also. I hope you told Cheryl where you were.'

Luke and Tessa exchanged guilty looks.

'Right, here's what you do. Leave her a retrospective note that states time left the office, where you've been, and time back in the office, then leave it on her desk. It might work, it might not, but it's worth a try. Or you could simply grovel.' He grinned.

He handed them their drinks and they sat down opposite him and told him about their morning.

'You think he killed our body?'

Tessa hesitated. 'Strangely enough, I don't. Obviously we can't probe as deeply as the police can at interview, like asking for alibis and suchlike, but I actually don't think he's got it in him. He's a jack-the-lad, no doubt about that, one for the ladies, but a murderer? His shock was so obvious when I mentioned Lorna's name, and it blew him away when I said Denise was dead also. I'm off to that book club tomorrow, see if we can add anything to what we already know. Denise was a member, as is Sharon Shaw, the postman's wife. Lorna, of course, ran it, so I thought I'd head there tomorrow.'

'And you still going to London, Luke?'

Luke shook his head. 'No, we got the information we needed this morning. I've cancelled my train ticket, so I'll get an extra three hours in bed. It was a bit of a long shot anyway, that they could identify the lingerie set from twenty-five years ago. It seems Synyer bought it for her when he was stealing her away from Alan Egerton. You got much on this week?'

Fred smiled. 'Big conclusion to a case tomorrow morning. Our couple who live at Great Hucklow won't be living there together for much longer. I do rather think Amy Barker will go for the jugular on this one and I could almost feel sorry for Tony Barker if I hadn't seen him screwing his sister-in-law in Amy's bed.'

Tessa laughed. 'Ouch. I'm assuming she knows about it.'

'She does. She stayed out on Saturday night specifically to see what he would do, and he fell for it. I'd put a couple of cameras in, plus I was on surveillance outside to take pictures, so we have a proper gallery of photos to take to the divorce court. I'm going up to Great Hucklow for ten tomorrow, to hand everything over, hence I'm in here today printing everything off and producing our final bill.' Fred looked across his desk at Luke. 'And what will you be telling your Mrs Pearson?'

'I'll be taking the lingerie back for a start,' he said. 'She'll come up with some excuse as to why the police didn't take it first time round, I'm sure. I am a tad worried about her reaction when I say Synyer's name. I think his testicles will be in grave danger of being crushed by two house bricks.'

Tessa laughed, then realised he wasn't joking. 'You think she'll take matters into her own hands?'

'I think it's why she came to us in the first place. She wants this name before the police can whisk him away, out of her reach. She's insisted all the way through that any information we get goes to her before the police as she's paying us. If I don't tell her first, it might not only be Synyer's balls in those two house bricks.'

Trying desperately to hide the laughter, Tessa looked at Fred. 'I'm so glad I didn't cop for this case, aren't you, Fred?'

'Too bloody right, I am. It's bad enough with the warring Barkers, but they're pussycats at the side of Harriet Pearson. Good luck tomorrow, lad, and don't forget to tell Cheryl your movements in case she has to retrieve your body.'

Luke secured the shutters and waved as the other two drove away. He felt it had been a successful day, even though it gave him additional problems. He would set up an appointment with Carl Heaton for Monday afternoon, but he needed to make it late in case Tessa wanted him to go to the book club with her. He would be passing on what they had learnt, but that meant definitely seeing Hattie before that meeting.

He sat in his car thinking things through, then drove around to Maria's home. He needed to tell her about his postponed London trip, and she came out to meet him as he was locking the car.

'You coming in?'

'If it's okay.'

She grinned. 'Oh it's okay. Mum's never shut up singing your praises. Come on, I'll make you a drink.'

'Water, please. I'll be bouncing if I have any more coffee today.'

They sat at the kitchen table, and he smiled at her. 'I could have texted.'

'Probably.'

'I've been working, had to interview somebody we think might have been a naughty lad, but it's solved one issue which means I don't have to go to London tomorrow. I didn't want you to spot me at the office and wonder what was going on.'

She laughed. 'I think I might have realised your plans had had to change. Yours is never going to be a regular job any more than mine is. I can be called into the vets at any time if there's an emergency, so we'll learn to live with the situation. And as you say, we can text when there's a change of plan. Having said all that, I'm really glad you called round and didn't text.' She leaned across and gave him a gentle kiss.

'And that made it all worthwhile,' he said.

Luke arrived home but called in to see Cheryl before anything else. He needed to tell her of his change of plans.

'You're not going? I'd be truly disappointed if that was me.' She smiled. 'Okay, it's no problem. What are you doing instead?'

'I'm going up to see Hattie, then I can either ask DI Heaton to call in, or go with Tessa to a book club. I'll speak to Tessa before I make a decision, I think. If I see Carl first, then we find something out at the book club...'

'Like who wrote Shakespeare's plays?'

'I've thought myself into the book club outing, haven't I? And surely they'll read crime. Please don't tell me they're likely to read romance or erotica.'

'If it's women, it could be anything. So where is this book club?'

'Bakewell library. Lorna Thompson was the librarian and she ran the club. Denise Jordan was a member, as is even the postman's wife. The postman found Lorna's body. The chap we went to see this morning...'

'Whoa! Rewind, young man. The chap you went to see this morning?'

Inwardly he cursed. 'It was a spur-of-the-minute thing. We've left you a note...'

'Stop digging, Luke. The hole's deep enough. What if something had happened to the pair of you? Nobody would have known where you were.'

'We left you a note.'

'When?'

He couldn't keep his face straight any longer. 'When we got back, and Fred told us we could leave a retrospective note. So we did.' Luke creased in laughter, and she hit him with the *Sunday Times*.

'Go home, Taylor, and all of you had better check your inboxes tomorrow. There will be a memo.'

He was still stifling laughter when he reached home, and trying to explain to his mum what the conversation with Cheryl had been like caused laughter to erupt once more. Naomi couldn't help but think that meeting Maria London had done him a power of good, had retrieved his sense of humour from wherever it had been following the road accident. Her Luke was coming back to her.

'You're in bother then?'

'Seems like it. Me and my big mouth. But it's not only me, we're all getting a memo. I'm sure I wasn't as strict as this when I used to keep track of everybody.'

'Then you've got a short memory, young man. You've grumbled many times that you couldn't find Kat, or Nan had disappeared, and clearly Cheryl takes her job seriously. She has to, so read her memo and take her a bunch of flowers to say sorry.'

'I can't blame Tessa?'

'She'll not fall for that. You're the one who's passed on the work she's expected to do, and she's trying to do it to the best of her ability, and you've thwarted her.'

'Thwarted her? Crikey, it had better be a big bunch of flowers.'

Luke went to his bedroom and placed his laptop on his desk. He stubbed his toe as he shuffled around his bed, and let out a curse.

Spending a few minutes tapping away brought his files on the Pearson case up to date, so he removed thoughts of work from his mind. He needed to leave home. Pulling a piece of paper towards him, Luke made some notes. A flat. He didn't want a house, he wasn't too fond of gardening. Two bedrooms so one could be used as his study. Near to work. He would prefer within walking distance. He liked having the choice of whether to take the car or not. Biggest plus – Rosie could move out of the bedroom she currently shared with Imogen, and they would have a room each.

He did a brief internet search, left his name with a couple of estate agents, and closed down the computer. A quick shower, then sleep. Perchance to dream. Damn Cheryl and her Shakespeare comment...

He laid his head back on the pillow, and when he woke at three it was only to pull the covers over himself to stop the shivering. He had his shower at seven, and was in work by eight, clutching a bunch of flowers picked up from the petrol station, along with a packet of jelly babies. That should sweeten up Cheryl, he decided, leaving them on her desk.

He headed up to hide in his office.

19

MONDAY 20TH JANUARY 2020

I t was sunny, and the drive up to Great Hucklow was extremely pleasant. Fred had switched on his radio, listening to news about the virus that seemed to be spreading outside the confines of China, and he wondered if he should be worried. The government seemed to be moderately concerned.

'Oh well,' he said aloud, 'I expect somebody will say if we've to take any precautions.' He pressed a different button and Gold radio filled the inside of his car. He listened to hits of the sixties for the rest of the journey.

'I'm off,' Tony Barker called from the bottom of the stairs. 'I'll ring before I leave the office tonight.'

'Fine,' Amy responded after stepping out of the shower.

There was a few seconds of hesitation, and then Tony spoke again. 'You okay?'

'Yes.'

He shrugged and headed outside to his Jaguar. He smiled as he sank into the leather driving seat. If there was one thing above all else that he felt told him he was a successful businessman, it was this beautiful car, his Jaguar, something he had craved since being a boy in junior school. He reversed off the drive and began his journey into Tideswell. Using his voice controls, he said, 'Ring Vee.'

Amy stood in the bay window in the bedroom, a towel wrapped around her, and watched as her husband pulled away up the road. She briefly wondered if it would have been easier to get somebody to kill him, rather than initiate the divorce proceedings that were definitely on the cards, as from this afternoon. She decided that she couldn't possibly end up in prison from filing for divorce, whereas taking out a contract on your spouse was probably frowned upon, but it was always an option. She carried her clothes through to the small guest bedroom, knowing Fred had put cameras in the two main rooms in addition to the lounge downstairs. She dressed quickly, then returned to the main bedroom to dry her hair and apply a touch of make-up.

Fred arrived promptly, and Amy smiled as he walked up the drive towards her.

'Amy, everything okay?'

'It is, and as a bonus, Mum and I had a lovely time at the theatre, and at the hotel, so all's good. Come in, the kettle's boiled.'

He smiled outwardly, frowned inwardly. She looked happy that her world was about to implode spectacularly, and he suddenly felt uncomfortable. Something felt off. He followed her down the hall and into the kitchen, then sat at the table. He said nothing until she handed him a mug of tea, then he took the envelope he had filled with still pictures from his folder.

'This holds copies of the camera footage from two of the three cameras. They didn't use the spare bedroom.' He handed her a USB drive, and she stood and took it to her handbag.

'Thank you. I don't think I want to look at it. I'll hand it to my solicitor this afternoon.'

'Are you okay looking at these? These are prints of photos I took as your sister arrived, and various stills from the films that clearly show both their faces. One or two show them having sex. You have more than enough here to guarantee the efficacy of your claim.'

'I'll look at them when I'm on my own,' she said, and sipped at her drink. 'You've brought your final bill?'

'I have.' He handed her the white envelope, her name on the front. 'While you're checking it, I'll go and take down the cameras, if that's okay.'

'It's fine, Fred. Do what you have to do, and I'll write a cheque for this.'

· Fred walked slowly upstairs, took down the camera from the spare room, then went into the room used by the about-to-be separated couple. It was a calm room, beautifully decorated in pale blue, and he had placed the tiny camera in the gap left by two of the three mirrors on the dressing table. It was angled towards the bed. He quickly removed it and dropped it into his coat pocket.

He turned to leave the room and saw the photograph on the chest of drawers – a happy, carefree shot of Amy and Vee, her sister. He stared at it, wondering how on earth she could leave that in situ, reminding her of the woman who was so clearly having an affair with her husband.

Fred shook his head, guessing he'd never understand women if he lived to be a hundred.

He rejoined Amy in the kitchen, where she handed him a cheque for the balance owing. He finished his drink, then stood.

'You have my number if you need me for anything. Good luck in the future, Amy. You're making him leave, or are you going?'

She smiled. 'Oh, he's going. I have someone coming to change the locks shortly, so he won't even get beyond the garage when he comes home tonight. I'll leave his stuff in there, and he can go find his solace wherever he can.'

Fred walked down the hallway and she followed him. 'Thank you for your custom,' he said. 'I hope everything works out for the best.'

Fred drove back to Eyam still deep in thought. His first meeting with Amy hadn't led him to believe she was the sort of person who buried her head in the sand and ignored everything going on around her, but her attitude this morning had been odd. It was almost as if it was happening to someone else, not her.

He shrugged. He could forget about the situation now. The job was done, he could concentrate on the one that could prove to be an extended one at Chesterfield, and the Wednesday morning staff meeting would get a job complete report from him.

He pulled up in Bradwell, called in the bookshop to ask them to order a book for him that he had seen recommended on Facebook, only to find to his delight they already had a copy of it. He paid for it, walked a few shops further along to the café and ordered a large latte.

He became immersed in the book, the true story of the Pottery Cottage murders in Chesterfield in nineteen seventy-seven. He could vaguely remember it happening, but his parents had spoken of it often as they had been friends with two of the victims through a local bridge club.

The bookshop had slipped in a bookmark, so he used it

before closing the book, drained his coffee cup and thanked the waitress as he left. It had been a pleasant half hour, something he needed after the slightly nasty taste in his mouth left by his thoughts about Amy and Tony Barker. How and why could a marriage have gone so drastically wrong in a short six months.

Cheryl smiled at Fred as he walked through the door. 'Good outcome?' she asked.

'Seems so,' he said, returning the smile. 'Is Luke in?'

'No, he's gone to see Mrs Pearson.'

'Brave lad. If he hadn't gone yet, I was going to offer to go with him.'

'He's okay. I don't think I've ever known such a confident young man. I guess it's because he's always been the man of the house.'

'Really? No dad then?'

'No, and it's much tougher than simply no dad.' She laughed. 'He'll not mind me saying this because he jokes about it all the time. His dad left when he was about eight, went off with some other poor woman. Luke now lives with his nan, his mum, and his two younger sisters, Rosie and Imogen. He's definitely the man of the house and I think that's why he displays such confidence and... cheekiness... in whatever he does and says. He was a rock for me when Keith was so poorly. The whole family was, I couldn't have wished for better neighbours. His mum works over the road in the Co-op. Naomi, she's called. She's the undermanager, but mainly works on checkout.'

'I'll look out for her. So if Luke isn't in, is Oliver?'

'Again it's a no. Luke went out the door, and Oliver followed him. They're inseparable. Makes me smile.'

'I've bought him a catnip mouse from the bookshop.'

To Cheryl's credit she didn't query why a bookshop would

sell catnip mice. 'That's nice, I don't doubt he'll be back soon wanting food anyway. Oliver, I mean, not Luke.'

Fred went towards his office and he heard Cheryl's follow-up words. 'And you've got a memo.'

Luke couldn't help but be impressed by Hattie Pearson's lounge. He had time to look around him while she made their pot full of tea and plate full of scones, and he realised what a true cottage it was. Her suite was a wooden one, with comfortably deep cushions. She had a small table of the same wood by each seat, the carpet was a caramel colour beautifully set off by the duck egg blue walls, and the patterned curtains reflected the colours inherent in the room. It seemed that the creative talents were present in both mother and daughter. Hattie didn't overfill with knick-knacks; the ones on display were clearly antiques with the exception of a little duck. He stood and walked over to where it had pride of place on the chunky oak beam above the wood burner.

He heard the door open, and he put down the duck before going to help her manoeuvre the serving trolley across the thick carpet.

'It's a duck,' she said.

He smiled at her. 'I was busy admiring your other things. They're old?'

She poured the teas. 'They are. I don't know if it's still there because I haven't been for a while, but there's a garden centre at Calver Crossroads. Part of it was an antiques centre, and I picked most of them up there. A couple I inherited from my mum. The duck is the odd one out, but my most precious item.'

'Evelyn made it,' he said.

'She did. She was only five when she asked if she could have some proper clay. I've always been quite creative and it was soon clear she was streets in front of me with her ideas. Anyway, I got her the clay, she spent a couple of days playing with it, getting the feel of it. The result was two ducks. This is one of them, and the other she gave to her teacher at school for a Christmas present. The teacher thanked her of course, but she sent a letter home to me telling me how talented Evelyn was, in every aspect of craft work.'

Luke walked across and picked up the duck. 'She was five when she made this?' He looked underneath and saw a barely visible EP.

Hattie nodded. 'I have pictures that she drew at that age, they are equally as amazing. But it was clay that she loved. Either moulding it, or sculpting. There is still a kiln in that shed at the bottom of the garden. The world lost a true talent when she was killed.' She placed Luke's tea and a small plate that held a buttered scone on the table by his chair. 'Come and get your tea, and tell me what you've found out.'

'Okay, it's not a lot, but it's a start. However, Hattie Pearson, seventy-four-year-old dynamo, I want your firm pinky promise that you won't attempt to find out anything further for yourself, and won't approach anybody I may mention when we talk.'

She thought about it for a moment, then held up her little finger. 'I've not heard that phrase since my Evelyn went. Pinky promise, Luke. But that only holds good until you tell me the name of the bastard who definitely killed my Evelyn. Then all promises are cancelled.'

'But it will hold for now?'

She nodded. 'It will.'

20

Granby Road was in the middle of Bakewell, and boasted many small shops selling artisan goods, books, clothes for tramping the hills and dales of the surrounding countryside; Luke and Tessa walked along admiring the items on offer, both feeling unsettled about going into the book group meeting.

Tessa had already had a difficult few minutes with the acting librarian who was devastated at the loss of her friends, and who was toying with the idea of cancelling the book club until February; Tessa persuaded her otherwise.

'We need to talk to everyone. They may know something that they don't realise they know, and to be honest talking about Lorna and Denise will help them come to terms with losing them.'

There was a lull while Faith digested that. 'They filter in about fifteen minutes early so we start promptly at one. I'll explain what's happening as they arrive, so they are prepared for your arrival. Is that okay?'

Tessa breathed a sigh of relief. Crisis averted. The group would meet.

. . .

The meeting room was on the first floor and Tessa and Luke climbed the stairs. They found the room easily enough, and walked through the already-open double door. There appeared to be around a dozen people there, all milling around with mugs of tea in their hands.

Tessa hesitated and Faith detached herself from the people in the room and walked across to them. 'You had an easy journey?'

Tessa smiled. 'We did, and thank you for accommodating us. This is a lovely library.'

Faith nodded. 'It is. Very well used, and we have all sorts of groups meet in this room. If ever you want to learn how to make lace, this is the place to come.' She turned and clapped her hands. 'Everyone! This is Tessa and Luke, from Connection.'

There was a general waving of hands in acknowledgement, and they followed Faith across to the refreshments table. They both requested coffee, and she handed them a mug each. 'They'll start to wander towards the table in five minutes or so, but from the bits I've picked up, they're only talking about Lorna and Denise. I had to tell one or two, they hadn't heard.'

'We'll be sensitive,' Tessa assured her. 'I'll be passing around a piece of paper so they can all add their names. Can you let me know who isn't here today who would normally be here?'

'Of course,' Faith said. 'You know, we're only a group of friends. This club has been in existence for about three years now, and they're all devastated that we've lost two of our members. Today is going to be hard for all of us.'

People drifted towards the table, taking their drinks with them, so Luke and Tessa followed their lead, sitting together halfway down one side. When everyone was seated, Faith introduced them. 'This is Luke and Tessa, who are here from the Connection Investigative Agency. They need to ask a couple of questions, so thinking heads on, everybody.'

Tessa smiled and waved a piece of paper. 'I'm going to pass this around the table. It would be helpful if you could put your name and phone number, so we know who we've spoken to. I'm going to give you what bits of information we have, so we'll all know where we are. Denise Jordan and Lorna Thompson were both our clients, although they weren't aware of that fact at the beginning. Obviously, the murders are now a police investigation, but we're still continuing our side of the job we've been paid to do. The police will no doubt be contacting all of you over the next couple of days.'

The door opened and a woman came in, apologising profusely for being late. Faith smiled at her, and reassured her she hadn't missed anything. 'This is Luke and Tessa, Phyllis. They're here to ask some questions about Lorna and Denise.'

Phyllis Synyer turned her head and stared at the Connection colleagues. 'We've met,' she said, and sat as far from Luke and Tessa as she could.

Tessa continued. 'We were originally brought in to investigate some threatening letters the women had received, and had only just started our work when they were both killed. The obvious link between the two women was this book club, so we're here today to ask for openness, and for you to think. Firstly, if you've had any notes of a threatening nature, can you speak with us later, please? I'll give each of you a business card before we go, so if you think of anything at any time, please contact either us or the police. The other clear link is that they both lived in Bakewell, and therefore it's nothing to do with the club. Sharon, is your husband okay?'

Sharon blushed slightly. 'He's fine. I made him put in for a week of compassionate leave, it knocked him for six. He's found people dead before over the past twenty years, but they've been natural causes. Lorna's has really upset him, but to hear about Denise has...'

'Please tell him we asked after him. I fully understand how he is feeling, I was a DI in the Serious Crimes Unit until a couple of months ago.'

Sharon gave a tentative smile. 'Thank you. I'll pass that on.'

The paper had passed around everyone, and ended up back in front of Luke, who counted the names, making sure they agreed with the number around the table. He added Phyllis Synyer, who clearly had decided she didn't need to be treated in the same way as everyone else.

'Have any of you seen Lorna since your last meeting here?'

One or two held up their hands, but both confirmed it was purely in the library setting when they had come in to stock up on books for over the Christmas period. Nobody had met up with her outside of her work.

'And Denise?'

This time nobody acknowledged having seen her. 'Denise was our quiet lady,' Faith said. 'She loved coming here because it finished at a perfect time for her collecting Alex from school, and she loved books. Sometimes we don't always manage to get the book finished that's under discussion, but Denise always did. She would always make some comment on it, but she never pushed herself forward. In view of your visit today, we won't be discussing this month's book, we'll work our way through two next month.'

'And what was this month's book?' Luke asked.

'It was an old one, written in the fifties, called *Flowers for Algernon* by Daniel Keyes. It's a book that I know we'll have plenty to say about, so we'll postpone our discussion. Everybody will have made notes on it, I'm sure,' Faith said with a soft tinkling laugh.

Luke wrote down the title. 'And do you have physical books?'

'Some of us do. We all have eBook readers though, in case we can't get enough copies of the book of the month. We take it in turns to choose the book, and it would have been Denise's choice today... I've chosen one for us, to get us through to next month, and we'll be working our way through *Circe* by Madeline Miller.'

Notebooks were produced and everyone wrote down the title, and Luke and Tessa heard a couple of people say 'YES!' quite loudly.

'That's a popular choice,' Tessa said with a smile.

'It's because we've already read another of her books, *The Song of Achilles*, and we loved it, almost unanimously. We need a guaranteed good one to lift us at the moment. I have managed to get four copies at short notice, so it's up to you how you get this one.'

Almost everyone said they would buy the paperback, they wanted it on their bookshelves, and Faith visibly relaxed.

'Tell me about Lorna,' Tessa said.

'I can tell you she was a good friend to have. Never pushy, kept herself to herself, had a strange relationship with her partner in that they lived in the same house, but weren't really a couple. She confided in me that she felt so much happier once he'd gone. She did hint there was maybe someone else coming into her life, but it was early days and she certainly hadn't reached any stage other than going out occasionally. I have no idea who it was, and I didn't ask. I knew she would say if it progressed.' Faith looked down. 'I'm really going to miss her. I've worked with her for a long time, she taught me so much.' Faith wiped away a tear.

One of the elderly ladies sitting directly opposite Luke spoke next. 'Nothing was too much trouble for her. If you ordered a book, she would ring to tell you when it was in, and one time I couldn't come because I'd had a fall, so she came round every other day to make sure I was okay. A truly wonderful woman. We've lost someone special. Denise was in the same mould. I never had to go and get my own cuppa at our break time here, one or other would always get it for me. As a group, we're really going to miss them.'

Phyllis stood. 'If we're not discussing the book today, I'm going to be on my way.' She put her notebook into her bag, zipped up the coat she hadn't bothered removing, and headed for the door.

Luke stood quickly, and walked towards her, opening the door for her. 'Thank you for coming,' he said with a smile, 'we'll pop round to see you soon.'

Faith decided it was time for the drinks break, and the group mingled with each other as they had earlier. Tessa took around her cards and handed one to everyone. An older man, with a beautiful head of thick grey hair and the bluest of blue eyes smiled at her. 'You've certainly livened up our afternoon,' he said. He looked at her card. 'I'll maybe give you a ring when I get home. I need to think about something first.'

'Anytime, Mr Fletcher.'

'You know my name!'

'I looked at the sheet, and I'm blessed with a photographic memory. It helps in my job.'

'I bet it does. But please call me–'

'Patrick.'

'Now I'm really impressed. Do you read?'

'A lot. It's my winding down activity. I must confess to not having read the book you intended discussing today. Is it good?'

'It's thought-provoking, fascinating, and one of the best books I've read in a long time. You should get it. I'm going to pick up our new one from WH Smith on my way home. I normally read on my Kindle, I have arthritis in my hands and it's easier, but *Circe* has a beautiful cover so I want that on my shelves.'

'It seems a pleasant group. You been coming since the beginning?'

'I have. I suggested to Lorna we have one, and she set it up within a week. A lovely woman, which is why I want to think before I speak to you. Is that okay?'

'It is, and ring anytime.'

21

'Good day?' Cheryl asked, as Luke and Tessa arrived back at the office.

'Excellent,' Tessa said. 'You ever read a book called *Flowers for Algernon* and apparently Algernon is a mouse?'

'I have indeed. One of my top ten books of all time. You've never read it?'

'No, I like horror and psychological thrillers. You reckon I should read it?'

Cheryl laughed. 'I'll bring my copy tomorrow. I want it back when you've read it though. By then you'll want to buy your own copy.'

'Has DI Heaton confirmed what time he's coming?'

'He has, he's due in half an hour. Your office?'

'Yes please. Luke, will you join us?'

'As our two cases seem to have blended effortlessly, I think I'd better. We telling him everything?'

'Luke Taylor! Of course we are unless I kick your leg under the table. That will mean shut up. Okay?'

'Okay. Cheryl, you'll find this out for yourself, but when

148

you're working with our lovely Tessa, it's like working with the lights out and a blindfold on.' Luke shook his head as if in disbelief, then he grinned and headed towards the lift. 'I'm off to write up everything we've done today. Beth working from home?'

'She is. Stefan promised to keep the noise down to a minimum, but every so often I hear some expletive from in there. They're cracking on though. The wall is up now, and they were about to start working in reception to fit the new door, last I heard. Beth no longer has the largest office. It's looking good. There's a big window between Beth's and her assistant's office, that will have blinds on it. It would have been quite dark in both rooms otherwise, I think.'

Luke disappeared, leaving Tessa downstairs with Cheryl. 'I'm half expecting a phone call from somebody called Patrick Fletcher. If he does ring, can you put him through even if Carl is still here? He's an elderly gent from the book club, and it seemed as if he had something to say, but didn't want to say it there. At the very least he wanted to mull it over first, before speaking to me.'

Cheryl made a note of the name. 'Of course. You know what, I've been here exactly a week today, and I can't imagine what I did with myself prior to this. We've had three dead bodies, sorted out a biggish divorce issue, and found out we all get on. Would you think I was crazy if I told you I chat to Keith's photo every night and tell him all about my day here?'

Tessa reached in and gave her a hug. 'Welcome to my world. I too have a photo I chat to every night.'

'Hannah?'

'Hannah.'

· · ·

'So now you know everything we know.' Tessa gently kicked Luke's leg. 'If anything else happens I'll give you a call. I suggest you make a bit of a thing about bringing Martin Synyer in, because he was rattled by us, so the police turning up, as we promised you would, will scare the living daylights out of him. Having said that, I don't think he's who you're looking for, but that's gut instinct.'

'Gut instinct got you through everything, Tessa. I'll go with that. We'll definitely have him in though. He seems to be the only lead, and to be connected to both crimes...'

Tessa spoke quietly. 'My gut instinct only goes as far as my two cases, it doesn't extend into Luke's case. Luke?'

'My gut instinct, which is nowhere near as honed as Tessa's, says he could be a person of high interest with Evelyn's murder, and it'll be heaven help him if Hattie Pearson ever finds out I'm thinking that.'

Carl stood. 'Thank you for all of this. I have somebody out interviewing Alan Egerton this afternoon, so we'll see what comes of that. If we have to interview him twice it will be formally at the station and under caution. That will also happen with Synyer. I'll keep you informed.' He shook Luke's hand, gave Tessa a kiss on the cheek, and they heard the lift start to descend.

'Glad that's over,' Tessa said thoughtfully. 'Oh dear, I forgot to mention Patrick Fletcher.'

'That's somewhat remiss of you, Tessa Marsden. Coffee?'

'You got chocolate biscuits?'

'I do.'

'I could be tempted then. Wish that lovely old man would ring. He seemed a bit... hesitant. As if he didn't want to get somebody into bother.'

'Good book club, wasn't it?' Luke pressed buttons on the coffee machine.

'Surprisingly so. They were all so enthusiastic. I used to go to one many years ago, and to me it seemed as if it was a group to share gossip. The books were a sideline. It was lovely to be part of that one even if it was only for a day. I thought Faith did a remarkable job keeping it all together, because she was hurting. As they all were. Life can be pretty shitty at times, can't it.'

Luke handed her a mug, and placed the packet of chocolate digestives next to her. He completed his own drink, and sat down. He carefully rested his left arm on the table.

'Sore?'

'A little. I think I slept on it, instead of the other side, and it doesn't do it any good. It's much better than it was, so one day I'll be pain free. Needs time, I suppose.'

The telephone beeped, and Tessa quickly reached across for it. 'Tessa Marsden.'

She listened for a moment. 'Thank you for ringing, Patrick. I wasn't sure if you would. How can I help? I'm putting you on loudspeaker because Luke is in the office with me. That okay?'

'That's fine. Hello, Luke. It was good to meet you both today. I've had to give a lot of thought to this, because I'm not one to gossip, and basically that's what it is, but somebody has killed our two lovely ladies. So let me tell you what I've observed simply by being the quiet bloke of the group who nobody takes much notice of, if I can.'

Luke grabbed a piece of paper from the printer, and clicked open his pen.

'Go ahead, Patrick. We're listening,' Tessa said.

'Okay.' He sighed. 'The woman who left early is a bit of a strange one. Phyllis Synyer is her name. That's the first thing you need to know. The second thing is that her husband, Martin, a smart-looking bloke, always brings her to the meeting, and I mean actually brought her into the lobby every month. Lorna used to greet us in there, and direct everybody to the appropriate room, because at first we occasionally had to change rooms. Phyllis used to head off upstairs, but then he would stay in the lobby talking to Lorna. I always went early, because the library itself is off there, and I used to go and have an hour in there either picking new books, or reading the papers, relaxing. About six months ago things changed. I could see the occasional kiss, a quick touch on her bum, that sort of thing. But they also changed in another way.' He paused for a moment.

'Tuesday nights I play dominoes at the pub. It's a big pub, several rooms, and I saw Martin Synyer at the bar one night while I was playing. I thought nothing of it until Denise walked up to him, pointed to something over the bar, and turned away. Ten minutes later I went to the bar in the room I was in, and could see them quite clearly in the other room, sharing a table, heads close together, laughing, smiling a lot.'

'And you've seen them together since?'

'Oh yes. Once you know it, you can't unknow it. I even saw him with Lorna at the Chatsworth Christmas Fair, although I scuttled out of the way rather than confront them. Maybe things would have been different if I'd actually liked Phyllis, but she's a nasty piece of work, looks down on everybody because of who he is. And, of course, of who she is.'

'So he was seeing both women. Do you think his wife knew? Has she ever indicated that she was aware of the situation?'

Patrick laughed. 'I'm not privy to her thoughts on the matter. Maybe she did, maybe she didn't, but I'd give the information I've given you, under oath. I keep myself to myself, Tessa, but this is murder, and I liked both the ladies a lot.'

'Thank you, Patrick. This has been really helpful. Please hang on to my number in case you think of anything else. You may be interviewed by the police at some stage because I will have to pass this on, you need to be aware of that. Take care, and go read your book now.'

'Thank you, Tessa and Luke, I will.'

He disconnected and they looked at each other. 'Two at once,' Luke said. 'Brave man.'

'Three at once,' Tessa corrected him. 'He has a wife, don't forget. This has been a funny old day, hasn't it?'

'Certainly has. I'm going to write this conversation up for the Pearson file. You want a copy for your file?'

'Yes please. I don't quite know what to do about my file. We've taken deposits from both the women, but they're no longer with us, so won't be paying for any further work. I don't think we can leave it there. The brief was to find the writer of the notes, and we haven't done that, so it's logical to carry on, isn't it?'

Luke shrugged. 'Who knows. Are you feeling that Evelyn's killer is the same person as Lorna and Denise's killer?'

Tessa shook her head. 'No. It's the handwriting on the notes. Look at that list of names we took at the book club. The women take care how they write, the men don't. These notes were written with care, and if you think that's a crazy reason for me thinking a woman killed our two ladies, then so be it.'

He laughed. 'It probably is a crazy reason, but I'm not crazy enough to say you're wrong.' He stood and picked up his piece of paper with the notes scribbled on it, and took his packet of biscuits.

'You're not leaving them?'

'Certainly not. There'd be none left.'

He placed the McVitie's packet and his notes on his desk, then went down in the lift to have a look at the changes being made to Beth's office. There had been a considerable amount of drilling during the phone call.

There was now an extra door leading off reception, and he carefully opened Beth's door to see what the internal changes were. Beth's room had shrunk, but appeared much lighter with the addition of the large window between the two newly-formed offices. Stefan was in the small room, and looked up to see Luke's thumb held up in approval. Luke backed out, not wanting to stop them, and headed back upstairs.

The biscuits had disappeared.

22

'Is Oliver in?' Maria mouthed the words towards Cheryl, through the plate glass window.

Cheryl waved her towards the front door, and pressed the lock release. 'Come in, it's freezing out there. I think he's with Luke in his office.'

Maria held up the cat carrier. 'I've come to organise him being chipped. Luke said last night he would bring him across, but we're quiet at the moment so I thought I'd offer a collection service.'

Cheryl picked up her phone. 'Visitor for Oliver,' she announced.

Maria grinned and headed for the lift. 'I'll be two minutes.'

Oliver clearly wasn't happy inside the carrier, and Maria ran across the road, dodging the traffic. She lifted him out, and made a fuss of him, before taking him through to the treatment room. The little cat was swiftly dealt with, and he was given a drink of water before being placed back in the cat carrier.

Maria braved the traffic once more and returned the newly

officialised member of the Connection team to his home. 'I'll take him up to Luke, he'll want to be pampered,' Maria said with a laugh. 'He was a brave boy, but I get the impression he thinks Luke is his dad.'

'Oh, he definitely thinks that. The hand that feeds him and all that. Go straight up.'

Luke met her at the lift.

'He's not heavy,' she said. 'You didn't need to be here waiting.'

'Did it hurt?'

'Of course not. He's been chipped, not castrated. However, we do need to talk about that...'

Luke looked horrified. 'He's not old enough.'

'He is.'

'But you want to take away his rights to be a father.'

'True, but he's hardly a pedigree cat where his kittens would be worth loads of money.'

Luke took him out of the carrier, and covered Oliver's ears. 'Don't listen to her, pal. Your kittens would be precious and loved.'

'Luke, he really does need to be done.' Maria laughed. 'Shall I book him in?'

'Soon.' Luke sat, placing Oliver on his knee. 'Let him get over this first.'

'Okay, but I'll remind you again in a fortnight. We didn't take his collar off, by the way. He didn't have it on.'

'I'll hunt around for it. He's always sliding it off, but I daren't make it any tighter. It'll be in somebody's office, I keep finding it placed on my desk so I can put it back on him.'

'He's chipped now, so if he strays he doesn't need his name on his collar. Leave it off, he clearly doesn't like it. See you later.'

He smiled. 'Definitely. I'll pick you up at six, and we can have a drink first. The table's booked for seven. That okay?'

'Certainly is.' She blew him a kiss and disappeared.

Tessa stood in Luke's doorway. 'I've been thinking. I've checked with Synyer's place in Sheffield and he's in today. Fancy a trip to the big city?'

He placed Oliver on the floor and stood. 'Definitely. I'll pack a bag.'

'It's Sheffield, not Las Vegas. Twenty minutes and we'll be there.'

'I meant my backpack with my notes and stuff, clever clogs. If we're seeing him I want to be prepared. I also want to ask him if he was the one who wrote that little note she slipped in that journal envelope. I'll take all the diary sheets. You think it's a good idea to confront him at work?'

'I do. Away from Phyllis.'

Luke nodded and unzipped his backpack. 'I kind of empathise with him chasing other women. Did we find out who owns the house they live in?'

'Beth messaged me last night. It was in her name only, but made joint ownership on their marriage.'

Luke looked up from what he was doing. 'So if she were to die...'

'He'd end up the sole owner of an expensive piece of real estate in one of the most sought-after counties in the UK.'

'And he's a prime suspect in...'

'Murder.'

Tessa drove, and Luke spotted the sign for the Synyer Medical car park. They found a space and pulled in, then sat for a moment.

'Are we going merely to cause him aggro, or do we think we'll get something from this?'

Tessa half-turned towards Luke. 'I've no idea. I'm going to wing it, see what happens. We didn't tell Carl Heaton till yesterday afternoon, so I don't think he'll have spoken to him yet. I think Synyer'll still be jittery, maybe we can catch him off-guard. Talk to me.'

'What about?'

'Gut feelings. When I first joined the police I didn't know what a gut feeling was. Everything had to be black and white. When I was made up to DS, my superintendent congratulated me, and told me to develop something he'd noticed in me and that was gut instinct. You feel anything about this man?'

'Yes, but I didn't put it down to gut instinct.' Luke stared out of the windscreen. 'I put it down to me being stupid enough to think it. I don't believe he killed Evelyn, and I don't believe he killed Denise and Lorna, although he has the obvious connections. Now shoot me down in flames.'

'I can't. I agree. The trick now to learn is how to follow your gut instinct, and yet keep an open mind. Follow my lead when we get in, I'm going to try to get him to give us an alibi. This won't be easy, but if he can produce an alibi for Evelyn, there's really only one other in the running, isn't there?'

'Alan Egerton.'

Tessa laughed. 'Alan Egerton. Or somebody who hasn't even appeared in the running yet.' She opened her door and climbed out, leaving Luke to stare at the space where her body had been seconds earlier.

Somebody not in the running yet?

. . .

The receptionist handed them two visitor IDs which they slipped around their necks. 'Mr Synyer can see you for ten minutes. He'll be down to collect you shortly.'

They moved around the reception area, looking at the various pictures on the wall that were all of Sheffield, but both turned as the lift door opened.

Synyer walked across to them and looked at the picture they were examining. 'It's the old Coles Corner. Do you remember it being like that?'

'Vaguely,' Tessa said. 'No longer, of course. It's a coffee shop now, I believe.'

'It is. These pictures were bought at various times by my father, and I've kept the collection because of that. Follow me, and we'll go to my office.'

As he passed the receptionist he asked her to hold his calls until told otherwise.

Martin Synyer's office was a direct contrast to his calming, quite sophisticated reception area. His desk was glass topped with a stainless steel base that was truly stunning in its simplicity. He had artwork on his walls, all Pete McKee originals, and the walls were a pale beige, setting off the thick dark beige carpet to perfection. In one corner was a small oval coffee table, with four low chairs around it and in the centre a framed photograph of a smiling Martin Synyer standing proudly by the side of a white helicopter. Luke immediately picked up the photograph.

'Wow. Is this yours?'

Synyer smiled. 'It is. We have a helipad on the roof here, and I have one in the grounds at home, so I occasionally use it to get to work. It's awesome for impressing clients. We also mainly use it for getting to our holiday home in France. That was my original idea for buying it.'

He told them to sit down, saying his secretary would bring coffee in.

Tessa was flummoxed. She had expected aggression, a refusal to co-operate... anything but what she was seeing.

They had taken their seats when the door opened and a smiling woman brought in a tray of drinks.

'Thank you, Kirsty,' Synyer said, and waited until she had left the room before sitting down opposite his two guests. There was a choice of tea or coffee, and both said coffee. He poured out their drinks, then sat back.

'How can I help this time? And I apologise for my behaviour on Sunday. Phyllis and I had had a hell of a row, and you took the fallout, I'm afraid. I haven't been approached by the police yet, by the way.'

'We only told DI Heaton yesterday afternoon,' Tessa said. 'He'll be here shortly, don't worry.'

'I'm not worried. I'm also not guilty. I held back a lot on Sunday because I was feeling so pissed off with the world in general, but I really didn't have anything to do with Evelyn's death. I wasn't even in the country.'

'You know when she died then?' Luke allowed a puzzled expression to cross his face, he didn't want this man to think he could tell them anything and they would take it at face value.

'I know she didn't return home on the Monday night, the twenty-first of August nineteen ninety-five. I think it's reasonable to assume it's because she was dead. She was close to her mother, and if Evelyn was doing anything to keep her away from home, she would have told Hattie.'

'And you have an alibi?'

'I do. Every year this factory closes down for two weeks from around the twentieth of August for maintenance of all the machines. Most of the employees take it as their annual holidays, and we work with a small skeleton staff. My father and

I always headed off to Spain for two weeks, to play golf. That year we left the UK on the nineteenth of August, the Saturday. I last saw Evelyn the Friday night before we flew, and she gave me a picture.' He stood and walked to his safe.

He removed a small framed picture and brought it across to the coffee area. He fiddled around removing it from the frame, then showed it to them.

The drawing was of Evelyn. She had captured the essence of herself, her eyes sparkled, her lips curved in a gentle smile. She had signed it EP, 19-08-95.

'Turn it over,' Martin said quietly.

To my Martin, I will cry from 20th August until 3rd September, then I will smile again. Everything will be sorted when you get home, I promise. I love you xxx

Tessa read it twice. She looked up. 'Everything will be sorted?'

Synyer nodded. 'She was going to tell Egerton she was calling off their relationship. We would have been together properly, not having to sneak around. I returned home after our two weeks away and she had disappeared. Alan denied all knowledge of her going, said maybe she had found somebody else, but I knew different. We were so right for each other, there couldn't have been anybody else. She wanted to wait until I had left with Dad before telling Alan, and I presume he was the last person she saw...'

'Mr Synyer, could we have a photocopy of this beautiful picture before we go, please? We have to give a report to our client, and she would love to have this last reminder of her daughter.'

'Of course. I'll do two copies, because no doubt the police will want one. I keep it locked in my safe, because it's my most treasured possession, and I wouldn't want jealous wives – or lovers – seeing it.'

'Evelyn was certainly a talented woman.' Tessa stared at the picture before handing it to Martin, who walked across to his printer to copy both sides of the picture.

Luke opened his backpack and removed the diary copies. 'What puzzles me most,' he said as Martin returned, 'is why she put nothing in her diary about you going.'

Luke picked up his copies, and flicked through to August. He stopped at the nineteenth. It was blank. As was the twentieth, the day of the alleged flight to Spain. He spun it around. 'Look,' he said to Martin. 'Absolutely nothing.'

Martin pulled it towards him. 'Look closer.' For the two weeks following the flight date, every initial letter of the month had a small pencil underline beneath it. 'You have to remember that when I told her I would be going to Spain for two weeks, our relationship was secret. She would have marked this so that she knew I would be coming back to her. She wouldn't have put in capital letters MARTIN IS GOING TO SPAIN FOR TWO WEEKS, trust me. It was really that secret, because she wanted to choose the right time to call it off with Alan. That was her nature. I loved her so much.'

Luke removed the final diary sheet from his copies. 'And did you at some point give her this little note?'

He smiled. 'I did. She kept it, clearly.'

'It was in the little envelope pocket at the end of the diary. Thank you for confirming you wrote it.'

'As I said, I loved her so much.'

23

They sat quietly in the car for a moment, both lost in their thoughts.

'Well?' said Tessa, eventually.

'Is that the same feller we saw on Sunday?'

'It is. And now he's a feller with an alibi, provided it can be confirmed. We'll leave that to Carl, because personally I believed him. I think you need to discount his involvement, assume it's a proven fact he was in Spain, and move on. To Egerton. I bet he hasn't got an out-of-the-country reason for not being near Evelyn.'

'First thing tomorrow I'm off to see him. You didn't mention Denise and Lorna, I noticed. Any reason for that?'

'That's for a second visit.' Tessa laughed. 'We'll let him get over this first, then tomorrow I'll be back. I actually think he's a womaniser, not a murderer, but we'll see. If he'd been aggressive with his answers, then I might have gone for the jugular, but he was quite amenable and helpful, so it was better to let him run with that, we got more from him. I don't see him tied in with the other two deaths, he had nothing to gain. My two ladies probably kept him sane in what is clearly a fraught marriage. I'll give this some thought tonight.'

'I'm going out...'

'So I gathered. Nothing's a secret in our office.'

'It's our first proper date. Saturday night was good, but it was a school reunion and a game of Uno. Tonight I've booked us in for an Italian meal in Bakewell.'

'Best behaviour then.'

He smiled. 'Maybe.'

Luke stood in front of his mirror, and straightened his tie one more time. He suddenly felt extremely grown up, a man, and a brief thought flashed across his mind as he wondered how he had got to this stage almost without realising. One second he was a teenager in school, studying for exams, knocking about with mates, and the next he was taking a beautiful girl, woman, to an Italian restaurant, dressed to kill in a suit and tie. His best suit and tie.

He closed the bedroom door behind him, and heard two wolf whistles. Rosie and Imogen were standing in their bedroom doorway, grinning.

'Get lost,' he said and turned to chase them back into their room. They disappeared, slamming the door behind them. He could hear their giggles as he walked down the stairs. Yes, he definitely needed his own place...

The candle in the centre of the table glimmered, and simultaneously Luke and Maria reached across and linked fingers.

'You're beautiful,' he said softly, and she squeezed his fingers in response.

The waiter slid up beside them and handed them a menu each.

'Can I get you drinks?'

'Water, please,' they said in unison.

'Thank you,' he said, writing it down. 'I'll leave you for a few minutes, and I'll be back to take your order.'

Maria tried desperately to hide her giggle. 'We certainly live the high life,' she said, 'both of us asking for water.'

'I'm driving, but you could have had anything.'

'I'm not keen,' Maria admitted. 'I don't really like the taste of alcoholic stuff. And I definitely don't like the way it makes me feel; wobbly and headachy.'

They picked up the menus and made their choices.

'Can we stop somewhere and talk for half an hour?'

Luke turned to look at Maria. 'We can. You don't want to go home?'

'Not yet. It's too... loud at home. And we couldn't really talk in the restaurant, as lovely as it was.'

He thought for a moment. 'I'll pull into the car park in Stoney Middleton. That okay?'

'It's fine. If the police come, I'll tell them you've kidnapped me.'

'Okay.'

Two minutes later he indicated right, and dropped down the small incline into the car park. After turning off the engine he reached into the back seat and grabbed at a blanket.

'We'll put this over our knees, it'll soon go cold.'

She smiled at him. 'You're so thoughtful.'

'Don't be fooled,' he said, smiling back at her. 'I was taught by an expert who went on many a night-time surveillance with me. Always have a blanket on the back seat, you never know when you might need it.'

'Doris?'

'Doris. Was there something in particular you wanted to talk about, or are we avoiding going home after such an awesome evening?'

'I wanted half an hour with you, only you.'

He lifted her hand and gently kissed it. 'Am I complaining?'

'Can I see you again?'

'I thought I was supposed to ask that.'

'Then ask it.'

'Maria, can I see you again?'

'Yes. I'm glad we've settled that. Now to the next bit.'

'The next bit?' Luke felt himself break out into a mild sweat.

'I'd like to be your girlfriend. I know I'm not supposed to be saying this, but we live in twenty-twenty, Luke, not nineteen-twenty. I've wanted to be your girlfriend for a long time, since being at school, and never thought you'd look twice at me. But you have.'

He pulled her close. 'Maria, I feel blown away by you wanting to go out with me. You're stunning. You could have anybody. I bless the day Oliver brought us together. Shall we stop all this men and women nonsense about who does what? We're boyfriend and girlfriend, right?' He kissed her. Then kissed her again.

'Right,' she murmured, and kissed him. For a long, long time.

Maria's father was standing in the front garden, smoking a cigarette and keeping an eye on the dog busy completing his ablutions for the night. He watched as Luke pulled up, then get out of the car and walk around it to open Maria's door. He didn't hear Luke whisper 'pretend it's nineteen-twenty,' to his daughter, but he did feel relief that Maria's first boyfriend did seem to be a nice lad.

Buddy, the little white Shih Tzu, ran towards Maria, so she planted a swift kiss on Luke's cheek. He knelt down and rubbed Buddy's head, called goodnight to her dad, and climbed back in the car.

Maria watched until his tail lights disappeared, and then turned to go into the house.

'Nice lad,' her dad said. 'You smitten?'

She punched him in the shoulder. 'Oh, Dad, don't be so old-fashioned. It's not nineteen-twenty,' she said, and tried to suppress her laughter.

Naomi Taylor was still up watching the end of an old Gently detective programme, and tried to pretend she wasn't waiting for her son to come home.

'Mum? Why are you still up?'

'I like Martin Shaw.'

'You're not waiting for me to get in, then?'

'Of course not. You're a man now.'

'I am. Okay – I've had a lovely evening, we went to that swish little Italian in Bakewell, we stopped to look at a non-existent moon in Stoney on the way back, had a chat and I delivered Maria safely home to the loving arms of her dad, who was standing in the freezing cold in the front garden, smoking a cigarette and waiting for Buddy, her little dog, to have a wee. Like you, he too was waiting for his offspring to come home. I wasn't involved in any traffic issues, nobody tried to run me off the road. I'm safely home.'

Naomi picked up the remote control and switched off the television. 'I have one thing to say to you, smart arse. One day you will have children of your own.'

She walked past him, sniffing loudly with her head in the air, and deliberately trod on his foot.

'Ouch,' he said.

Fred stood outside his own home, staring up at the same moonless sky. There was the faintest of glimmers behind thick clouds, and he hoped Luke had enjoyed his night out.

Fred's had been a cold and a fruitless one. He suspected he could look forward to several nights of the same ilk, because it felt as though his current investigation could be classed as a slow burner, but deep inside he knew it would come to fruition.

The man he was watching, Harley King, was thought to be involved in what would have been termed industrial espionage in bygone times, but Fred knew it was pure and simple theft.

His three meetings with Connection's client had seemed a little bit tentative at first, but that afternoon he had been shown proof that someone was passing on precision work from the small engineering company based in Tideswell. Ernest Lounds and Company had been in existence for over thirty years, specialising in making precision components for Formula One cars alongside high-end luxury cars, and they had recently lost a large order from a major customer because they could get it elsewhere at a much lower cost.

The meeting had been a long one, and one name had emerged as the fore-runner for the man Ernest believed to have taken blueprints. Harley King was the husband of Ernest Lounds' daughter, Ursula.

Fred had been a little surprised to learn that Ursula and Harley had met when Harley started to work for the company, some twenty years earlier, so he was clearly someone of importance in the company, and not a newcomer.

'Why?' he had asked Ernest. 'He's obviously going to get the entire company one day, so why would he do this?'

Ernest sighed. 'I don't know. That's why I don't want the police involved. This is family, and I need to know what's going on. Do what you have to do, Fred, find me the answers.'

The answers didn't come from the moon, that was for sure. Fred stayed outside for a few minutes longer, finished his cup of tea and went back inside. He ran his thoughts through what he already knew; nothing was being passed electronically directly from the data held by the company on their computers, and all incoming and outgoing calls were, and had always been, carefully monitored. All mail was opened by the receptionist before being distributed to the intended recipients – which left mobile phones.

Mobile phones with their bloody cameras that could take pictures of anything and have them sent anywhere in the world within seconds. He needed to get hold of Harley King's phone and give it to Beth. He knew she would be able to do something magical with it, and give him answers.

How hard could it be to steal a mobile phone? And how much harder would it be to return it without the owner actually knowing it had disappeared in the first place?

Fred refilled his cup of tea, and went to bed. He took his book with him, guessing it was going to be a long night. His brain would be churning, working out how to get hold of that phone – and wondering how much or how little Ursula King knew of what was happening in her dad's company.

Fred opened his book. The Pottery Cottage murders book was showing itself to be a fascinating insight into the theory of

Stockholm Syndrome, where the captives bond with the abductor, and the family who had lived at Pottery Cottage had all proved how manipulative a kidnapper could be. He couldn't remember how many of the family actually died, and he settled down to delve further into the story.

His tea went cold, his book fell to the floor, and eventually he slept.

And Harley King took advantage of his wife being away for the night. Two bottles, one full of whisky and one full of sleeping tablets, did the job. By morning he was dead, and Fred no longer had to worry about stealing Harley's phone, Ernest Lounds handed it to him.

24

They met in Luke's office for the weekly report meeting. Beth was the last to arrive, and brought with her a tall young man. A guess would have placed him around twenty-two or three; he looked smart, wore a suit and tie, and he stayed by Beth's side as she introduced him.

'Okay, everybody, this is Simon Reynolds. We've sorted everything over the last couple of days, and he will be starting next Monday. He isn't on the investigative side, he's on my side, and no, you can't borrow him. He's a bit of an expert on finances, comes highly recommended and while I may have been supposed to be recruiting him for someone else, I managed to persuade him he'd be better off here at Connection.'

Luke held out his hand. 'Welcome, Simon. Has Beth mentioned the dead bodies?'

Simon laughed and instantly the scared look disappeared from his face. 'She has indeed. I'm aware this is an investigation agency that has morphed into other things, and I'll go with the flow and do whatever I'm told to do. I'm certainly looking forward to next Monday, and getting to know everybody.'

Cheryl placed her mobile phone on the table. 'I've put all

calls through to my phone, so nobody has to panic at leaving a voicemail. Does anybody want a drink before we start? It's all made.'

Everyone said coffee, and five minutes later they were all seated around the table, waiting for Beth to open the meeting.

'Luke,' she said. 'I know you and Tessa have sort of amalgamated, so do you want to start?'

Luke nodded. 'Our two cases came together when we found people involved in both the Jordan and Thompson murders, and the Evelyn Pearson murder. Simon, Evelyn Pearson was our lady we found in our outhouse. It's made sense, and saved duplicating work, to go to interview them together. We had a tottering time initially with Martin Synyer, but our second interview showed us a different side of him, one that was away from his wife. He definitely has an alibi for the night Evelyn went missing, he was in Spain for two weeks, so we're going back to talk to her fiancé, Alan Egerton. I've kept Hattie Pearson fully informed.'

'Tessa?'

'What he said,' she smiled, 'but he's not told you about our trip to Bakewell Library and the Book Club there. We learned all about Martin Synyer's penchant for other women, finding out he "knew" our two victims in the biblical sense.'

'Both of them?' Beth looked surprised.

'Both of them, but knowing them doesn't mean he killed them. There's no motive. They certainly weren't telling tales out of school, our two deceased ladies, neither of them mentioned him to me, nor him to each other, so it made no sense for him to feel threatened by them to the extent that he had to bump them off. I think we possibly have to delve deeper into our Mr Synyer, because if he had these two women then I imagine he's had others as well.'

'Mrs Synyer?'

'A strange lady indeed. She really didn't want us in her home, which was why we headed off to the business premises of Synyer's for our second interview. He was much nicer, helpful, and was clearly deeply in love with Evelyn.'

Beth nodded. 'And Fred?'

'The case at Great Hucklow is closed, final invoice paid. I believe the divorce is underway, and I've saved all the films to my computer. Mrs Barker has copies of everything, but we need to hang on to them for a short time. It's a just-in-case situation.'

'Something not sitting right?' Beth asked.

'I don't know... on the surface it went fine. Anyway, I'm covering our backs by saving this footage. I'm now working with a company at Tideswell, bit of old-fashioned industrial espionage, but again, something's not sitting right. I can't say what yet, because I don't know what's troubling me, but it's a family situation, and it doesn't make sense. I've only recently started with it, so watch this space.'

'You need extra help?'

Fred shook his head. 'No, it'll all work out, I'm sure. I'll keep you informed.'

'Cheryl?'

'Oliver's lost his collar so can I employ the skills of the company to track it down, please? He's been chipped, and he's going to be castrated shortly. Everybody is checking in and out properly, almost.' She cast glances at Tessa and Luke. 'I've sussed out the telephone system, and the new offices downstairs are nearly finished. They were finishing fitting the new blinds when I came up, and that was the final job. All looking extremely good, I must say.'

'We have a cat?' Simon said, backtracking to Cheryl's first point.

'We do. Luke found him and we've taken him in. If you feed

him, he'll love you.' Beth smiled at her assistant. 'Please don't say you're allergic.'

'I'm not. I love cats. We've recently lost ours, he was thirteen. I look forward to meeting him.'

'Okay, my turn,' Beth said. 'I've found Simon, we have acquired two new medium-size clients since last Friday, and Simon will be taking them on. His remit is to go out and visit clients, in addition to being desk based when he needs to be. Does a Wednesday morning meeting suit everybody?' They all nodded. 'Then I think we'll make this a regular thing, so all reports by Wednesday morning, if you need help ask for it, we can all juggle our schedules, I'm sure, and thank you everybody. Is it time for biscuits now?'

Oliver joined them as they were partaking of second coffees, and Luke's biscuits. He instantly went to investigate Simon, who bent down to stroke him. 'So you're the boss, then,' he said to the little black cat. 'I'd best keep on your good side. Are you open to bribes?'

'He definitely is,' Luke said. 'He'll do anything for some Dreamies.'

Cheryl's phone rang, and she scooped it up and answered it, trying desperately to swallow her biscuit. 'Connection Investigation Agency. How can I help you?' She listened for a moment. 'Thank you, I'll put you through to him.' She muted her phone and turned to Fred. 'It's for you. A Mr Lounds.'

Fred took the phone from her, and unmuted it before speaking. He listened for some time, and then said, 'I'll be there in half an hour.' He disconnected before handing the phone back, and saying, 'Shit.'

'Bad news?' Luke asked.

'The man at the heart of the case at Tideswell, who we

thought might be the one handing over blueprints, has allegedly committed suicide. I'm heading there now.'

'You need company?' Tessa asked.

Fred shook his head. 'No, I'll be fine. This kind of clarifies things in my mind. Maybe not with the family, but it didn't make sense that this chap was jeopardising something he would most likely inherit one day in the future.'

'Blackmail?' Luke suggested.

'Possibly. I'll know more when I get there. I'm meeting our client at his son-in-law's house. Cheryl, I'll let you know what's happening when I know.'

Cheryl gave a brief thumbs up, and made a note. 'Take care, Fred. See you later.'

Simon accompanied Beth downstairs, and Beth unlocked the door to her office. He followed her in, then smiled as she handed him the key that had been left on her desk.

'That,' she said, pointing through the window, 'is your office. We'll keep the blinds closed, because it can be distracting if you need to work quietly on your own and there's someone in your peripheral vision, but the alternative was to put you in the outhouse.'

He laughed. 'That would be the famous outhouse where you found your body, would it?'

'It would. I'll show you the building, and then you can be suitably grateful that I gave you part of my workspace. We keep stationery in it, plus spare chairs so we don't have to clutter our office space up. I originally intended putting in a connecting door as we will obviously be working closely together, but decided against it. We have to go outside into the reception area, where we can check if the other one has the engaged light, before we go interrupting. Cheryl will direct us, anyway, she's taken over control of our working lives.'

'And I thought she seemed nice.' Simon winked.

'She's lovely, but she calls it keeping us safe.'

He stared at his key. 'So can I go in my office?'

'Help yourself, and I'll make sure you have an access fob and everything else you need by the time you start on Monday. You looking forward to it?'

'You could say that. I was so ready to move on from my last job, and when you approached me it felt like a load had been taken off my shoulders. I'd already handed in my notice, as you know, so Monday morning will be a new start.'

'I'm really glad to have you join us. Go and inspect your office, then I'll show you the kitchen and outhouse.'

The rain spattered on the windscreen in a sudden heavy downpour, and Fred upped the wiper speed. He tried to stop thinking about the case, and concentrated on his driving, slowing down to accommodate the bad conditions.

He saw the police cars and ambulance outside the property from a fair distance, and he parked in the entrance to a field. There was no way he would get anywhere near the house.

He pulled on a hat, turned up his collar, and trudged up the road. He was stopped at the gate by a police officer, who asked his name.

'Fred Iveson, Connection Investigation Agency.'

'Ah, yes. Mr Lounds asked that you be admitted. I believe he's in the kitchen with his daughter, sir. If you go through to the end of the hall...'

Fred nodded and walked up the stone steps to the open front door. He could hear sounds of movement from upstairs, and walked down the long narrow hallway until he reached the end door. He knocked and opened it.

Ernest Lounds and Ursula King were seated at the table, close together. Ernest had his arm around his daughter's shoulder, and she was leaning into him, her eyes red from the tears she had shed.

Ernest looked up. 'Fred, thank you for coming. The kettle has boiled, make yourself a drink and come and sit with us.'

Fred nodded, and two minutes later joined them at the table.

'Mrs King, I'm so sorry to hear of your loss.'

She sniffed and nodded. 'Thank you. Can I call you Fred?'

'Indeed you can. Did you find your husband?'

Her sigh seemed to come from the bottom of her ribcage. 'I did. I stayed last night at Mum and Dad's place because Mum and I went out. I had to return home early because a friend was arriving to pick me up to go to Meadowhall, and when I got here...'

She grabbed for a fresh tissue from the box.

'Take your time,' Fred said.

'I thought he'd overslept because his car was still here.' She choked back a sob. 'He's not been sleeping, something's been troubling him for a while, but I couldn't get him to talk about it. He said it was pressure of work, the business was growing, that sort of thing.'

Fred sipped at his tea, and waited. He could tell the scene was unfolding in her mind, a scene she must have already had to explain once to the police.

'I ran upstairs shouting him to get up, it was gone nine, but he didn't answer. I was half tempted to leave him to wake up naturally, he was so tired every day, but I had to go in the bedroom anyway to get changed for my shopping trip. I shook his shoulder and I knew. I read the note he'd left on the bedside table, then rang Dad because I didn't know what to do, couldn't think straight at all. He rang the police for me, then came over. Everybody seemed to arrive at once.'

'Thank you,' Fred said. 'I'm sorry I had to take you through it all again. Mr Lounds, when did you last see Harley?'

'Yesterday. We didn't speak much. I had no idea at all that anything like this might happen.' He reached for his daughter's hand. 'Sweetheart, I had asked Fred to investigate something at work, and I believed, although Fred hadn't really got started on the ins and outs, that Harley was responsible for stealing blueprints from work and selling them to our competitors.'

25

Ursula stared at her father. 'Don't be so ridiculous, Dad. Harley lived for the company. Good God, it would have been his one day! Why would he want to do that?'

'My thoughts exactly, Mrs King,' Fred said. 'Those thoughts kept me awake last night, and the only answer I reached was that he was possibly being blackmailed.'

'It's Ursula,' she said, her voice almost robotic. 'Blackmailed? What about? What could he possibly have that someone else wanted? What could he have done or said that would give anybody ammunition to blackmail him? None of this makes sense.'

The kitchen door opened, and a PC popped his head around. 'Can I ask you to remain in here, please, while we place Mr King in the ambulance. I'll let you know when you can come out.'

Ursula reached again for the tissues. 'Dad...'

Ernest clasped her hand, unable to speak. His most precious daughter, his only child, was hurting so badly.

.   .   .

Once some semblance of normality had returned, Fred made them all a second drink, and they moved into the lounge.

'This was our peaceful place,' Ursula explained, clearly wondering how she would ever find peace in it again. 'We sat here most evenings, doing whatever we felt like doing. Sometimes watching television, sometimes doing a jigsaw, sometimes reading, and Harley loved crosswords. The harder the better.' She held her mug of tea tightly. 'Dad, please be certain of your facts before you accuse Harley of committing any criminal acts. He loved you. He loved me, and he damn well loved the business.'

'Ursula,' her father began, 'let's leave this to Fred. Harley's note was quite ambiguous, and therefore nothing needs to come out, it will be kept in the family. And then I will deal with it.'

'What did the note say?' Fred looked towards Ursula but it was Ernest who responded.

'I will send you the picture. I took a photo while it was still on the table. The police have it now.' He pressed send, and Fred's phone pinged.

I'm sorry, this every day blackness and despair is too much. I can't do it anymore. I'm sorry for all the hurt and pain this will cause you, my love, but it's time for our goodbyes. I love you, Ursula, but I'm no good for you. xxx

'Is this your husband's handwriting, Ursula?'

She nodded. 'Why didn't I know he was feeling like this? I knew things were a little out of kilter, but suicide?'

Ernest joined in. 'The awful thing is, if he'd come to me and told me what was going on, we would have sorted it. Selling on those blueprints wasn't his idea, somebody must have had something on him to force his hand. How can anybody of his intelligence be left with no option other than a bottle of whisky and a tub of tablets?'

'I will have to delve really deeply into Harley's life,' Fred warned. 'Has anything changed recently? Would you know, Ursula, if anything extra went into your bank account?'

She shook her head. 'Not really. We've always had a joint account that was for household payments, but we have separate accounts for ourselves. I wouldn't know what was happening in Harley's, any more than he would know about transactions in mine. We don't have money worries, Fred, and never have had. I've always had a salary from Lounds, as Harley did.'

'So the obvious inference from that is that it is something in his personal life.' Fred frowned. 'I'm sorry to ask this, Ursula, but have either of you ever had an affair? Or have you even suspected Harley might be seeing someone else?'

Shock passed across her face. 'Good Lord, no. If anything, I would say we're closer now than ever. Were closer,' she corrected herself, and reached for another tissue.

'He had no skeletons in cupboards that you were aware of?'

'We met when we were twenty, and we were open books with each other. We told each other everything, never seemed to stop talking, and six months later we married. Fred, believe me, we were as close as close can be. If there is something, it's a recent thing and I'm not aware of it.'

'Ernest?' Fred probed gently.

'Fred you know how puzzled I've been by the whole situation. Even when I was giving you Harley's name, I was astounded I was giving it. He's been my right-hand man for so many years, and yet logic told me it could only be him.'

'Have the police taken his phone?'

'Why would they do that? It's not murder is it? And he did leave a note. I'll go and look.' She stood, but Fred stopped her.

'Leave it until later. There are still police here, and they may decide they want it. I don't want to alert them to me having an interest in it. I'm going back to the office now. Ernest, when the house is empty will you let me know? If the phone is here, I'll collect it. Ursula, are you going back with your dad?'

'I am. Mum isn't too good, and Dad made her stay home, but she'll be worrying about me. I'll pack a few things and go stay with them for a couple of nights. I... I don't want to be on my own.'

'And you shouldn't be. I'm so sorry everything's such a mess for you, Ursula.' Fred spoke quietly. 'We will get to the bottom of it, I promise, but you should prepare yourself to be even more upset. It must have been a really strong reason for Harley to have decided there was only one way out of the chaos in his life.'

Fred smiled at Cheryl as he closed the office door. 'Everything good?'

She nodded. 'Tessa and Luke are out, Beth is in her office, whisking a duster around, and Simon has gone, to return next Monday. I've organised his set of keys, so he's good to go. Beth's been telling me his qualifications – impressive. How've you gone on?'

'It seems it was definitely suicide, whisky and tablets, lots of, but as to the why... no idea yet. I'm hoping to get hold of his phone, see if that tells us anything. I imagine the police will have his laptop, so I think I can rule that out as a source of information. His wife is in a state, she'd no idea how low he was.'

'I feel for her,' Cheryl said. 'Losing a much-loved husband is... hard.'

Fred gently squeezed her shoulder as he walked past, heading for his office. He started his coffee machine working, then opened up his laptop. He typed in *Harley King*, and waited for the information to appear.

Luke knocked on Hattie's door – her car was parked nearby, so he hoped she was in. It had been a spur-of-the-minute thing to call, following his trip out to see Alan Egerton.

'Luke!' she said, a huge smile lighting up her face. 'Come in. You want a drink?'

'No, I'm good thanks, Hattie. It's a quick visit. I want to ask you about something, and I'm hoping you can remember.'

The smile changed to a frown. 'That's asking a lot, I'm in my seventies, you know.'

He followed her through to the lounge and sat in the armchair. 'Okay. I want you to think back to the week before Evelyn disappeared. Talk to me about Alan.'

Wrinkles appeared on her forehead as she concentrated. 'He was a bit of a wimp.'

Luke laughed. 'You've said that before. No, I don't mean that. Did he have some sort of accident during that week?'

She hesitated. 'I didn't want to tell you about this, because I knew it would rule him out straight away. He fell.'

'And?'

'Broke his leg. Quite badly. He was on crutches for months. He was in a climbing group, the Hope one I believe, but I'm not sure about that. They met up on the Wednesday, and he came tumbling down the rocks. Really smashed his leg up. He was in hospital for a while, then on crutches for ages, as I said.'

'Why didn't you tell me this?'

'I wanted you to look at everybody in case it was him who killed my Evelyn, but really I always knew he wouldn't have been physically capable of it. And he certainly couldn't have carried her, not while he was using two crutches. Am I in trouble?'

Luke laughed. 'No, but I think you should make this clear to DI Heaton. It appears both our obvious suspects have strong, unbreakable alibis, so it's back to the drawing board.'

'You have nobody else in your mind?'

'Do you?'

'She knew lots of people. What about that woman she worked for?'

'She's been dead five years. Don't worry, Hattie, I'm not letting it drop. If our two suspects are out of the running, somebody else did it, and I'll find them if it's the last thing I do.'

He stood to leave. 'You know, Hattie, if you ever want to come down to the office and have five minutes where Evelyn was found, I can be there with you. Don't be afraid to ask.'

'I've thought about it, but I'm not sure I'm strong enough yet. I will, one day.'

'Let me know.'

He left her standing at the front door, watching his departure, and walked up the road to his car. He needed to see Tessa.

'So you've managed to lose both suspects now?'

Luke grinned at Tessa. 'Don't say it like that. Why didn't Egerton tell us at the time that he had a cast-iron alibi, anybody normal would have done.'

'He was playing with us. He knew he could produce it whenever he felt like it. It's some sort of phenomenon in the criminal world. If they've got proof positive that they didn't do something, they don't mention it until they have to. So, it's not Egerton and it's not Synyer. She disappeared on a Monday, didn't she? What did she do during the day?'

'Hattie said she went to work, but I can't get proof of that because the shop owner died five years ago. They don't keep records going back twenty-five years anyway.'

'I wonder if Carl's come up with anything I don't know about. Think he'd tell me if I asked?'

'He might, but you'd be better asking Beth. I don't pretend to know how Beth and Doris worked this, but they always knew more than we did. Oh, we'd get there in the end, but it was always after they did. Beth said this morning to shout if we needed any help, and I think you do. You need to know what information the police have uncovered, if any, and then you need to sleep on it. That's when the best ideas are born, before you drop off to sleep.'

'Is Beth in?'

'I believe so. Sweeten her up with a doughnut.'

He stood. 'Thanks, Tessa, you're a star. I asked Hattie if she wanted to come down and have five minutes in our outhouse, to be where we found her daughter, but she wasn't sure. I don't think she's ready yet, but I said I'd be with her when she was.'

'You're a lovely lad, Luke. Now go and see what Beth can tell you.'

26

Beth thanked Luke for the two doughnuts, then raised her eyebrows. 'A two-doughnut problem?'

'Could be,' he said. 'If your nan wanted to know anything that the police might already know, she always found out. Can you do that?'

'Of course not.' She winked and pulled a piece of paper towards her. 'What is it you want to know, and how quickly do you need it?'

'I want to know if the police know any more than I do. As far as I was concerned, there were really only two people who could have killed Evelyn, and they both have solid alibis. I wondered if they'd come across anybody else in her life who needed to be investigated, because honestly, it's baffling us. I can't really ask Carl, it's not fair to put him in that position, so I thought...'

'You thought two doughnuts would crack it. Get out, Luke Taylor, I'll let you know what they've found out as soon as I know. And this is between us, yes?'

'Of course.'

. . .

'Ernest Lounds,' the man said, smiling at Cheryl. 'Is Fred in? It doesn't matter if he isn't, I can leave this for him.' He waved a phone in the air.

'He is. I'll let him know you're here.'

Fred handed Ernest a coffee, and they sat down on opposite sides of the desk. 'You're my first client to visit,' Fred said, and Ernest gave a brief nod of acknowledgement.

'Then I'm honoured. I've taken Ursula to her mother, they were having a good cry when I left them. I got the phone soon after you left, didn't want the police getting it. His code to access the phone is 071100. It's the date of their wedding day. I really don't want this to become a criminal investigation, that won't do Ursula any good at all. Whatever you discover needs to be confined to members of the family. Me, my wife and Ursula. You have any theories, Fred?'

Fred shook his head, slowly. 'None yet, but now I have his phone I'm hoping something will ring alarm bells. What did the forensic team say?'

'Very little. They have the note he left, the empty bottle of whisky, and the empty bottle of tablets – these were quite old, prescribed for Ursula by her doctor when she was having difficulty sleeping, but she didn't take them, feared they would be addictive. It was twenty-eight tablets. He meant it, didn't he?'

'I don't doubt it was suicide, but this is more than a person being depressed, isn't it? He's taken this way out to stop something else happening. As a family, are you prepared for fallout, or is it between the two of us? And are you prepared for possible police involvement if I find serious criminal activity?'

Ernest sipped at his coffee. 'My daughter is hurting so much. She knew nothing of my suspicions that Harley was selling our blueprints, or giving them away to keep somebody quiet, she thought he simply became depressed and felt he couldn't carry on. Now she knows about the blueprint issue, and I need to keep the truth as soft as possible, for her sake.'

'Ernest, we may find nothing at all. You have to be prepared for never finding out what has created all this mayhem in your life, but with Harley's death I suspect no more blueprints will go missing. Things will eventually get back onto an even keel, and life will go on. I know that's a load of cliches, but that's what will happen. If this phone shows contact with some toerag, you can bet your life it will be by using a burner phone, and we will find nothing from that.'

Ernest placed his cup on the desk, and stood. 'Do your best, Fred. Keep in touch. I'll get back to my two ladies now. You know, Harley was more like a son than a son-in-law, I'm going to miss him on a personal level as well as a leader in our business. If I wasn't such a stubborn bastard, I'd be crying myself. If you do find who's caused this to happen, I'd appreciate knowing first if it turns out you have to tell the police.'

'Understood. My first priority is to you, you're paying for my services.' Fred followed him to the door. 'There'll be nothing left undisturbed with this one, I promise.'

Beth gathered together the printouts of the items she had accessed, which to her seemed very few, and walked up the stairs to Luke's office. He was staring out of his window, rocking gently back and forth on his chair.

He turned as she placed the papers on his desk.

'Thanks. They've not got far then?'

'Seems not. I imagine the concentration is on that gang murder that's going on at the moment – they've two dead with that, plus they have Lorna and Denise's murders. A twenty-five-year-old mystery is at the bottom of the pile. There's Martin

Synyer's statement, a much shorter one from Alan Egerton, and one from Hattie. I can't see any of it being a help, I reckon you've probably done more on it than they have.'

'That's what I thought. It's sort of ground to a halt. Evelyn didn't seem to have girlfriends, she was all about her craft. A definite loner. She worked in that shop which has proved a dead end, and she did her sculpting and stuff at home getting things ready for the craft fairs where she sold the items she'd made. She must have had customers, possibly regular ones, but she didn't keep records. None have come to light anyway. I'm hoping these from the police show something, but I'm sure there was nothing in her room, and if Hattie had known of anything, she would have passed it on to me.'

Beth walked around the room to look out of Luke's window. 'You were lost in thought when I came in. About what?'

He frowned. 'It's a bit of a jungle. That grass has probably been uncut since Evelyn was put in the outhouse. It was a passing thought, that's all.'

'You think something relevant could be in that grass?'

'No, it would have rotted after all this time. It was a bit of a contemplative thought really, didn't mean anything. I do think we should have it tidied up though. Will we get a combine harvester round the back?' he asked with a laugh.

'Possibly not, but can't you use a scythe?'

Luke collapsed dramatically onto his desk. 'Oh, my shoulder... the pain, the pain...'

She scuffed the top of his head. 'Wimp. I'll ask Stefan if he knows somebody, it won't take long to smarten it up, and you're right, it's a bit of an eyesore. Thanks for the doughnuts, hope there's something in there worth looking at.'

He smiled as she left the room. Did he look as though he could do gardening? He didn't know a dandelion from a daffodil – they were both yellow, weren't they? Pulling the paperwork towards him, he flicked through it, then straightened it and began to read.

Fred was another colleague lost in deep thoughts. Accessing the phone contents had been easy, and he began with text messages. There were many between Harley and Ursula, all ended with kisses, and most of them were affectionate. His last message to her had been, in view of everything that happened overnight, overwhelmingly poignant. **Always remember I love you. xxx** She had responded with **And I love you too. xxx**

There were no suspicious words of any sort, nothing that made Fred stop to investigate. Harley had a fishing friend, someone called L, but every text was about them meeting, whose car they were taking, having a weekend of fishing, and nothing made Fred's brain go into overdrive. The texts between the two men went back for a long time, and Fred thought he would read them on a second visit. To make sure…

The pictures were mainly family photographs, and it was only when Fred went into an album called Favourites that he realised what he was looking at. Blueprints. Diagrams. Sheets and sheets of words. He soon realised that these pictures meant nothing unless he could find out who they had been sent to, so he moved on to Messenger.

There was nothing to unnerve him there, and he realised that Harley King rarely used his phone other than for texting his wife, and the sporadic texts from his fishing friend. Calls were few and far between, personal emails almost non-existent and in the end Fred put down the phone with a sigh. There had to be some other method that had been used…

Royal Mail.

'No,' Fred said aloud. 'Surely not…' It dawned on him that it was possibly the best way of moving anything around that you didn't want tracing, and Harley had been moving A4 printouts that would probably have gone into an ordinary envelope with a first class stamp, untraceable everyday mail. He could simply slip it into an envelope, address it by hand, stick on a stamp and put it in a postbox. Who would know? Only the recipient.

Harley King wasn't a stupid man. Why had he left the pictures in his favourites folder for someone to find? To show Ernest Lounds the loophole? None of this explained why Harley had done it, simply how. Printing off the pictures and popping them in the post had to be the easiest thing ever.

Fred waited for some time, then rang Ernest. He needed to talk.

Luke read through the initial observations of the crime scene in their backyard jungle, and found nothing to disagree with; the door had been forcibly opened in the absence of a key, a body had been found and the body was subsequently removed for investigations to continue.

The report about the visit to Hattie's home to see the two rooms kept waiting for the return of Evelyn had yielded little, although there was mention of a diary in the safekeeping of Connection Investigation Agency pending collection by DI Heaton.

Alan Egerton's statement was short, sharp and to the point. His broken leg was his alibi – he couldn't walk, hadn't seen Evelyn Pearson, and she had neglected to contact him despite being his fiancée. Luke smiled. Alan had thought it expedient to give his alibi to the police, not to them.

It was as Luke was reading Martin Synyer's statement that he did a double-take. He went back to the beginning and read slowly, wondering if he had glossed over anything, but decided he hadn't. It seemed when he and Tessa had visited Synyers they had neglected to ask one important question. And similarly, Martin Synyer hadn't thought to mention one tiny little fact. But Carl Heaton had asked it. The issue now was, had Carl acted on it?

Luke thought not...

27

THURSDAY 23RD JANUARY 2020

I t had rained overnight, but the brightness of the sun woke Tessa early. She lay in bed for a few minutes contemplating putting her feet on the floor, then had to anyway as her mind drifted to her thoughts of the previous night, thoughts that had appeared as she floated off to sleep. She slipped on her dressing gown, felt at the radiator not quite believing it was on, and headed downstairs.

Cup of coffee by her side, she opened up her laptop. She typed in the name *Phyllis Ashford* and waited for the results.

There was little to see; she had been Phyllis Ashford until the age of thirty, when she had changed to Phyllis Synyer after marrying the CEO of Synyer Medical, with the happy couple choosing to live at Alport, in Derbyshire, in the bride's former home. Following the untimely deaths of her parents within six months of each other, she had inherited the Ashford chain of hotels. The Synyers had no children.

Tessa drew a quick family tree, and looked up Orville Ashford. It seemed he had worked hard, his wife giving birth to their only daughter Phyllis late in life. They had bought the house at Alport for their daughter's twenty-first birthday, and one night they had visited her for a meal, only to be in a road accident as they drove home later. Orville had died immediately, Wanda had tenaciously clung on to life for a further six months, but then succumbed without ever leaving her hospital bed, or indeed waking up.

The coroner deemed accidental death, after it was revealed Orville had complained of migraine symptoms during the evening, and his daughter had given him a box of paracetamol to take two tablets immediately, and then to take the packet home with him. She confirmed he had looked grey when he went home, and in fact they had left earlier than originally planned so he could get home to bed. It was concluded he had probably closed his eyes while driving, possibly to keep headlights from blinding him, and he had veered off the road. An exceptionally large oak tree stopped any further travel, and Orville died immediately. Six tablets were missing from the packet, and his daughter confirmed it was a new pack of sixteen tablets she had given him.

With Wanda's subsequent accidental death findings, Phyllis became an extraordinarily rich heiress.

Tessa leaned back in her chair, picked up her coffee and sipped thoughtfully. Had it really been accidental death, or had Phyllis spotted an opportunity with a severe headache? It was only her word that she had given her father a full packet of tablets. Suppose she had given him two to take but had crushed another four and put them in his meal, or in a drink. Six paracetamol would certainly make him drowsy...

Tessa made a few notes on the family tree and closed down the laptop. Had Phyllis known about the presence of Denise and Lorna in her husband's life? Or were they simply what they appeared to be, fellow members of the Bakewell Library Book

Club? If it was the former, did this mean that Martin Synyer was in some danger?

Tessa felt she needed to talk further with Martin; she closed down her laptop and headed upstairs for her shower. Time for some pro-activity, she reckoned, after she'd checked if Luke wanted to accompany her.

Luke was in his office, contemplating the sheet of paper in front of him, the yellow highlighter pencil glowing from the page. He needed to speak to Martin Synyer. Luke looked up as his office door opened.

'You got a minute?'

'Several. You okay, Tess? You look frazzled.'

'My brain's in overdrive. I shouldn't have major thoughts as I'm dropping off to sleep. I've been digging into Phyllis Synyer. Maybe I'm seeing stuff that isn't really there, and I really shouldn't be arguing against a coroner's findings, but you know when you get a little niggle and it won't go away...?'

'Yep, I also know about little niggles turning to bigger niggles. What's wrong?'

Tessa explained about her research work of earlier, and the horrible feeling she had about the deaths of the Ashford couple. 'It's infuriating I can't remember anything about it, I was in the police force at that time, but not with the Derbyshire force. I was doing a two-year stint on secondment to Kent, so missed this altogether. I don't think for one minute Martin was in any way involved, he didn't meet her until four years later, and it may have been simply accidental death, but would an intelligent astute business man really take six paracetamol all at one go? Especially as he knew he was driving.'

'You planning on asking her?' Luke said, his eyebrows raised. 'The thought terrifies me.'

'Not asking her at this point, but maybe getting Martin's take on it.'

'I'll go with you,' Luke said, and pushed the paper in front of him across to Tessa. 'Look at the highlighted section. This is Martin's police statement.'

Tessa laughed. 'The two doughnuts worked then.' She read the yellow section then lifted her head. 'Shit. How did we miss asking him this?'

'I think there's possibly other stuff we missed asking him, we were so gob-smacked at the change in him, and the information he was giving us. He kind of controlled it, and we didn't pick up on this. We've got it now, though, but even seeing this in print I'm not sure what it means if anything. I'm leaving it at the back of my mind and going back through everything we have.'

'You got any biscuits?'

'Chocolate digestives. You want one?'

'I'll make the coffee.' She stood and walked towards his door. 'I'll ring Synyer and see if we can pop down and see him today. Let's hope he's in work, I don't want to see him at home with Phyllis there.'

Cheryl listened to the messages left overnight and smiled as she heard Fred's voice. 'Hiya, sweetheart. I won't be in until later, I'm going to Ernest Lounds' place first, then maybe to his daughter's home, so hang on while I find the addresses.' There was a brief noisy pause, then he read out both addresses. 'That okay? I don't think you'll have to send out a search and recover party. See you hopefully around twelve.'

She listened once more to the message, scribbling down the information he had left for her, then checked who was in and who wasn't. Both Tessa's and Luke's lights were showing green. Beth's, like Fred's, hadn't yet been lit.

Cheryl put a drop of water onto the plant and spotted a new bud forming. She felt inordinately pleased that she hadn't managed to kill it so far, and settled herself into a comfortable position. There was a small pile of post, and she sorted through it. There was only one with a designated name, for Beth. Using her letter opener after sustaining a nasty paper cut three days earlier, she went through the remaining mail. Two were queries for Beth, from companies wanting quotes on recruitment issues, one was a general query for surveillance work which she put aside for Fred, and one was a handwritten one, no stamp, with one sheet of paper in it. The words were stuck on, and obviously from newsprint and magazines.

One BIG Fat LIE FROM Start to FINISH. I KNOW.

Cheryl stared at it, then rang through to Luke. 'Can you pop down for a minute?'

'No problem,' he said, and pointed to the packet of biscuits. 'Do not steal my biscuits, Tessa Marsden, I'll only be a minute. Cheryl needs me for a second.'

'That statement doesn't make sense,' Tessa said, reaching across for the packet. 'I'll save you a biscuit, don't worry.'

Luke didn't even glance at the biscuits when he returned. He was holding the letter in the grip of Cheryl's tweezers, and he placed it in front of Tessa. 'I kept my fingerprints off it, but Cheryl has touched it. What do you think?'

She quickly scanned it, then looked up. 'It wasn't addressed to anyone in particular?'

'No. Hand-delivered, said Connection on the front. That was handwriting.' He handed over the envelope.

Tessa stared at it. 'This could mean anything. It could refer to any of our cases.' She looked up at Luke. 'We'll copy it so we all have one, and file this original. It may become apparent one day who it's intended to help.'

'I think it's intended to help me. It's hand-delivered, so that suggests it's local. But let's keep our minds open on that one. Somebody obviously thinks they know something.'

Fred and Ernest were closeted in the study, but spoke sporadically while waiting for Ursula to bring them drinks. She looked drawn, had obviously had little sleep, and was still dressed in her pyjamas proclaiming she loved Mickey Mouse.

Fred thanked her as she handed him a mug of tea, and she gave a quick nod. 'The teapot is full, so help yourself whenever. Dad, I need to go home at some point, I didn't really bring anything with me.'

'That's fine, sweetheart, we'll go down later. You okay for the moment?'

'I am. Good to see you again, Fred. Find out why, will you?'

She left the room, and Ernest shook his head. 'There were many tears last night,' he said. 'If only I'd picked up on this sooner, the blueprints and stuff, all of this could have been avoided.'

'I looked through the phone, found the pictures of everything he passed on. They were kind of hidden in plain sight. In the favourites folder. I have no idea why he didn't delete them, but suspect he knew it would come to this one day. This is probably his way of trying to stop an investigation. He's protecting you, your family and the business. "You have your proof he did it, now drop it" sort of thing. Do you get what I mean?'

'Unfortunately I do. And we should leave it at that, but for my peace of mind I need to know why. Who had something on him that meant he had to give away our future? It's already caused a lot of damage financially to the company. I'm taking over his side of the business until we can get our heads around this, but I don't want to do that. I'm ready for retirement. I would have been out of here in six months and Harley and Ursula would have had full control. Was there really nothing else on his phone?'

'Very little. He didn't make many calls, mainly text messages to Ursula and arrangements for his fishing trips.'

'Fishing trips?'

'Seems so. He had a friend called L, only used an initial, but they texted a lot about fishing spots. It did seem friendly, and really that's why I'm here to see if you know who L is. He might be able to shed some light on this.'

'I've never known Harley go fishing, ever. Give me a minute.'

Ernest walked to the bottom of the stairs and Fred heard him call Ursula's name.

When she responded, he said, 'Where did Harley keep his fishing tackle?'

'What fishing tackle? He doesn't have any. He wouldn't know how to fish. He likes his salmon en croute, not in a river. Liked,' she corrected herself.

'Thank you, sweetheart,' Ernest said, and returned to Fred.

'So who's L and what's the significance of all these messages? I'd brought the phone back to you, but I'm taking it with me again, to the office. This needs a much-deeper investigation.'

Ernest stared at him. 'You think the messages between them could be a sort of code for whatever Harley was involved in?'

'I don't know yet. I'm going to get them transcribed, then I'll email them to you. I need you to look at them, particularly with regard to the dates they were sent, and see if anything jumps out.' He stood. 'Thanks for the tea, Ernest. I'll be in touch as soon as I can. It's quite possible this L doesn't know of Harley's death, so we may get further communications. Fingers crossed.'

28

'I thought you were here to talk about Evelyn?' Martin Synyer's forehead creased into a frown, not an attractive look, Tessa thought.

'Not necessarily,' she said. 'We represent different clients. Luke's case is Evelyn Pearson, my case involves Lorna Thompson and Denise Jordan.' She watched him carefully, and the frown disappeared to be replaced by a glance at both of them, as if worried about what was coming next.

Luke opened his folder. 'You have a perfect alibi for the night Evelyn disappeared, but can you tell us where you were on Thursday evening, say between nine and midnight, on the sixteenth of January this year. And also on Saturday morning between ten and twelve on the eighteenth of January?'

'You asked me this when you came to my house.'

'No we didn't. We simply checked that you knew both women.'

Okay, Thursday evening I stayed home until about nine, then went to the church in Bakewell to pick up Phyllis. I had to wait a bit. Phyllis had taken some stuff round to one of the elderly churchgoers, and I also gave a lift to her friend so it would have been around ten when we got home. We had a drink, then went to bed. We were in bed for around half ten, I would think. Saturday I was at the hairdressers for nine thirty, and from there went straight to Crosspool in Sheffield to my friend's house. We're season ticket holders at Sheffield Wednesday and every home match we have lunch at his, then go to the match from there.'

Luke smiled. 'And this week you wished you hadn't bothered?'

Martin gave a deep sigh. 'I take it you saw the result.'

Luke nodded. 'Lost 5–0 to Blackburn Rovers. Even I said ouch.'

'After the match we headed back to Crosspool, and I picked up my car and drove home. The police have verified it, so I don't think I need to give you my friend's address.'

'What does your wife do when you're at the matches? She doesn't go with you?'

Martin gave a short bark of laughter. 'She'll watch a horse race, glued to the screen, but football leaves her cold. She usually asks how we've gone on, but I think she must have seen the score this week, because she said nothing. Probably figured it was for the best. She did say she'd been out to do some shopping, which was pretty normal for a Saturday for her.'

'You were seeing both Lorna and Denise, so we've been told. Was there anyone else?'

'For God's sake, no! They were both free agents, you know.'

'But you're not.'

'No...' Martin looked down. 'Since you arrived on my doorstep telling me Evelyn's body had been found, my life's been in turmoil. It was always in turmoil really. Evelyn and I were so right together, and I feel as though I go through life thinking the next one will be the right one once again, but it doesn't happen. I think you picked up on my unhappiness at the present time. I don't suppose anything would have come of my seeing either Denise or Lorna, but someone's taken away any chance of that.'

'You met them through the book group?'

'I did. My wife doesn't like driving, so I always drop her off at the library. I bumped into Denise in a pub one night, we had a drink and went out a couple of times. Lorna and I used to chat at the library. We talked mainly about books, but she was also fun to be with. That's why I took her to Chatsworth, and hoped we wouldn't be spotted.'

Tessa finished her coffee and placed the cup on the table. 'Thank you for clearing up these last little niggles, and I'm sorry Wednesday lost.'

Luke packed away his notes, picked up the recorder and shook Martin's hand. 'Thank you, Mr Synyer. And I hope they win next time.'

Luke and Tessa walked down to the car park unaware that Synyer's eyes were on them every step of the way.

'You didn't ask the question?' Tessa glanced sideways at Luke, as they settled back into the car.

'I didn't need to. I have his police statement. I came with the intention of asking it, but then realised I didn't need to, and I didn't want to trigger any thoughts in his mind that it was the most important question of the lot. I don't want him taking matters into his own hands, any more than I wanted Hattie doing that. If there's one thing I've discovered in my twenty years on this earth, it's that people are unpredictable when love comes into the equation, so things will be released when they're ready to be released.'

. . .

Where the fuck are you? Fred stared at the text from L. How to respond...? Beth had checked the number in Harley's contacts, but had confirmed their suspicions that it was a burner phone. If he responded in any way that would ring warning bells with L, they would lose this lead and probably immediately.

In the hope of buying some time he texted back **In bed. Flu.**

He waited with a degree of trepidation and then the phone beeped. **Two days. We need trout.**

He stared at the message, wanting to laugh. We need trout? What the hell did that mean? It was clearly a code between the two men, but he didn't think for one minute it was anything to do with fishing in one of Derbyshire's beautiful rivers. This was something much more sinister that had ended with a man taking his own life rather than face up to what he had done.

Fred went into contacts and rang Ernest, who answered immediately.

'Fred?'

'A text has come through from L. Hang on, I'll send you the screenshot.' He waited, giving Ernest time to read it.

'Trout?'

'So it doesn't mean anything to you? I hoped it would.'

'You going to text back again?'

Fred hesitated. 'I don't think so. We run the danger of him guessing it's not Harley if we get into a conversation with him. I've bought us a day or two to think things through by saying Harley's got flu...'

Ernest sighed. 'If only it was flu. Ursula and her mother are in bits. Call me anytime, Fred.'

Luke sat at his desk realising that today he didn't like his job. It was the first time since he started work at Connection that he had had that feeling, but today it was a shitty job.

He sorted the various papers into order that would form the report he would be giving to Hattie, making sure that the photocopied picture of Evelyn's drawing was in there. He double-checked the photograph taken by Tessa of the body in situ before the forensics team's arrival, and placed that behind Evelyn's drawing. He hadn't shown either picture to Hattie yet, but it was a major part of his job to present everything that had been discovered to the client, and so he would do that. He needed a picture of the outside of the outhouse to complete that section of his report.

He stood and looked out of his window towards the overgrown grassed area and saw to his surprise there was a man with gardening equipment, and a little black cat watching every move he made.

He went down to join cat and gardener, and was soon making cups of tea and a saucer of milk.

'Your lady on reception let me in,' the gardener explained. He held out his hand. 'I'm Vic. I'm here to sort this lot out.' He waved an arm to indicate the whole area.'

'Thank heavens for that,' Luke said. 'I'm Luke. It was casually mentioned I could use a scythe. I'm glad common sense prevailed.'

Vic laughed. 'This'll take a bit more than a scythe. My instructions are to clear it, get all the grass back to ground level, so to speak, then discuss planting. It'll be an ongoing thing, so don't worry. It's too early to get any flowers in, but I can prepare the ground once I'm given a thumbs up.' He took a sip of his drink. 'Stefan's done all the refurb, hasn't he?'

'He has. Brilliant job. He's done it twice now, in two years. We needed to expand, so he expanded us. He recommended you?'

Vic nodded. 'He did. Told me about the body in the shed. I'll try not to find you one in the long grass.'

'Thanks. The first one was enough.' Luke had a quick image of the file on his desk. 'Will there be somewhere out here we can put a cat shelter?'

'For that black cat? I'm sure we can. I'll knock something up at home, I've loads of stuff I can use in the shed. We can fit it on the end wall of that outhouse. It lives here then?'

'He's called Oliver, and he adopted us. Sometimes he stays out overnight, and I'd feel happier about that if we had some sort of escape for him from bad weather.'

'I'll sort some stuff out when I get home.'

They sipped at their rapidly cooling drinks, and Luke took out his phone. 'Need to get a picture of the outhouse for our client.' He took three pictures, finished his drink and went inside. 'Thanks, Vic, and bill me for the cat shelter, will you? Not the business.'

'No problem. I'll enjoy building it. Only thing is, the missus will want me making one for our cat.'

Luke printed off one of the pictures, and added it to the now-complete file. He then finished off the invoice, which revealed only twenty-five pounds to be owing, as Hattie had insisted on a hefty deposit.

He double-checked the file contents, closed it, and put it into his lockable drawer ready for the morning. He rang Hattie to check she would be in, arranged to see her at ten, then rang Carl Heaton.

Beth stared at the figures that weren't adding up. Work on her primary case had been ongoing for a couple of weeks. The initial request had been a simple one, to check some figures that didn't seem to agree with other figures. For the first time a potential criminal investigation had intruded into her corporate work, and it seemed that it was much worse than the CEO at Goldex had feared when he had asked for her help in solving his problem. Money was definitely being siphoned off, and she suspected it was disappearing offshore. Everything would have to be double-checked; it would do Connection's reputation no good at all if she was wrong, and it was proving to be a much bigger task than she had initially thought.

She looked at her screen and then down at the scribbles on the piece of paper in front of her, and called Simon.

'You busy tomorrow?'

'No, I told you I could start immediately.' He laughed.

'I need you to check up on me.'

'Wow. That's not what I expected. Nine o'clock?'

'I'll be here for eight.'

'Then so will I.'

During the night, Harley King's phone pinged. Fred didn't hear it despite it being on his bedside table; he was deeply asleep.

Ring me tomorrow. A picture was attached of a naked Harley King, on top of a naked blonde woman with his head turned towards the camera flash.

The second message that pinged through was **The next one goes to your father-in-law. Third to your wife.**

29

Luke was surprised to find the shutters up and lights on. He glanced at the indicator board and saw that both Beth and Simon had amber showing, so he knocked and popped his head around Beth's door.

'Morning. Couldn't you sleep?'

'No. Couldn't you?' she responded, glancing at her wrist watch. 'It's only quarter past eight.'

'I know. Too much on my mind. And Simon's in?'

She smiled. 'He's my cavalry. I need him to check my figures before I jump into something with big welly boots on. For the first time it seems my side of our business has a criminal element that's surfaced accidentally. I'm supposed to be finding a way of splitting a company's finances into three, to get maximum benefit from the split regarding tax and other issues, and instead I found what appears to be some siphoning off. I need to sort it as quickly as possible, but I need to check I'm correct, so Simon has come in to help. You're in early.'

'I'm going up to see Hattie Pearson in a bit. I need to fill her in on everything to date. Then I'm seeing Carl later.'

Beth put down her pen. 'You want to talk?'

Luke brought a chair towards her desk and sat. 'I do.'

Simon could see Luke and Beth deep into a discussion, and marvelled at the level of sound-proofing that must have been installed when Beth's office was split. Nothing could be heard of their conversation. He returned to checking the figures, and following the cash, but so far had found zero to reverse Beth's findings. Someone smart had been feeding money into an offshore account for quite some time; Beth had gone back three years and it had been happening then. Now all they had to do was work out exactly how much was involved without alerting whoever had done it, because it would disappear fast if he or she discovered Connection were investigating.

It seemed his new job was going to be extremely different to his old one, which had been pure accountancy – balancing books for small businesses, auditing, and general accountancy work. Working for Beth at Connection would be a complete change in direction – she delved deeper, worked with businesses to improve cash flow, recruited the right people for them, and her reputation was sky high. He hadn't even had to think about it when she had contacted him to ask him to talk to her.

And here he was, a day earlier than expected, being asked to check the boss's findings!

He saw Luke stand and leave Beth's office; he looked unhappy.

Luke went to his own office after feeding Oliver, and sat for some time, thinking. What came next had to be handled carefully and he had no idea how Hattie would react to what he had to tell her. He stood and walked to the window, hoping the sight of the outhouse where his case had started would ease his thoughts; he saw Vic manoeuvring a wooden structure along the side wall of the small building.

A diversion was Luke's initial thought, and he went downstairs and unlocked the back door.

'Cup of tea?'

'My saviour,' Vic replied. 'This didn't feel half as heavy when the missus helped me put it in the van, but I thought it would be easier bringing it around the back than through the office.'

Luke knelt to inspect it, then looked up. 'It's a cat mansion.'

Vic laughed. 'That's what the missus said. She's made the cushion for inside.' He handed Luke a carrier bag. 'And there's two more in there for when you need to wash this one. I painted the whole structure black so it would deflect the sun, and it hopefully will be cool enough for Oliver to get some shade. It'll also make it warmer in winter.'

'He's even got his name over the door.'

'Again that's the missus. I'm the builder, she's the creative one.'

'It's brilliant. Don't forget to invoice me, not Connection.' Luke looked around at the already much-improved cleared space. 'Can you build me one, on this bit of land?'

'What? A cat house?'

They both laughed at the thought, and Luke said, 'No, an adult house. I've got move out asap, my sisters are growing up and need their own rooms, but it's not as easy as it sounds finding somewhere in Eyam. I have to stay local, for work and for Mum. I'm not straying too far, simply freeing up the bedroom they need.'

'I might have the answer. If you go up Hawkhill Road, past the museum, there's three houses set back from the road. Big front gardens. I do all three there, but the end one has a granny annexe in the back. The granny in question died last year, so they've had it completely refurbished, and I'm working with Stefan Patmore redoing the driveway to it next week. It's then going to be available for rent. I'll give them a ring if you like. I'm sure they'll jump at the chance of a professional like yourself moving in. One large bedroom, one small one that the overnight carer used that could be an office, all ready to move into in about a month or even earlier.'

'Sounds perfect. Don't bother building me my own cat house if I manage to get this one.'

Vic glanced at his watch. 'It's a bit early to be ringing them, I'll do it in an hour and let you know. About this cup of tea...'

'On its way,' Luke said, and went back inside.

He punched the air, and said 'Yes!'

Tessa arrived in Bakewell at a little after half past nine, and headed straight for a coffee shop across from the library. She ordered a toasted teacake and a latte and settled back to enjoy the treat before starting work for the day. She liked Fridays; Fridays had always held the promise of the weekend to come, although that no longer seemed to count now she had moved her investigative life into the private sector.

She wasn't really sure why she was here. Her intention was to have a word with Faith, to see if her version of the relationships between Martin and Denise and Martin and Lorna were the same through her eyes; or had Martin understated the situation. Could it be that things had progressed to the point where Martin felt he had to get rid of two needy women...

Tessa finished her teacake, wiped the crumbs from her top and around her mouth, then took out the folder from her bag. She reread the transcript from the last interview with Martin, and accepted that his alibis for the Thursday evening of Lorna's death and the Saturday morning of Denise's death were pretty solid, not so much his wife. He had gone to collect her from church but she hadn't been there, and he had had to wait for her return. On the Saturday morning Phyllis Synyer could have been anywhere, he was on his way to his football match at Hillsborough. Phyllis could indeed have been breaking a lock on a garden gate, and squeezing through, to return five minutes later at some speed, escaping the same way she had arrived...

Tessa shook her head. Her imagination was running riot. Was this what a latte and a teacake did to a woman? But to add fuel to Tessa's fiery thoughts, Phyllis had been limping on the Sunday morning when they had first met her. Perhaps they needed to ask the question why the limp? Had she injured her ankle in her rush to escape the bloodbath in the kitchen of Denise Jordan's home?

She sipped at her coffee, one eye on the library door, and when Faith eventually arrived, Tessa finished off the last of her drink, replaced her file back in her bag and left the café with a thank you to the girl behind the counter.

Walking across the road, Tessa let her brain run through what she already knew, and entered into the peaceful atmosphere of the library. It was a couple of minutes before ten, and the outer doors were open. Not so with the inner doors to the library, and she could see Faith putting some books on a shelf; Tessa stood patiently, watching and waiting.

She didn't recognise the young assistant who eventually opened the doors, but she could see Faith at the far end of the room. Faith's face lit up with a smile as she spotted Tessa walking towards her.

'Hello! Is this a library visit?'

'No, although I do love a good rummage around. I like finding authors new to me.'

'Then you should come next Friday evening. We have a local

author giving a talk for us, his debut novel comes out next month. He writes crime. Should be a good night.'

'Actually I came to talk to you. Have you got time to spare me quarter of an hour or so?'

'I have. I'm in charge now...'

'Of course. It's been made official, has it?'

'Yesterday. Let's go into my office.'

'You've changed your hair,' Tessa said with a smile.

'I had streaks put in and a shorter cut. I decided it was time for a new me. I've been in Lorna's shadow for far too long.'

'Oh?'

'Ignore me,' Faith said, with a nervous laugh. 'It's been a difficult time. What did you want to see me about?'

'Lorna. And Denise, but I guess you knew Lorna better. You knew that she was seeing Martin Synyer?'

Faith sat a little straighter. 'I did. It was obvious. He always stayed downstairs for a bit once Phyllis had headed up to the meeting room, he never went home straight away. And Lorna stayed down there with him. There was a clear attraction. And then his eyes started straying again with Denise. It was like he was collecting his own harem from the book club. His wife, the leader, and a member.'

'And you?' Tessa said softly.

'Don't be so ridiculous.' The anger burst from Faith. 'Why on earth would I want Martin Synyer?'

'Because he's quite a nice man, wouldn't hurt a fly, and has a lot of respect and liking for women. He really shouldn't be married, that's a fact, and my job is to track down any other women in his life. I think you're a possible contender in that category.'

Faith stood. 'I have to get back to work now. I'll see you to the door.'

Tessa sat in her car feeling slightly shocked. That hadn't gone in the way she had envisaged at all, she had anticipated Faith denying all knowledge of everything. The woman had seemed to be quite retiring, quiet and of the non-gossip variety, but suddenly the anger had shown.

She took out her phone and scrolled through until she found Patrick Fletcher's number. He said he would put the kettle on, and gave her directions to his home.

Patrick not only put on the kettle, but he also provided biscuits, and Tessa thought maybe a couple of weeks of a strict diet was looming. They sat in the lounge, and chatted while drinking the tea.

'My wife instilled in me that I must always offer guests a drink and a biscuit. She's been gone five years now, but I've never let her standards slip. I miss her, but we'll be back together soon enough. She'll be waiting for me.'

Tessa smiled. 'I don't doubt. I wanted to discuss with you what you told us over the phone. We have had everything you said confirmed by Martin Synyer himself now, but I really wanted to talk about the new head librarian, Faith.'

'They've given her the job then?'

'They have. I would have thought it was a sensible appointment, but...'

'Still waters run deep,' Patrick said with a laugh. 'I know it's a cliché, but it describes her exactly. One minute she's as nice as anything, the next minute she's snapping. I honestly thought they would bring somebody new in altogether, but she obviously had her good head on when they interviewed for the job.'

'Okay, Patrick, here's the killer question. Was there ever anything between her and Martin Synyer that you were aware of?'

He laughed. 'Not recently, but he dumped her for Lorna. And I suppose for Denise as well.'

30

Luke pulled up outside Hattie's house and sat for a moment. He had brought everything with him: the statements he had collected, Evelyn's sketch, the final bill, and Luke knew today it would be done. There were questions to be answered, but the answers he felt he already knew. Hattie herself would be able to confirm them for the most part; DI Carl Heaton would take them from there.

He glanced in his mirror and saw Carl's car pull up behind him. His initial thoughts had been that he would go alone to see Hattie, in accordance with their terms and conditions, but further thought had deemed that might be a stupid move. Carl got out of his car and came to Luke, who gathered up his paperwork and joined the detective inspector.

'You're ready?' Carl asked quietly.

'I am. You've organised your side?'

Carl nodded. 'I have.'

They walked down to Hattie's cottage, and Luke knocked on the door.

Hattie opened it with a smile, which froze on her face as she recognised Carl Heaton. 'You need back-up to visit me, Luke?' she said.

'Not at all. DI Heaton is the lead investigating officer on the case. Can we come in?'

She held open the door. 'You want a drink?'

'No, we're good thanks, Hattie.'

She showed them into the lounge and Luke and Carl shared the sofa. Hattie sat across from them in the armchair, and waited patiently. Her face was inscrutable; lips set in a straight line, eyes open yet almost unseeing, and her hands were balled tightly into fists.

Luke took out his file, and placed it on the coffee table. He also placed his recorder on the low table.

'Okay,' he began. 'This sketch, Hattie, is one that Evelyn drew the Friday before she disappeared on the Monday. This is a photocopy but I knew you would want it.' He handed it to her and she took it, taking a long time to look at it. She ran her fingers across the face she knew so well, touching the eyes, the nose and the mouth with a display of reverence that was heartbreaking in the simplicity of the actions.

She lifted her head eventually. 'This is beautiful. My daughter was so talented.'

'She was. This piece of paper is the photocopy of the back of that portrait.'

Hattie read the words. She said nothing, merely lifted her head and stared at Luke.

'Hattie,' Luke pressed, 'what did Evelyn say to you on that Monday? I believed at the beginning that she had to see Alan Egerton to tell him it was over, that she had found a new love. But she had someone else to tell, didn't she, Hattie?'

There was a silence in the room, and Carl let it carry on, reluctant to interfere in what Luke had carefully worked out. He knew he could step in if it became necessary.

'Hattie, what did Evelyn say to you?'

'I told you, I didn't see Evelyn. She went to work that Monday morning, and I didn't see her again.'

'She told Martin Synyer that she would be with him once she had told Alan Egerton and you. And she would do it before Martin returned from his golfing holiday with his father. Isn't that the truth? And didn't she come home from work and tell you? She didn't tell Alan Egerton because she was dead before she could get to see him. Where did she die, Hattie?'

They watched as Hattie Pearson visibly crumpled. 'It's over,' she whispered. Suddenly she looked every one of her seventy-plus years.

'What is, Hattie?' Luke spoke gently.

'Twenty-five years of regretting one split second.'

'What happened, Hattie?'

'I... she came home early from work. I had taken some tablets because I had a thumping headache, and when she came in I was asleep on the sofa. She woke me, said she had something to tell me. She didn't reveal his name, only that she loved him and she was going to live with him. I couldn't let that happen, but I also couldn't really take in what she was saying. I felt really ill. I stood up to try to talk to her, to stop her from leaving me, and she pushed me away when I tried to put my arms around her. I was suddenly so angry it felt like flames running through me, my head was pounding so hard, and I picked up the paperweight she had bought me.' Hattie turned and pointed to a large glass item on her sideboard. 'I hit her head with it, and she went down. I hit her and hit her and hit her until she was dead.'

'But why did you employ us to find this out?' Luke kept his voice low; Hattie was distraught.

'I didn't know what else to do. When Nora told me they had found a body, I knew with DNA and stuff they'd soon find out who she was, so I tried to get a head start by muddying the waters. I should have known you'd work it out, but I had to try. I thought you would think it was either Alan or this new man she'd got in with who killed her. I waited until it was dark, then put her in the boot of the car and took her down to your outbuilding. I knew how to get in the little shed, I used to go there as a teenager to smoke with other kids from school, and the key was under the bottom tile on the roof. After I put Evelyn in there, I threw the key into the grass.'

Carl stood. 'Mrs Pearson, I have to stop you there for your own good. I am arresting you for the murder of Evelyn Pearson, but my advice before you say anything else is you need a solicitor. Please wait here. We will formalise proceedings at the station.'

He left the room, and Hattie looked at Luke. 'I'm so sorry for lying to you. There isn't much left of my life, and I didn't want to see it out in prison. I thought it was too long since she died for anybody to work out what happened, but you did, didn't you?'

Luke reached to the table and switched off the recorder. 'I did. Hattie, please don't say another word until you have a solicitor to guide you. DI Heaton will have a copy of this recording. If I can do anything to help you I will. What was so bad about Evelyn leaving home?'

'She was all I had. It had always been the two of us, and then this new chap arrived on the scene, and I lost her to him. I couldn't bear it, and I felt so ill. Everything exploded, and I couldn't stop hitting her with that damn glass thing.'

The lounge door opened, and two PCs accompanied Carl. 'Please put on shoes and a coat, Mrs Pearson,' he said. 'You'll be going in a car with these two officers.'

. . .

Luke watched through the window and Hattie turned as she reached the garden gate. She inclined her head slightly, and he knew what she was saying to him – that it was as she expected it to be.

As the car pulled away, Carl spoke. 'Thank you for your help with this. She would have denied everything to me, and to be honest we haven't given this investigation the concentration it needed. We're overworked, underpaid, understaffed – and this was a twenty-five-year-old crime that held no priority.'

'It holds no satisfaction for me.' Luke's voice was grim. 'I know she's done wrong, that it's murder, but she's in her seventies, Carl. And what's worse, she's confessed.'

'Did you expect that?'

Luke nodded. 'I did. I've got to know her, and to like her, and she's basically really honest. I knew she would recognise when it was all over, and she couldn't hide any longer from what she'd done, but even so...'

Carl looked around the room. 'I've asked Forensics to come back here. I know we won't get any physical evidence from the paperweight after all this time, but we can probably match the indentations in the skull to its shape. It's a hefty piece of glass, isn't it?'

They stared at the murder weapon for a few moments. It was truly a beautiful piece of artwork. Inside the rounded glass was a rose, sealed in forever, beautifully preserved from all angles. Luke knew the late Evelyn Pearson would have appreciated every curve of every petal. And she would have known her mother would love it.

'Why on earth did she keep it?' Carl asked.

'To remind her every day of what she'd done, what she'd lost. Her punishment, I suppose. Do you want me here any longer?' Luke needed a few moments alone.

'No, I'm going as soon as Forensics get here, I have to leave the key with them. You get off. I'll want a statement from you, and can you send me the recording as soon as possible?'

'Tess, where are you?'

'On my way back to the office. You okay?' Her voice sounded tinny and Luke could tell she was in the car.

'No. I need doughnuts.'

Tess sighed. The diet was creeping ever closer. 'I'll get us some. I'll be there in about ten minutes. Sort out the coffee.' She disconnected and increased her speed.

Luke handed her a coffee as she walked through his door, carrying the white box of goodies.

'I got a mix of things,' she explained, 'because it's Friday. Beth and Simon are coming up for a break, Cheryl's staying on reception so she's got her bun.'

'Fred?'

'He's out. According to Cheryl, he's at the Lounds' place. He thought the job would be over when the main culprit under investigation died, but it seems that's not the case. I've taken one out to Vic. Have you seen Oliver's new house? And that back garden area is looking much better. We planting it up or leaving it to grass?'

Luke laughed. 'I've no idea. I'm not a gardener. I think if we have it grassed properly, we could put a table and chairs out there for us to have coffee breaks in the summer.'

Tessa placed the box in the middle of the desk and turned to Luke. 'You okay? Is Hattie with Carl?'

'She is, and I'm not okay. But we knew, really, didn't we. As soon as we saw the answer to the question I didn't think to ask... who did Evelyn have to tell before Martin's return from Spain.

We, or rather I, closed my mind. Unforgivable. I assumed there were only two people in the mix, Martin and Alan. But she had to tell her mother, the mother she knew would be devastated by her leaving home. I missed it, Tessa, I missed that fact.'

'You got there quickly though, Luke, and it's you who's delivered the end result to Carl.'

Luke's laugh was bitter. 'At what price, though. It would have been so much better if we'd simply swept the bones up and put them in a black bag for the binmen to take away.'

'Oh, Luke.' Tessa walked around the desk and put her arms around him. 'And you could have lived with that, could you?'

He didn't answer.

31

Luke parked his car on the main road, and headed back a few yards to the bottom of the driveway that was partially excavated. He kept over to the left and walked by the side of the adjoining house and round to the back door.

There was a woman by the bin store sorting recycling.

'Mrs Yates?'

She turned with a smile, threw in the last two empty bottles, and said, 'You must be Luke. And call me Jenny.'

'I am.' They shook hands.

'Hang on while I get the key, and I'll take you to see the annexe. Has Vic explained about the driveway?'

'He has. He said I'll be able to park my car outside the annexe because you're widening the access to it.'

'I'm assured it will be finished in two weeks, but if the property is what you're looking for, you can move whenever you want, you will have to leave your car on the road until the drive is finished, that's all.'

She opened the back door and unhooked a key from the wall.

'My mum lived here until she passed last year, and was very

happy. It's a lovely little place. There's a small second bedroom where her carer used to sleep overnight, but really it would make an ideal office. Will Maria be moving in with you?'

Luke knew the shock must be showing on his face. 'Erm... no... I mean...'

Jenny laughed. 'Luke, there are less than a thousand people live in Eyam. Everybody knows everybody else, we all know who is seeing who, and I chat to your mum most days in the Co-op.'

Once again Luke decided he had to find a new job for his mother.

He gave a half smile before speaking. 'Then you'll also know I've only been seeing Maria for a little over a week, so we're not getting married yet. No, this place is for me, it's so I can leave home and let my two sisters have a bedroom each. I do need to be close to Mum, though, in case she needs any more furniture building.'

Jenny's laughter tinkled in the air. 'I'm quite sure your mum needs you there for more than furniture building.'

They reached the door of the annexe, and Jenny handed him the key. 'Go ahead.'

He opened the door which led directly into a small hallway. They both went inside and Jenny pointed to a door on the left. 'That's a little cloakroom, keeps everyday coats and shoes out of the way. This is the lounge.'

They stepped into a bright room, a neutral colour on the walls, vertical blinds at the windows, and a log burner with logs laid waiting for a match. The floor was carpeted in a deep beige, and Luke slipped off his shoes before stepping on it.

'This is lovely. I could have a sofa bed in here, because you can bet your life either Imogen or Rosie, or both, will want to stay occasionally.'

'We threw out all of Mum's furniture, it was a bit old-fashioned, so you'll need to furnish, but the kitchen lacks for nothing. It's brand new, with all the white goods built in. You'll only need saucepans, crockery and stuff. Let me show you.'

The kitchen was white, gleamingly so. He walked around opening and closing doors, said wow several times, and turned to face Jenny who was trying not to laugh.

'Do you need references? I am a partner at Connection, and I'm sure ex-DI Tessa Marsden and Beth Walters will be happy to recommend me. So will Reverend Kat Heaton.'

'No, Luke, I don't need references for you. We were delighted when Vic rang and said you needed a home, we've watched from afar how you've done. We also know Maria's family – in fact, there's not many people in Eyam we don't know. Come and look at the bedroom. We had wardrobes built into the long alcove, so I think you'll only need a bed and a couple of bedside tables.'

They sat in Jenny's kitchen, and he signed the tenancy agreement. He transferred the requisite amount of money, and they shook hands once again.

'Thank you so much. I didn't expect it to be signed, sealed and delivered this afternoon. I've had a rubbish morning, and this has totally made my day. I'll move in as soon as possible, so we can get the girls sorted in their bedrooms. Tonight I need to tell Mum. I'd like to bring Maria to see it over the weekend if that's okay.'

Jenny passed the key across to Luke. 'It's your home now. I hope you're happy here.'

Tessa hugged him. 'That's awesome, my lovely friend. It's exactly what you need. And it certainly sounds as if Rosie and Imogen are going to benefit from the move as well. You need a reference?'

He laughed. 'No, apparently I'm perfect. Jenny seems to know every one of the thousand or so people who live in Eyam, so she didn't need anybody to tell her what a special person I am. She's really nice, and the annexe is amazing. I need to buy lounge furniture and a bed pretty quickly, but everything else can be got as and when I need it.'

'I can supply pots and pans...'

'Really?'

'Yes. When Hannah and I moved into my home together she already had her own home, so we ended up with double everything. Most of Hannah's stuff like that went into the loft until we needed to replace my equipment that was already in situ, so if there's anything I can help with...'

'You're a star, but it's still early days since Hannah died, Tess, so leave things in your loft. It's too soon. But I love you for the offer.' He kissed her gently on top of her head.

She wiped away a recalcitrant tear. 'You told Naomi yet?'

'No. I'd best go buy a bunch of flowers to sweeten her up first. The idea of me leaving home hasn't even been mentioned, so it's going to come as a shock.'

Luke handed his mother the flowers and kissed her cheek.

'Are these to say you're sorry for not mentioning you were thinking of getting your own place and you would possibly be moving into Jenny Yates's annexe?'

When he told Maria the story later that evening, she howled with laughter. 'That'll teach you to try to get one over on Naomi. Was she annoyed?'

'Not at all. She'd spoken to Jenny's husband Mike at the checkout, and he mentioned he was pleased I was thinking about moving into their annexe. By the time I arrived home to tell her she'd realised the pros to the move, and was trying to ignore the cons. She's fine about it, and I'm only a five-minute walk away from her anyway. So if you've nothing better to do tomorrow, I'd like to show you the place, and then maybe we can go look at some furniture. I can't move into it without something to sit and sleep on.'

Tessa said goodnight as both Beth and Simon left shortly after four, and went and sat for a while with Cheryl.

'I need to talk,' Tessa said. 'If I talk things through, they sometimes become clearer.'

'There's nobody else here,' Cheryl said. 'Fred's not been in yet, and the other three have gone home. Talk away.'

'It's this damn case. It started as a potential stalker issue with the notes that Denise and Lorna received – I'd only recently begun the investigation when they were murdered. I didn't have chance to get to know them, to understand their lifestyles, to find anything to give a reason for their deaths, so I've had to find what I can by talking to people on the periphery of their lives.'

'And that's led you somewhere?'

'Kind of. This morning, as you know, I headed back out to Bakewell to talk to the librarian who was in temporary charge following Lorna's death, thinking I might find out more about Lorna. I found out more about her instead. When we went to the book club she was helpful, upset at the loss of a colleague and a book club member, and really quite nice. I think this morning she showed her true colours. She's now been promoted on the back of Lorna's death...'

'Motive?'

'Possibly. I don't know how desperately she wanted the job. However, I can't really link Denise's death to that motive. Killing Denise, and according to the autopsy report they were both killed with the same knife, wouldn't have helped in any way to get her promoted. There is something else though. After she'd basically banished me from the library I called around to see that lovely man who rang me, another book club member. It seems that Faith was dumped by Martin Synyer in favour of Denise and Lorna. He's an absolute womanising pest.'

'Is he a murderer? And being dumped by him certainly gives Faith a motive.'

'I'm absolutely certain he isn't. He's actually quite a pleasant man, which is why he seems able to get any female he decides he wants at that moment in time. And his alibis for both murders are unbreakable. However, his wife doesn't have an alibi, as far as I can see, and if other members of the book club were aware of Martin's philandering ways, then it follows that Phyllis Synyer probably knew he was seeing both women. On the Thursday night when Lorna was killed, she was supposed to be at the church, but when Martin went to collect her and her friend, he had to wait because she had slipped out. On the Saturday morning when Denise died, Martin's alibi of going for a haircut, then straight to Sheffield to his friend's house prior to their regular football match outing took away any alibi for Phyllis. She was free to do whatever she wanted.'

'You're going round in circles, aren't you?'

'I am indeed. I needed to talk it out instead of thinking it out. So, Faith whatever her name is and Phyllis Synyer both currently have no alibis, and both have motive, which means I have to pass all of this on to Carl, because Faith is sure as hell going to clam up completely with me now, and Phyllis, I'm pretty sure, wouldn't talk to anyone below the rank of Chief Constable.' Tessa gave a deep sigh.

'Talk to Carl. He may have already spoken to Faith – and then you'll know her surname. Isn't it on her name badge?'

'No, it only says Faith. And she didn't put anything other than Faith when we passed the piece of paper round at the book club.'

'Leave it with me. I'll find it out for you.'

'Thank you. If I asked I don't think she would answer me now.'

32

Ursula had been devastated to hear the full story behind her husband's death, but Fred and Ernest had realised pretty quickly that as they couldn't send any further plans and blueprints to buy them time, they had to show Ursula the picture of Harley with the blonde woman. Whoever L was, presumably the photographer, would send the picture first to Ernest and then to Ursula. Ernest felt it would be easier to manage the total wreckage the picture would cause if they told her the full story behind Harley taking his own life.

At first she hadn't believed it; they tried to tell her without showing her the picture, but she demanded to see it. And then she believed.

'Do we know who this tart is?' she sobbed.

'No. And neither do we know who L is. Did Harley ever mention a new acquaintance with a name beginning with L? Did you meet anybody new with Harley?'

'No. I can't get my head around anything. Three days ago my life was perfectly normal. And L isn't necessarily the name of a person. It could be a letter they used. Or a company. You say the messages come from a burner phone?'

'They do.'

'Then my suggestion,' she said, wiping her eyes on a screwed-up tissue, 'is to message back and say up yours, Ernest and Ursula have seen the picture and it's now been passed to the police for action.'

Fred looked at Ernest. 'Your decision, Ernest. I always thought it was a police matter, Harley was driven to suicide by the actions of this L.'

Ernest closed his eyes for a moment, deep in thought. He opened them and looked at Fred. 'You available to come into the office?'

'I am.'

'Then let's open up the books to you, see if you spot anything. If by the end of this weekend we've hit on nothing at all to suggest who this L is, then we'll hand it over to the police. I'm trying to save Harley and Ursula from being dragged through the media circus and the mud that will be flung.'

'And if we find who has caused all of this?'

'Then I'll deal with it,' Ernest said. 'And now I need to find some way to explain all of this to my wife. Let's hope she's having a good day today, and can take it in.'

'Faith Cox,' Cheryl announced.

'Really? How did you find that out?'

'I rang the library and asked. Told them I was a reporter doing a piece on Derbyshire libraries.'

'Smart arse. Thank you, although I'm not sure it helps. I'm seriously thinking of going back to the library and browsing the books, picking a couple up to bring home with me, generally rattle her. I've not worked out how to rattle Phyllis Synyer yet.' She laughed as she replaced the receiver.

The phone rang again. 'Tessa Marsden.'

'Go and see Phyllis. That'll rattle her,' Cheryl said.

Bakewell library felt busy; the children's section had a number of schoolchildren who all seemed to be around five, and all wanted to speak at the same time. Tessa walked through the doors and strolled casually across to where she hoped the crime section was. It proved to be historical, so she moved on to the next bay.

Eventually she found what she was looking for, and began pulling books off the shelves that she had never heard of, authors she didn't know, and after reading various blurbs settled on three she hoped she would enjoy.

While choosing the books, Tessa had put Faith Cox out of her mind, but now Tessa moved across to a table surrounded by four chairs, and opened the first of the books. She tried to take in the words, but her eyes were constantly roaming around the library, searching for the elusive Faith.

The children were lining up at the two checkout machines, and Tessa sat back with a sigh. It would be some time before she could check out her own books, so she continued to people watch around the large room. It was a good library, well-stocked, warm and inviting. There seemed to be several people sitting in various places, reading books or newspapers, or simply chatting quietly, and there was a group of four men at a table near the end wall, who were discussing Charles Dickens books.

And then she spotted Faith, stepping down from the elevated area that was the children's section. She must have been there all the time, Tessa mused. Had she been letting the children know who was in charge now?

The smile on Faith's face disappeared the second she spotted Tessa sitting at the table. She walked across and sat down on one of the spare chairs.

'You're here again.'

'I am indeed. I realised when I got back to the office I hadn't collected a ticket for the author talk you told me about. Next Friday, isn't it? And I need some books, so I'm killing two birds with one stone, so to speak.'

Faith stood. 'I'll go and get my receipt book, that acts as your ticket.'

'Thank you.' Tessa's smile was beatific. 'That's good of you.'

Faith walked across to the central information desk, rummaged in a drawer and returned to Tessa holding a Silvine receipt book, circa nineteen-sixty, Tessa thought.

'One, is it?'

'It is. Did you say £5?'

'I did.' She sat down and inserted the carbon paper before beginning to write.

An evening with Charles Warsop, Bakewell Library, 31ˢᵗ January 2020, 7pm.
One ticket only. £5.

She signed it with her name, handed the top copy to Tessa and closed the book. 'You're number thirteen,' she said, her face devoid of expression. 'Unlucky for some.'

'Only some,' Tessa said with a smile.

'Don't forget to bring that with you, I may not be the one on the door, and you won't get in without it.'

'Don't worry, I'll keep it in my purse.' Tessa handed over the five-pound note, and folded the small receipt carefully. She placed it in the note compartment of her purse and then took out her library card. 'I rang my own library to check I could borrow books from here and they said no problem, and I can return them to any Derbyshire library. That's right, is it?'

'It is. You're going now?'

'I'm waiting for the last of the children to check out their books, and then I'm taking these three.' She patted the pile in front of her. 'I've a quiet weekend coming up, so I shall enjoy these.'

'Good. Maybe take them back to Chesterfield library, somewhere closer to home,' Faith said, and walked away.

Tessa stifled her laughter, waited a further five minutes, then moved across to the machines. She waved her library card at the red beam, and she was soon on her way.

'Is Luke in?' Tessa asked as she shut Connection's front door behind her.

'He is,' Cheryl confirmed. 'Probably checking out furniture stores. It's nearly five, though, home time to us mere mortals.'

'I know, I know. I went to the library, and managed to upset the lovely Faith all over again. I want to show him something before I pass it on to Carl. I need to go home, I've got three library books to read. It's a busy little place, loads of youngsters in being taught how to use a library. I'd have been back half an hour ago if I hadn't had to wait for around thirty five-year-olds to check out their books. Good afternoon, though.'

She entered the lift and went up to the floor she shared with Luke. She knocked on his door, and was surprised to see Beth and Simon in with him.

'I'm leaving some instructions with Luke for Monday, because Simon and I are off to Northumberland. It's possible we'll be back Monday night, but also possible we may have to stay over, so I thought I'd better tell him as well as Cheryl.' Beth laughed as she said it, but fully aware of the sense in Cheryl's instructions.

'You've done the report for your client?'

'We have, and it's definitely going to have to be passed to the fraud people, so I don't know if we can simply present it and leave, or if they will want us to go through it with the relevant authorities. I'll keep Cheryl informed, so if you need me, check with her.'

Beth and Simon edged around her as they left, and Tessa sank down into a chair. 'Give me a minute to recover from my afternoon, and I'll go fetch my file.'

Luke stood. 'I'll get it. Coffee?'

'Thanks,' she said, and closed her eyes for a few seconds. 'It's in the top drawer on the right of my desk. And coffee would be lovely.'

He returned with the file, handed it to her and turned to pour them both a coffee.

'Successful afternoon?'

'I think so. We'll know in a minute. And I got three library books. Think there's a possibility I might have to see Carl tomorrow, though, Saturday or not.'

'You know, Tess, nothing you say ever surprises me.'

'I might be wrong.' She pulled her file towards her and took out the photocopies of the original threatening notes Denise and Lorna had received, and placed them on the desk. Then she opened her purse and removed the receipt written by Faith Cox.

She only needed a few seconds to confirm what she thought, and she twisted them around so Luke could look.

'Bingo,' he said quietly. 'I don't doubt Carl will get these to a handwriting expert to verify these are all written by the same hand, but I think your job is now done.'

'Even so,' she said, a frown on her face, 'it doesn't prove she killed them.'

'That's Carl's job. You're giving him the proof of who wrote the notes, let him take it from there. We can't go around demanding alibis, as you know, but Carl can. Show him these tomorrow, and we can close another case.'

'You're right. I find it hard to accept I don't have to take everything to a conclusion, and we're not getting paid on this one beyond the deposits we took. Without power of arrest I can take this no further, so good luck with DI Heaton, Faith.'

'His clear up rate's going to be impressive, after Evelyn Pearson this morning and Denise Jordan and Lorna Thompson tomorrow. Fred seems to be heavily embroiled in this suicide case, but it seems obvious it is suicide, so we can't pass anything from that on in Carl's direction. I don't think it's probable Beth's fraud issues could end up with him, even though he used to be in that specialised department before he moved to major crimes. If Beth is heading to Northumberland, it will most likely stay with their fraud squad.'

'Think he'll send us a thank you card?' Tessa grinned.

'Doubt it. Is there a card with the message "Why can't you lot be quiet?"?'

Tessa placed the notes and the receipt back in the file, and sighed. 'Let's hope next week is a bit quieter. This Coronavirus thing that's on the news is becoming a bit worrying, so maybe we need some sort of a plan. We certainly need to bring it up at Wednesday's briefing.'

'You think?'

'Ah, the joy of being young. You haven't considered it at all, have you?'

He laughed. 'Not really. I'll listen more carefully from now on. When they say it's centred in Wuhan, you kind of think it's a long way from here, and nothing to worry about.'

She finished her coffee and stood to go to her own office. 'Thank you for that. I'm going home shortly, but I'll see if I can meet Carl here tomorrow. I don't want to wait till Monday, Faith could have killed someone else by then. Probably me. She really doesn't like me.'

. . .

Fred rang Cheryl to report he was on his way home, and he was going to take the weekend to think things through on the Ernest Lounds case. She said she would ring him Saturday morning to make sure he hadn't weakened and gone into the office. And then she asked him if he would like to have Sunday lunch with her and the kids.

He said yes.

33

Tessa and Carl both arrived at Connection at the same time, and Tessa quickly put a pot of coffee on to brew. 'I want to take you through everything I've followed in this damn case, Carl, and if you find my body somewhere, start your investigation with Faith Cox, at Bakewell Library.'

'I didn't realise you were still following up on it, as both your clients are deceased.'

'It's partly because it linked into Luke's case with Mrs Pearson, it's all become a little interwoven, and we did take a deposit from our clients. I felt we needed to follow it as far as we could, and I think I've reached that point. Almost.'

Carl sighed. 'Almost?'

'Yes. I'm certain I've found out who wrote the original notes to Denise and Lorna, but writing the original notes doesn't mean the person of interest is the killer, as you will be quick to point out. As far as I've been able to ascertain, there is another person also possibly without a good alibi for the murders of both women. I've not asked for an alibi from this first person I'm going to talk about, because she definitely won't tell me

238

anything. I can't think why, but she really doesn't like me.' She laughed.

Carl groaned. 'I hope you've got biscuits to go with that coffee. This looks like being a long morning.'

Carl was on his third sheet of paper. His writing was deteriorating by the second, as he tried to annotate everything Tessa was telling him.

'You haven't spoken to Phyllis Synyer at all?'

'Not really. She made it clear on that first visit that we were beneath her, which was why we were so surprised by the way Martin Synyer was with us, when we went to his office. He quite happily gave us his alibis for both killings. It leaves Phyllis without one, but that's only as far as we are aware.'

'You think this is all about jealousy, whoever the killer is?'

'I do. I've handled enough murder cases to know it's about the most powerful motive there is. Martin dumped Faith, to take up with both Lorna and Denise. She knew without him having to spell it out. I believe Phyllis also knew as she was in the same book group at the library. On the night when Lorna died, she was supposedly at church, but when he went to pick her up he had to wait for her to come back from somewhere. I think he said she'd had to take something to somebody who was also a churchgoer. He was a bit vague about it, and I don't think he could remember the details. What if there were no details? What if she'd nipped round to Lorna's but because of the blood it took longer for Phyllis to clean herself up than she had anticipated.'

Carl scribbled further notes.

'And on the Saturday when Denise was killed, Martin left home before nine to go get his hair cut before heading straight for his friend's house in Sheffield. He didn't get back home until after the match, so that would have been after six. She had the full day to herself. You have confirmed that the killer forced that back gate open after breaking off the padlock?'

'We have.'

'When we saw Phyllis on the Sunday morning, she was limping. It might be worth asking her why.'

Carl leaned back, and ran his hand through his hair. 'You seem to be a couple of steps in front of us.'

Tessa laughed. 'That's because this is my only case at the moment. How many are you handling?'

'These stabbings are running us ragged, and we're getting nowhere fast, I can tell you. I will be bringing in Phyllis Synyer first thing Monday morning, along with Faith Cox. This can't be allowed to carry on, we need to close it. Is there any more of that coffee?'

Tessa stood and poured them both another drink. 'You want my thoughts?'

'I've got nearly four pages of your thoughts. You got some more?'

'Only my feelings, not facts.'

'I'm listening.'

'Find out how closely they know each other, Faith and Phyllis. If they're working together, they only need an alibi for one of the murders, as it was the same knife used in both. Ergo, same knife, same killer – but if Faith has an alibi for the Saturday morning it basically rules her out for Lorna. Likewise for Phyllis. I bet she has an alibi for Lorna, but not for Denise when her husband couldn't vouch for her. Am I making sense?'

He frowned. 'I think so. How did you know it was the same knife?'

'I think you might have mentioned it.'

He gave a slight nod. 'Yes, I'm sure I must have done.'

'When you have them brought in on Monday, make sure

they see each other. My Lord, I wish I could be there,' she said with a grin.

'You mean you haven't got a direct connection to the camera that videos the interview?'

'I'm working on it.' She pushed the plate of biscuits towards him, and he took one with a sigh. 'I love chocolate digestives. Put them away before I empty the plate.'

'It's okay,' she said. 'They're Luke's.'

Luke had no idea of the theft of biscuits from his office. He had shown Maria around his new home, and now was sitting on the lounge carpet, sharing a picnic with her.

'This is awesome,' she said, nibbling on a ham sandwich. 'Should we go buy a kettle or something?'

'Don't need to. Tessa's bringing me pots and pans and stuff, so I'll wait to see what she has spare before I get anything. I need as much money as possible for furniture.'

'You can have my TV.'

'What TV?'

'The one that's leaning against my dressing table. Mum and Dad have bought that new enormous thing in our lounge, and they're wanting me to have the old one on the wall in my bedroom, but I don't want it. It's too big for that size room, and I wouldn't watch it anyway. You want that?'

'If it's okay with them, that would be awesome.' He poured her another coffee from the flask, then handed her a cupcake. 'It's pretty urgent I organise something to sit on and something to sleep in, though. And a desk, although if Rosie doesn't want my desk that's in my room, I'll bring that. If she wants it, I'll have to get a new one. There's a lot to think about, isn't there?'

Maria laughed. 'I think it's amazing. And you've managed to get a lovely landlady.'

'She knew about us seeing each other.'

'Your mum?'

He nodded. 'Always my mum. But nothing's secret in Eyam anyway. I wonder how everybody's reacting to the Hattie Pearson issue.'

'You're such a softie, Luke Taylor. Hattie Pearson killed her daughter, and then came to you hoping you would be able to find somebody else to pin it on – it didn't happen. Was she counting on the feller her daughter was running off with being untraceable now?'

'I think so. She certainly didn't know who he was, and I reckon she hoped we could say it was him. She knew we couldn't pin it on Alan Egerton, he couldn't even walk. I still feel sick about it, though, it was a moment of anger and madness, combined with her being ill at the time. But murder is murder, no matter the circumstances.' He took another sip of his coffee. 'I've got an appointment lined up for Monday morning, let's hope it's a bit more straightforward than a body in our outhouse.'

'Dad, will you be okay if I go back home?' Ursula King took hold of her father's hand. 'You know we're going to have to make some decisions about Mum soon, don't you?'

'Your mum is fine.'

'She's not fine. She asked me who I was.'

'But she knew you yesterday. She's okay, only the odd lapse.'

Ursula shook her head. Her father was obviously burying his in the sand.

'Why do you want to go home?'

'I need some time out. Time to think. Dad, I want you to talk to Fred and ask him to drop it all. It's obvious Harley was being blackmailed, but now that little line has died with him, we've put much higher security in place and nothing will be gained by this coming out. It will damage the business, certainly damage us as a family, and destroy Harley's previous good name. My in-laws will be even more devastated than they are at losing Harley if they find out why – we have to put a stop to this now. Ask Fred for a final bill, let's pay it and close the investigation. Please.'

He stood and pulled her into his arms. 'If that's what you want, consider it done. I don't think we've any hope of finding things out now, so I'll speak to Fred this afternoon. Would you like me to go home with you?'

'No, I'll be fine. I've to go in the house on my own some time, so I'll go today. Thank you so much, Dad, for your support. Let's put it all behind us. And let's get that phone back from Fred and smash it to smithereens.'

Ernest stood outside his home and watched his daughter drive away. His heart ached for her. She had loved and respected her husband so much, and that one photo had destroyed it all. She would mourn his passing, but there would be anger there also.

He walked back into the house, and saw his wife standing in the doorway to the kitchen.

'Who are you?' she said. 'Don't come near me! Are you a burglar?'

He walked quickly towards her and took her in his arms. 'Hush, lovely. It's me, Ernest. Let's get you in the lounge, and I'll make you a cup of tea.'

He tried to lead her, but her reluctance showed. 'Come on,' he said. 'You know who I am.'

'Harley? Is it you, Harley? I've got something to tell you, Harley.'

Ernest stared at her. 'What have you got to tell me?'

Her whole body seemed to shake. 'Who are you? Tell me who you are.'

Ursula locked the door behind her, then leaned against it. It felt strangely cold, bereft of all life. Of all warmth and love.

She walked around the house, touching things, bringing everything back to life in her mind before going upstairs. She held her breath before going through into the bedroom she had shared for so long with Harley and knew that from now on she would sleep in the guest bedroom. This one would be deep cleaned to lose the smell, redecorated and refurnished. Maybe then she could think about sleeping in it, but that was some time down the line.

She gathered some clothes and carried them through to the pretty lemon bedroom that overlooked the front of the house. She put the clothes away in the wardrobe, then went back downstairs to begin a new life. And that life began with an exceptionally large whisky.

34

'E rnest? Is everything okay.' Fred was surprised to hear from anyone in the Lounds family, they had decided to put it all to one side over the weekend.

'All good, Fred. Ursula and I had a discussion this morning, and we've decided there's no point carrying on with the investigation. It will only cause more heartache all round and Ursula is at breaking point. Thank you for everything you've already done for us, but can you send me the final bill along with Harley's phone, and I'll pay it immediately?'

'Of course I can, Ernest. And I think you're probably right in this decision. It won't do you any good for this to reach the papers, and if we continue to investigate there's every chance that could happen. How's your wife, by the way?'

'Ursula and I also discussed this in a roundabout way this morning, and I can see Pamela is getting worse. She thought I was a burglar as I came in the front door from seeing Ursula off. She isn't really recognising either of us, and to be perfectly honest, Fred, I'm going to be resigning from work, probably as from now, and leaving Ursula to step into my shoes. I had, of course, always planned to do this, but with Harley as joint CEO, and in six months' time, but I fear I have to escalate my retirement. It seems we've halted the damage being done to the business, so I'm calling that a win situation, and concentrating on the things that matter.'

'I think you're probably sensible, Ernest, but keep my number handy in case there are repercussions. I'll call round on Monday with the phone and the bill.'

'Thank you, Fred.'

They disconnected, and Fred stared at his phone for a minute. His ex-policeman head said a crime had been committed, but his private investigator head said the client was the priority.

'Let it develop, Fred,' he finally said aloud, without expecting a response.

With the remnants of the picnic tidied away, Maria and Luke left the annexe and walked down the driveway to Luke's car.

'Apparently,' he said, 'the driveway will still be fairly narrow, but they can gain a couple of feet by taking the tarmac or whatever they're using right to the edges, and getting rid of the slight banking of weeds that's always been either side. There'll be a hardstanding for two cars at the side of the annexe, and that little top area,' he pointed to a small enclosed part of the Yates garden, 'is my garden. Jenny suggested I might want to put a small set of furniture there in the summer. She said it's a real suntrap, and her mother used to love to sit out there.'

'So what do you want to do now?'

'I need to organise furniture. I need a bed and a suite of some sort. Preferably with a sofa bed in case the girls want to stay. And I'd like a small table in the kitchen with chairs that fit inside it. Do you know what I mean? There's not much room, so it has to be compact, but I don't really want to be eating off a tray on my knee all the time. Occasionally I'd like to be civilised and sit at a table with a candle on it when I'm entertaining my best girl.'

'That me?'

'Could be.'

'Better be.'

They laughed, exchanged a kiss, and he started the car.

'Sheffield or Chesterfield?'

'Darley Dale?'

'Never thought of that,' he said. 'One-stop shopping at its finest. Come on, let's go spend some money.'

They brought the small compact table with four chairs that slid inside its legs home with them in the car. Maria bought him a candlestick and a box of candles. The bed and two armchairs would be delivered Tuesday, the sofa bed would be some time in the future, but the salesman had ordered it as an urgent requirement. Luke suspected that meant nothing, it would arrive when it arrived.

He had listened carefully to Maria's oohs and aahs, and together they had known that the beautiful dark green fabric for the sofa bed was right, and the checked armchairs with the same dark green in the pattern matched perfectly.

Luke called in at the garage on the way home for petrol, and came out with two fold-up garden chairs and a small fold-up matching coffee table. He knew there was no chance of closing the boot with the new acquisitions inside it, so he carefully wedged the items around Maria's legs.

'We can sit on these in the lounge until some furniture arrives, then use them in the garden in summer,' he grinned. 'Who's a smart cookie then?'

'If you say so,' she said, trying to wriggle her feet so she could move more than five centimetres. 'Thank heavens we haven't far to go.'

Jenny Yates met them as they struggled up the driveway with their packages. 'There's four boxes of stuff in your bedroom, Luke. Somebody called Tessa left them for you, said they're pots and pans and suchlike. I saw you go out, so I let her in before she collapsed. Nice lady. She was saying she works with you.'

'She does. That probably means we've now got a kettle! And some cups...'

'I guessed as much. The boxes rattled a bit. She said to tell you to wash them, because they've been in her loft for some time.'

'Thanks, Jenny. I'll give her a ring and thank her. She liked the place?'

'She did. She was saying she's hoping to buy in Eyam eventually, so I said I would keep my ears open for her. I'll leave you two to it. Shout if you need anything.'

'We will. I'm going to dump the stuff we've bought and call it a day. Maria's mum is feeding us, and we'll be back tomorrow to sort everything.'

Carl spent his afternoon at home sorting out the collection of Faith Cox and Phyllis Synyer at seven Monday morning, giving them no time to organise themselves, no time to get their brains into gear, and no time to contact each other if Tessa's thoughts proved to be valid.

He felt a little surprised to realise it was a possibility, that the two women had worked together. The sticking point was that Faith had been involved with Martin until Lorna and Denise had appeared on the scene, but maybe Phyllis hadn't realised that. Maybe Phyllis had assumed that Faith needed to get rid of Lorna in order to take her job, and she had seen it as an opportunity to get rid of both her husband's bits on the side in a clever way. The same knife to be used, but only one alibi needed. Faith, on the other hand, knew the full story...

Carl annotated the questions he would need for both women, but he intended interviewing Phyllis Synyer. He wanted to be the one who told her Faith Cox had also slept with her husband.

He would have Ray Charlton in with him, and DS Susan Ridgeway, recently returned to his unit after a serious road accident, would lead the Faith Cox interview alongside DC Nigel Glossop.

He contacted all three of them to inform them they needed to meet with him at eight on Monday morning to go through the planned questions, and he knew he could finally rest. Hattie Pearson had been charged with murder the previous night, and he hoped her confession would help her case, and now this one was potentially coming to a close. If only the stabbings would end soon...

Martha stood in the office doorway. 'Daddy.' She held up Patty, her doll. 'You play with me an' Patty?'

He laughed. This was what he needed. 'I will, sweetheart. Shall we make her a cup of tea?'

Tessa felt a sense of relief that she had passed everything on to Carl. She had been experiencing pangs of frustration at not having the power of the law behind her, but with the discussion that morning she had reached the end of her commitment to the two women who had died before she had had chance to help them. And she had none of the hard work to go through following up on it...

Her thoughts that she had passed on to Carl had been simply that – her thoughts. No proof, only feelings that there was something off-kilter with both women, and Phyllis had certainly not hung around at the book club meeting, disappearing out of the way as soon as she could. Faith had been quiet, but Phyllis had left. Unable to handle the stress? And if it was proved that they had worked together to get rid of two inconveniences, who had approached who? Had it started as a joke that turned serious?

Apart from her thoughts, Tessa had also passed on Patrick Fletcher's name to Carl, and knew that if Patrick did know any more, Carl would wheedle it out of him. She felt that Patrick could be a little gold mine of information, but it would take time for his memories to surface. Carl would give him the time to talk, would share tea and biscuits with him, as per Patrick's wife's instructions. Tessa had always rated Carl highly and been delighted every time she had managed to get him seconded to her team whenever they had found themselves in a major investigation. He had an approach to people that was quiet, measured, friendly, and they responded in kind. She knew he would be gentle with Patrick.

And when it was over and the killer or killers of Lorna and Denise had been charged, Tessa would go back to Patrick's little cottage and share tea and biscuits with him once again, and talk of things unconnected to murder.

The night passed peacefully for the Connection team – suddenly everything seemed out of their hands, and that made for a better night's sleep.

Except it didn't. Cheryl had explained, somewhat hesitantly, that Fred would be having Sunday lunch with them, and had known she was going a bit over the top with her explanation that he was only a friend from work who she really enjoyed talking to. Both her kids had laughed at her, and had spent the rest of Saturday taking the mick out of her, and now she was in a state of panic that they would inadvertently say the wrong thing when Fred arrived.

So now she was lying in bed reading, hoping that sleep would come soon and she could stop worrying.

Fred was also struggling to sleep because he was unconvinced by Ernest's decision. Something felt off, and he could do nothing about it. The only positive in his mind was that he would be having a decent meal at Cheryl's home, and would get to meet her two kids who he only knew from her chat about them over coffee at work. They had clearly been her rocks after she lost her husband.

Fred picked up his book, and for the hundredth time wished it had been available for his eReader. It was difficult to read a real book while lying down. Finally, the story of the Pottery Cottage murders caused his eyes to close, and he drifted away while trying to decide if he would have handled it any differently to the way it was dealt with at the time. He came to no conclusion as he slept soundly.

Saturday flowed gently into Sunday, by tradition a day of rest.

35

SUNDAY 26TH JANUARY 2020

F red woke early, fed Angel who didn't seem all that bothered about breakfast, made himself some toast and coffee and picked up his book. He was so near the end he wanted to finish it. He could take it with him to Cheryl's later, she had expressed a wish to borrow it.

Angel climbed onto his knee and settled down to sleep. He softly stroked her head and thought he might take her to the vets to get her checked over. She seemed to be sleeping most of the time, and not eating much. She was getting on a bit...

She lightly snored, and he stopped stroking her, and picked up his book.

Half an hour later Fred closed the book, lifted Angel and put her in her cat bed, then wandered through to the kitchen with his now-empty cup. He washed his breakfast dishes and headed down into the cellar where he chose a bottle of wine to take with him. He decided also to pick up a couple of bottles of Schloer from the supermarket, as he couldn't begin to second-guess

Cheryl on her stance with alcohol for her children, teenagers or not.

He was looking forward to the unexpected treat of having a meal cooked for him; he knew he'd become introspective after losing Jane but this job at Connection was changing him. They made him talk! It was a remarkably inclusive atmosphere in the office, and everyone discussed their cases between each other, confident in the knowledge that nothing would go outside the front door. He needed to talk to Luke, whose logical brain would work through what Ernest had said, and he would then chip in with his twopenn'orth of advice.

But today he would talk to Cheryl, who always brought a smile to his face with her chatter. He stopped for a moment to look at Angel as he went by her bed, and pursed his lips. Laid on her side, he could see she was losing weight. Definitely he would book an appointment with the vets as soon as he could.

He headed upstairs for a shower, pleased that at fifty-two he was still able to climb the stairs two at a time, and hadn't put on a pound in weight since his twenties.

Fred handed flowers, the wine and a carrier bag containing Schloer to Cheryl and she smiled her appreciation. 'Wow. These are beautiful. Thank you so much. Come through, Fred, let me introduce you to my kids.'

She led him into the lounge. 'This is Tyler on the iPad, and the one with her nose in a book is Eleri. It says everything you need to know about these two – one on an iPad, one in a book.' She laughed.

'Pleased to meet you both,' Fred said, and they stood up.

'You too, Mr Iveson,' Tyler said, and held out his hand. Fred shook it.

'It's Fred. Eleri? That's a pretty name.'

Eleri smiled at him. 'Nobody's ever heard of it, can't spell it, can never get anything personalised in a shop. It's a Welsh name, because my dad was Welsh.'

'Ah, I have a niece called Cerys who moans about that same issue. On the plus side, Eleri, you'll always stand out when it comes to job interviews and suchlike.'

'I have to go to work? I can't laze around and read all day?'

Cheryl laughed. 'You two are meant to keep me in luxury in a few years' time. Best get that into your heads now. Fred, come and keep me company in the kitchen. Let's leave these two reprobates to their Sunday chill day.'

The meal was a complete success everyone decided, and Eleri and Tyler loaded the dishwasher before making coffee for Fred and Cheryl, who had returned to the lounge.

'Thank you so much, Cheryl, I haven't laughed so much in ages.'

She smiled. 'They're real characters, my kids, but that's how we brought them up. They've never been told to go away because they're only kids, they've always mixed with adults and can relate to adult things. When Keith died it knocked them for six, but they're coming round. They've even understood the concept of you being a man friend, not a potential boyfriend, if you know what I mean.'

'Oh, I do. I had a woman friend when I was in the police who is still a woman friend now some twenty years later, but the nudges and winks used to drive us mad. And Tessa is also a friend from that time. Since I lost Jane I've steered clear of relationships that could develop into more, and I don't think I could ever see a time when I would want somebody else.'

Cheryl sighed. 'I know. It's a little over a year since I lost Keith, and to be perfectly honest, he still lives with me. You remind me of him. He was a quiet man, but with an underlying sense of humour that even now, when something springs to mind that he said or did, still makes me break out into laughter. I talk to him a lot, as I'm sure you do to your Jane.'

Fred smiled. 'I tell her all sorts of stuff. I'll be talking to her tonight, because I'm not convinced stepping back from this Lounds case is the right thing. I know there's no choice in the matter because Ernest has said stop, but even so...'

'I'm always there to bounce thoughts off, Fred, whether it's about work or personal stuff. I hope you know that.'

He finished his coffee and stood. 'I'm going to leave you in peace now. I imagine you've never stopped all morning, and I've brought you the Pottery Cottage book to read. I'm also a little concerned about Angel, my cat, so I'll see if I can tempt her with some milk. I picked some cat milk up while I was in the supermarket, so we'll see if she goes for that. I know she's getting old, but she's definitely out of sorts.'

'Maybe you need a vet.'

'Ringing tomorrow. I'll let you know if I'm going to be late in. It's a pity she's not with the Eyam vets, but she isn't. Say goodbye to Tyler and Eleri for me.' Cheryl followed him into the hall and he shrugged on his jacket. He removed the book from his pocket and handed it to her. 'The police side is a bit of an eye-opener,' he said, 'but Stockholm Syndrome was a blast in this one. And this is real life, not crime fiction.'

'I'll start it right now. The kids are both upstairs, so it will be quiet. Take care driving home.'

He placed a kiss on her cheek. 'Thank you, see you tomorrow at some point.'

He opened the front door and looked into eyes that were exact copies of Luke Taylor's. The woman in front of him smiled with Luke Taylor's smile.

'Hi, you must be Fred. Is Cheryl in?'

'I'm here,' Cheryl said from behind him.

'Oh good. Fred, I'm Naomi, Luke's mum.'

He smiled. 'You think I didn't guess? You're so alike, he couldn't be anybody else's son. Let me get out of the way, and you can get to Cheryl.' He stepped outside, and once again looked into her eyes. His heart gave a small lurch. 'Good to meet you, Naomi. I hear a lot about you.'

She smiled with Luke's smile again. 'And I you, Fred. Don't be a stranger, I only work across the road from the office, in the Co-op.'

He laughed. 'I'll make sure I pick up the doughnuts in future.'

He heard Cheryl say 'Hussy' to her friend before laughing as she closed her door.

The drive home only took ten minutes, and he picked up the carrier bag from the boot that contained the cat milk, a new book and a bag of mints.

'I'm home, Angel,' he called as he went through the front door. He hung his coat in the cloakroom, and walked through to the lounge. Angel was still in the same position, and he walked over to her.

He knew without touching her that she had gone, and he sat on the floor by her side. He stroked her head, and allowed tears to fall, not moving for some considerable time.

Fred stood by the side of the deep hole and looked at the wooden crate nestled inside it. He covered it with the excavated soil, knowing the ache inside him would go, but he would miss Angel. She knew his secrets, his torments; he had played for hours with her and the little white catnip mouse on the end of a string and she had been there for him at the end of every day, waiting for his attention. The little mouse was with her in the box.

He covered the earth mound with some stones, straightened up and walked back into the kitchen. The day that had started with happy expectancy of being a good day had soured into a day of blackness.

Luke and Maria sat in their garden chairs, and looked around. The television was on the wall, the fire was burning brightly, and it was a beautifully warm room. A small lamp, part of the haul from the boxes left by Tessa, was standing on the floor in the corner, in the absence of anything to stand it on, but it gave off subdued lighting that added to the ambience.

The dishwasher had never stopped and now the kitchen cupboards were well stocked with crockery. The drawers held all manner of items on the cutlery side, and they decided to order in a pizza. They ate it at Luke's mini table which fitted tidily into the kitchen, and the candle in the middle finished everything off to perfection.

Maria reached across to hold Luke's hand. 'It'll be better when it's a sofa,' she said with a laugh. 'It's not exactly romantic sitting on garden chairs.'

'It's better than sitting on the floor. Remind me tomorrow to organise a television licence.'

They sat in silence, watching the flames, mesmerised by the beauty of firelight.

'This is so good,' Luke said.

'Certainly is,' Maria said. 'Think your chair will bear the weight of two people?'

.   .   .

DI Carl Heaton read through all his notes and statements once again, checked in with the two teams he had organised to bring in Faith Cox and Phyllis Synyer, and sat back to let his mind roam. He trusted Tessa Marsden's intuition implicitly; she had an uncanny knack for seeing through lies and denials, and he wished she was still working alongside him and hadn't defected to the private sector.

Tomorrow would be crucial in solving the killing of the two women, but judging which woman would crack first was something else. He was relieved Ray Charlton would be alongside him; the man was a stalwart of the interview room, knew when to step in, when to retreat, and when to cover his senior officer's back.

Carl guessed Phyllis Synyer would use a high-handed attitude, and they would have to break it down pretty quickly. He had taken on board what she was like from Tessa, and knew Tessa would have read her properly. Phyllis had money, she had property, she had businesses, and she would feel she was above being questioned by the police. She was due for a real shock.

He put his papers away, checked the house was locked up and headed upstairs to join Kat, who had gone to bed early feeling overtired. He opened Martha's door slightly, checked she was okay, and smiled. There wasn't much wrong with a world that had beautiful children like Martha in it, he mused.

36

The collection of Faith Cox went reasonably smoothly, partly because she wasn't really awake, and partly because she couldn't believe it was happening.

She was allowed to get dressed and to organise her mother's medication, but the female officer accompanied her everywhere she went. Cox reached for her mobile phone to take with her, but was told to leave it, it would be collected for forensic examination when the team moved in to search the property.

Hardly any words were spoken, and they held her head while she ducked to get in the car. The female officer sat beside her, observing how much Cox was shaking. She asked her if she was okay, but Faith simply glared at her, refusing to speak.

On arrival at the police station she was put into the first interview room. The male officer remained with her, without speaking. Her right foot tapped continuously, and she picked at the skin surrounding her fingernails. She only came to life when the door to the room opened for a moment, and the officer asked if the PC knew where DI Heaton was. Standing behind him was Phyllis Synyer.

It had been carefully orchestrated that the two women

should know they were both in for questioning, but although Faith Cox half stood, neither she nor Synyer said anything.

Faith sank back down onto the chair, and her foot resumed its tapping.

Phyllis Synyer was so angry she felt as if her head was going to burst. She had been manhandled at seven in the morning, and into the back of a police car! Her ineffectual husband, his face deathly white and his hair looking not quite so groomed as normal, had done nothing to help beyond saying he would ring their solicitor. And then to see Faith Cox sitting in an interview room... suddenly she realised this was a bit more than a police interview.

She sank onto the chair and watched as one of the two officers left the room, leaving the other one in with her.

'Why am I here?' she demanded.

'I'm sure I don't know, madam. I was simply told to collect you.'

'It's not good enough. I'd like a drink.'

'I'll mention it when the DI arrives, madam.'

The room was cold and uninviting. She imagined that at some time in the distant past the walls had been white, but they now had a grey tinge to them, with chunks missing from the plaster in several places. The door opened and her solicitor was admitted; the police constable moved outside the room to give them the privacy demanded by Yvette Garside. 'I need to speak privately with my client,' she'd said, and he inclined his head in acknowledgement.

'Martin rang in a bit of a flap. He's not sure why you've been brought in, but he doesn't want you here without help from me.

Have they said anything?'

'I think it's in connection with the deaths of two women I was acquainted with through the book club I go to in Bakewell. They haven't mentioned charges or anything, but they have threatened me with a house search warrant. I've already been here for ages, and seen nobody.'

'They would have been waiting for me. I rang as soon as Martin rang me, and told them under no circumstances could they interview you without legal representation.' She glanced at her watch. 'They picked you up at seven so Martin said. It's now nine thirty, so they'll not be much longer. Okay, tell me about it.'

'Tell you what? There's nothing to tell. Two members of my book club have been murdered. I had absolutely nothing to do with it. I only saw them once a month, so we didn't exactly have a close relationship. For God's sake, I don't think we even liked the same sort of books.'

Yvette gave a slight laugh. 'That will go down well with any jury.'

'What?'

'I'm joking. Lighten up, Phyllis, we'll have you out of here in a couple of hours. Now, if I want you to say "No comment" I'll touch your ankle. The police are good at twisting things that are said, so the best way of dealing with stuff is not to say anything. That way we'll find out what they think they have, and we can deal with it.'

'There's another issue. They've also brought in Faith Cox, the new librarian and current leader of the book club. She's replaced one of the two dead women, Lorna Thompson, who was head librarian there. It can't be coincidence that she's here, they've presumably got us in for the same thing.'

'Are you friends with Faith Cox?'

'No, I don't really know her, other than on the periphery of the book club. She dished out cups of tea, but she's sitting in the room next door.'

Yvette made a note of the name, and gave a slight nod. 'We're clearly going to have to wait this one out, find out what they want you for, and take it from there. I'm assuming you didn't kill one or both of these women?'

'Of course I didn't,' Phyllis snapped, 'but I can't guarantee murder won't happen if they don't hurry up and get this bloody interview over with.'

Faith was introduced to the duty solicitor, Barclay Wright, and her PC was despatched to stand outside the door.

'Do you know why I'm here?' she demanded as soon he sat by her side.

'For questioning about the deaths of Denise Jordan and Lorna Thompson,' he answered smoothly. 'Do you know anything at all?'

'Only that they're dead.' Her words came out almost as a snarl.

'Ouch. Touchy, aren't we? I suggest you don't respond like that when they question you or we'll be here for a long time. Tell me what you do know, without any clever comments.'

'Very little. Lorna Thompson was my boss. She was head librarian at Bakewell Library. She was killed on Thursday evening, I think the sixteenth of January.'

'And where were you that evening?'

'I was at home. I live with my mother, who needs help physically, but there's nothing wrong with her mentally. We play Scrabble, we read, we watch crime shows on television, we knit and crochet, and I rarely go out after I get in from the library.'

'You don't have a husband or partner?'

'No. I had a bit of a relationship, but it didn't last because I can't commit to being able to go out at night. It's difficult...'

'And your mother will vouch for you?'

'Of course. My journal will also probably do that. We document our Scrabble scores, along with start and finish times for the games. We've done that for years.'

He nodded. 'And the other death? Denise Jordan.'

'She was murdered on the Saturday morning. I go shopping on Saturday mornings. I'll still have the timed receipt because I save them all to balance my bank account at the end of the month. I haven't killed either of these women,' she said, her voice becoming more strident.

'Let's leave it there. I'm sure things will become clearer as we progress with the interview.' He checked his watch. 'They're already playing silly buggers, keeping you waiting. If I touch your hand at any point, reply with a "no comment". I'll see if I can get us a drink. You want a tea?'

'Please. Anything. I haven't had a drink at all this morning.'

Carl Heaton stood with Susan Ridgeway looking into the interview room where Phyllis Synyer and Yvette Garside were deep in conversation, both drinking from bottles of water presumably brought in by the solicitor.

'I haven't spoken to her yet and I don't like her,' Heaton said.

Susan took a sip from her coffee mug before answering. 'I know what you mean. Sour-faced, I'm guessing it's going to be a day of no comments.'

'Have we heard anything from the team with the warrant for her home?'

'Yes. The cleaner apparently arrived five minutes before they did, and she let them in. Martin Synyer wasn't there, and the cleaner seemed to think he'd already left for work. They've found nothing of any significance, but are bringing in two laptops, one iPad, and a mobile phone. The phone belongs to Phyllis, according to the cleaner. It seems the cleaner tried to contact Martin to tell him what was happening, but got no response.'

'And the team at the Cox house?'

'Taking it carefully. The mother is not too good, suffers with severe arthritis, so they've put her in the kitchen. There's only a phone on the technology side to bring in, but they've found a journal. They're bringing that. No bloodstained clothing from either property.'

'We'll give it another half hour, let them both stew for a bit longer, then go in.'

It was close to eleven when DS Susan Ridgeway and DC Nigel Glossop entered the room to begin their interrogation of Faith Cox.

They checked in all names that were present, and Nigel opened up his file.

'Faith, can you confirm your date of birth, address and your employment status, please.'

Faith did so, her voice muted, her face with a fixed expression that they hoped didn't promise a refusal to answer any further questions. 'Why have you kept me waiting for almost four hours?' was her final remark.

'Have we?' Nigel glanced at his watch. 'We were waiting to hear back from the search team at your house. It seems you don't own a laptop or an iPad. Or indeed any sort of tablet. Is that correct?'

'It is. I have a section full of computers at work. I don't need one at home. And I sincerely hope you haven't caused any distress for my mother, she isn't fit enough to cope with stuff like this.'

'She's been well looked after. Our forensics team have left your property now, and ensured she was safe before they left.'

Faith made no reply.

Susan coughed. 'Okay, Faith. Can we go back to the evening of Thursday, sixteenth of January. Can you tell me what you were doing that evening.'

'As it's a Thursday, I would have finished work at five, then headed straight home.'

'And?'

'And what? That's it. I would have headed straight home. I rarely have to go out in the evening, especially during the dark nights. I don't leave my mother. She can cope during the day because I leave her a flask of coffee and a sandwich for her lunch, but in the evening we have a meal, and usually a game of Scrabble, or we read, or crochet. We're making a new bedspread for Mum's bed at the moment, and do a little of that each evening. It helps keep her fingers moving a bit easier, half an hour of crochet. It depends how long our game of Scrabble lasts as to how much of the bedspread gets done.'

'So you didn't go out that Thursday evening?'

'Which part of the description didn't you understand? I can repeat it all, but it can get a bit boring hearing it through for the second time. My life is pre-programmed, DS Ridgeway, it never varies and I couldn't cope with the fallout if it did.'

'So your mother will vouch for you?'

'She will.' Faith's voice was firm. She'd suddenly realised that all this was simply to prove she didn't have an alibi for the evening of Lorna's death. And she did.

Susan reached into her file, and pulled out two evidence bags. 'Can you explain these?' Inside the bags were the handwritten notes and the handwritten receipt given to Tessa Marsden.

37

F aith stared at the notes and lifted her head. She glanced at her solicitor, but he didn't touch her hand.

She reached across the table and pointed to the receipt. 'That's a ticket I wrote out myself for an event that has been organised at the library. I gave it to Tessa Marsden, from Connection. The others are notes I sent to Denise Jordan and Lorna Thompson when I felt in the deepest of despair. I can't explain it any differently to that. A man I was seeing, and had quite fallen for, dumped me because I could rarely get out to go out with him. To go to bed with him, I should say. And he started seeing Lorna and Denise, both of them at the same time. It was obvious. I used to watch him at the library, always touching them. He couldn't keep his hands off them.'

'And what did you hope to gain by sending these?'

'I hoped they would be frightened off seeing him. They were notes, they weren't promises I was going to turn violent or anything. I hoped the power of words would scare them. But somebody else got to them.' Her head dropped. 'I didn't want them dead. I simply wanted them out of Martin's life.'

'Martin?'

'Martin Synyer, the man who I was seeing until he moved on. Don't pretend you don't know. You have his wife here.'

The two officers looked at each other, and suspended the interview. 'I'll arrange for hot drinks for both of you. We'll be back shortly.' Nigel Glossop spoke firmly, and accompanied Susan from the room.

Carl Heaton opened his file and stared at Phyllis Synyer.

'Mrs Synyer, can you tell me where you were between eight and midnight on the evening of Thursday, the sixteenth of January.'

She looked at Yvette Garside, who gave a small nod. 'If it was a Thursday I was at church. And if we're talking about the evening Lorna Thompson was murdered I was definitely at church. My husband dropped me off before seven because I open up for the group, and I nipped across the road to take some stuff to one of our congregation who'd had a fall and couldn't walk. We're making new kneelers for the church, and I took her supplies to sit at home and sew. I was back in the church for about quarter past seven and my husband called to pick me up at nine, as usual. We dropped a friend off on the way, and were back home for about nine thirty. He made me a hot drink, Horlicks I believe, gave me my sleeping tablets and I was in bed, alongside him, for ten. I'm sure he'll confirm that.'

'Your husband's statement doesn't confirm that. He says you went to see someone at the end of your group meeting, and he had to wait for you coming back.'

Phyllis looked perplexed. 'But that's simply not right. Do you have a piece of paper? I'll give you the lady's name and address who I went to at seven, not nine, and also the name and address of my friend who had the lift home.'

Carl handed her a pen and a piece of paper. She scribbled

furiously and pushed it back to him. 'Ask my bloody husband again. He'll have been confused by you when he told you that pack of lies.'

'Were you aware of his relationships with Lorna Thompson and Denise Jordan?'

'Hardly relationships, DI Heaton. He spoke to them at the library.'

'And were you aware of his relationship with Faith Cox?' Carl was relentless.

For the first time he saw shock on Phyllis's face.

'Faith Cox? The little mouse? Never in a million years.'

'He was seeing Faith Cox on and off for quite a while before he gave up and moved on to the other two, who he was seeing at the same time. Busy man, your husband.'

Before Phyllis could respond, the door opened and Susan Ridgeway entered. She didn't say anything, and Carl stood, suspending the interview.

'We'll be back,' he said.

Ray Charlton followed him out of the room.

'We need Martin Synyer arresting and bringing in as soon as possible.' Carl's voice was harsh. 'These women aren't killers, their stories don't match up with what he's said, and I bet Faith Cox has an alibi for both murders, doesn't she?'

'She certainly has for the first one, and I'll lay odds on she has for the second one by virtue of timed shopping receipts. That's why I've suspended, so we can tell you where we are with it. She admits to sending the notes, but with no intentions other than to frighten them away from Martin Synyer. We need Synyer in here, boss.'

'We certainly do. He's lied on his statement it seems, and at the very least we need to question him. He'll be at work according to their cleaner, let's have some lads there with Susan and me to bring him in.'

The receptionist smiled as she saw Carl, Susan, and two uniformed officers enter through the impressive glass doors.

'Can I help?'

'I need to speak with Mr Synyer, please. Mr Martin Synyer.'

'Oh, he left about eight.'

'Left? Where is he?'

'He didn't say. As I arrived he was down in the bay where we keep the skips, then he walked back up here to say he would be away for a while. He took the lift up to the roof, and I heard the rotors start.'

Carl looked at Susan. 'Susan, go with these two lads down to the skips, see if there's anything in them we need to know about.' He watched as they disappeared through the doors, then turned back to the receptionist.

'Rotors?'

'He came by helicopter this morning. His car wasn't in its usual place. And when I heard the rotors I knew.'

'He has a helipad on the roof?'

'He does. And one at home in their grounds. It's handy for him to fly into work, no traffic jams in the sky he always says. And he loves flying.'

'I'm going up to his office.'

'I'll advise his secretary you're on your way.'

Carl picked up the picture from Martin's desk. He was standing proudly by the side of a helicopter, white with a blue flash down the side, a nod to his favourite football team, Carl surmised.

'This is still his current helicopter?' he asked.

The woman hovering in the doorway nodded. 'It is. He bought it for their visits to their second home in France, it's quicker flying than by road, obviously.'

'You have an address for this home?'

'I do.' She disappeared and reappeared a minute later. She handed the address to him.

'Thank you. Could he have gone there now?'

'I have no idea. There was a note on my desk that said he was going to be away for a while, and that's all I know.'

'Okay, I'm sending a forensics team in, and I'm leaving one of my men here until they get here. Do not touch anything in this room. I'm taking this picture with me. Does he file his own flight plans?'

'Yes. I know nothing about that.'

Carl gave a slight nod. 'Thank you. I'll send my man up now. Please lock the door.'

She did, and he held his hand out for the key. 'My officer will return it when forensics have finished.'

He took the lift back down to reception, and arrived as Susan and the two officers burst back through the glass doors, one of the men carrying a holdall.

'Found in the third skip along,' Susan said, somewhat breathlessly. The bag was placed on the floor, and Susan bent to unzip it, revealing its contents.

It was filled with sports clothes, jogging bottoms and hoodies, shoes, socks, boxer shorts – all of them soaked with what appeared to be blood.

Carl stared at it for a moment and took out his phone. 'I want a forensics team at Synyer's Medical, and I need to know how to file flight plans by the time I get back.'

He handed the key over, explained he'd told the secretary she wasn't allowed in the room, and the officer nodded his understanding. 'I'll take this bag back to the station and log it in.

Good work, you three. It's definitely looking as though we brought the wrong ones in this morning.'

They released Faith Cox half an hour before they released Phyllis Synyer. Faith was allowed home to care for her mother, but Phyllis was told her house was a crime scene, and she would have to go elsewhere.

'Before you go, when you fly to your home in France how long does it take?'

'It's not a jet,' she said. 'I suppose a couple of hours. But don't go fretting about my husband, he's had a hell of a start on you, he could be anywhere now. You'll not see him again. And I don't suppose I will. I'd better retain the services of Ms Garside for a bit longer, and sort out my future. I don't want him back, and it seems he's killed off anybody else who might have wanted him. Except the little mouse of course, she might still fancy her chances. She'll have to find him first.'

38

L uke walked down the driveway towards his car, his mind fixated on the news that had come from Carl the previous evening. It seemed everything was cleared up, even if there was no sight of the killer of the two women. He knew Tessa had been shocked by the revelation that it was Martin Synyer after all, but Luke also recognised he had been completely taken in by the man, had quite liked him after that first disastrous meeting with him.

Phyllis had even explained the reason behind her limp on that Sunday morning – it was nothing to do with escaping from Denise's back garden, she had simply slipped down the stairs while going to answer the door when they had rattled her lion's head knocker.

All Carl had to do was wait for the forensics results on the bloodstained clothing, and find Synyer. They could find no flight plan that had been filed, and therefore had no way of knowing whether Synyer had left UK airspace or had simply flown the smart helicopter a few miles, and switched to more normal transport like a car. He would need money, that was for sure, but Carl had said during their conversation that there was a lot more to Martin Synyer than they had at first thought, and Luke had no doubt the money would be spirited away somewhere ready for when he might need it.

Luke got into his car knowing he would be back later to build up a bed. It was arriving between two and four, so he had asked Jenny if she would be around to take the delivery for him. He was about to drive off when there was a tap on his window.

He wound down the window. A small, rotund elderly lady was standing there, and she leaned on his sill. 'You got my note then?'

'What note?'

'I said I knew. I told you it was one big fat lie.'

'You wrote the note with the cut-out letters?'

'I did. She lied, that Hattie Pearson. I heard the argument that night, and then Evelyn disappeared.'

'And you didn't tell the police?'

'No, my hubby said to leave it alone. But when that body come to light, I needed to say summat, didn't I?'

'Thank you...?'

'Nora. No need to thank me, I had to do it.'

She walked away and he smiled. So that was Nosy Nora. That solved that little mystery of who had sent the anonymous note. Another minor thing cleared up.

Cheryl was waiting for him when he reached the office, with an old ice-cream container sitting on her desk.

He looked inside it when she pushed it towards him. 'What's this?'

'Vic's finished sorting out all the long grass, and he's picked up bits and bobs of stuff he wants you to check you don't need. There's hinges and screws and all sorts in there. He wanted everything out of that grass so he can mow it properly when the time is right.'

Luke laughed. 'I reckon we can probably throw it all away. Vic's a hoarder, keeps everything, but I don't. I'll have a look through it, then recycle the metal. Guess what I've discovered. That note we got that was all letters cut from a paper, it was Nosy Nora who sent it. Don't know her surname, Hattie called her that. Nora apparently heard them rowing the night Evelyn disappeared, so put two and two together.'

Cheryl grinned. 'Did she think we'd act on it?'

'I think she thinks we've solved it because of her careful cutting.'

'Bless her. Any more news?'

'My bed's being delivered today, so I've been to tell Jenny. She'll let them in. I can sleep there tonight!'

'Brilliant. Your mum okay about it?'

'She's fine. The girls are really giddy as you can imagine. The second I move out one of them will be in my bedroom. I'm not asking who's having it in case world war three breaks out.'

Luke picked up the grubby white box and took it with him up to his office. He made a coffee, and sat down with a large piece of newspaper spread in front of him. He tipped everything out, and separated the finds into recycling and dumping. When he came to the key he stopped. He knew exactly what it was, who had last touched it twenty-five years earlier, and he felt sickened, and saddened.

He had no doubt at all that it was the old key to the outhouse, and instead of putting it into recycling he placed it in his top drawer. He quickly went through the rest, and carried it all downstairs and outside to the bins, where everything was disposed of into the correct receptacle.

. . .

Fred finished work at four after a really early start, and decided to nip down to Meadowhall where he needed to buy himself new shoes. He thought he might grab a meal while there, and people watch for a while.

The shoes were easy, as were the three T-shirts, the hoodie, and the two pairs of jeans. He headed back towards the Oasis where he decided to sit above the main area, and enjoy an Italian meal. He called in the newsagents and picked up a newspaper, intending to sit and read for a while, until his meal arrived.

However, his plans went awry as he recognised an old friend who was leaving the restaurant, and by the time they had finished chatting his meal had arrived. He quickly finished it, suddenly aware of how hungry he was, and left some twenty minutes later, heading downstairs towards the main Oasis eating area, and the Lanes exit. That was when he saw a familiar face. Two familiar faces, although he remembered the rear area of one of the women rather more than her face. Amy Barker and Vanessa Noone.

He stood and watched them for a while, surrounded by bags from various designer shops, laughing and joking as only sisters can. He felt an anger mounting, and he knew he had to speak to them.

He stood by their table and the light died in Amy's eyes.

'Mrs Barker, Mrs Noone. How strange to see you together. And how strange to see you with clothes on, Mrs Noone.'

'And you are?' Vanessa said, her voice icy.

Amy leaned forward. 'Vee, it's Fred Iveson.'

Fred pulled out a chair that didn't bear evidence of their spending spree. He sat down.

'Well? I take it you used me to set up this divorce? And you used your body with Amy's permission to ensnare her husband?'

Neither woman spoke, merely looked at each other.

'And your husband, Mrs Noone, does he exist or was he a figment of Mrs Barker's imagination?'

'It's not like you think...' Amy began.

'I suspect it's exactly like I think. You used me, you used my company and you will ultimately be lying in court. But I've taken photographs of this little meet up, so remember that when you get to court. I will make the pictures available, and I'll make me available if they need me to tell them about this. I think they will.'

Fred stood, gathered his bags together and walked away. He didn't look back, simply walked out of the exit, and to his car. He sat for a moment, not wanting to drive, only to relax.

He picked up the newspaper, glanced at the front page, then turned to page two. Facing him was the headline *Millionaire Boss Suspicious Death,* and a picture of Harley King.

Fred felt sick that by the following day it would be front-page headlines, and he pulled out his phone to ring Ernest Lounds.

EPILOGUE

Martin pulled the woman closer and kissed her. He ran his hand down her body, and smelt the perfume, still so familiar after all the years of knowing her, after all the years of golf trips with his father, then alone.

'Thank you,' he whispered. 'Thank you, my lovely Paloma. There was no hesitation was there?'

'Why would there be? I have waited for you for nearly thirty years, my Martin. Why should I hesitate when you needed my help? And you know I will never desert you but I have to know why you killed these two ladies you have spoken of.'

She coughed, a deep hacking sound, and she clung to him. He soothed her, and turned to reach a glass. 'Have some more water,' he said gently, 'and we will talk. Both wanted me to themselves, exclusively. They wanted to tell Phyllis, and I couldn't let them do that, or find out about each other. In the end, I thought I had no choice but to kill them.'

'You're here to stay? With me?'

'Definitely. I can't go back to England, so I'm here for good. No more Spanish golfing holidays, now it's a Spanish life.'

Again the cough drained her.

'How long have you had this cough?'

'Today. I feel ill, but I'll take some tablets...'

He moved away from her slightly, remembering the news from earlier. The increased hospital admissions, the death rate mounting on the Spanish mainland...

And everybody in England watching with trepidation.

'Paloma, have you been in contact with someone with this new virus?'

She nodded. 'Si, my uncle and aunt. He in hospital. My aunt at home, but I need to take care of her. She is struggling to breathe. I am so worried.'

He pulled her towards him. 'And I'll take care of you. We can begin our life together now, no having to go back to England.' He bent down and sealed his words with a long kiss...

THE END

ACKNOWLEDGEMENTS

As always I begin my thank you 'bit' by mentioning my awesome publishers, Bloodhound Books. As the oldest (both in length of service and years!) author on their books, we have a close relationship, and Betsy and Fred, along with their team of Tara, Alexina, Heather, Maria and Ross, have endlessly supported me and my writing. My eternal thanks, guys. *Blood Red* is my eighteenth book produced by this wonderful team.

This book would be nothing without Morgen Bailey, my long-time editor, who takes my original, tells me where I went awry, and puts me right. I am slowly teaching her how to speak and read Yorkshire, and she is amazing. Ey up, lass!

My thanks are also extended to Cheryl Dodd, who allowed me to use her name without realising it meant it would be in three books! I hope I did it justice, Cheryl. I've given Oliver extra cat treats for letting me use him, and Buddy the Shih Tzu is also very real, an awesome little dog.

And now we come to my teams. I have a team of beta readers, Marnie Harrison, Alyson Read, Sarah Hodgson, Tina Jackson and Denise Cutler. Their feedback is exemplary, and without them I would be lost. My ARC reading team currently has forty members, and they read the book three weeks before launch day so they are ready with reviews pre-launch. A wonderful group of people, and I have been known to cry at their comments. Thank you to all of you, beta readers and ARC readers alike, you're an essential part of whatever success I have with each book.

There are other authors in this crazy writing world who give me comfort when I am down (usually when I've just killed a favourite character), strength when I need it, and general support when I have questions. Some make me laugh (which ALWAYS helps), some give information, and some are simply there, so a shout-out to them – Patricia Dixon, Judith Baker, McGarvey Black, Diana Wilkinson, Rob Ashman, Mark Tilbury and Liz Mistry; and a special mention for a dear friend who isn't an author but a stalwart of the writing community, Susan Hunter.

And lastly I have to thank Dave and the rest of my family who give me space and time to write. I love you so much, and your support is everything to me. Thank you, my loves.

Anita
Sheffield, UK.

A NOTE FROM THE PUBLISHER

Thank you for reading this book. If you enjoyed it please do consider leaving a review on Amazon to help others find it too.

We hate typos. All of our books have been rigorously edited and proofread, but sometimes mistakes do slip through. If you have spotted a typo, please do let us know and we can get it amended within hours.

info@bloodhoundbooks.com

Printed in Great Britain
by Amazon

70551003R00169